D1519975

# Patriotism, Inc.
## and Other Tales

S'press

ST. MARY'S COLLEGE OF MARYLAND
ST. MARY'S CITY, MARYLAND

058472

# Patriotism, Inc.

## and Other Tales

PAUL VAN OSTAIJEN

Edited & Translated by E.M.Beekman

The University of Massachusetts Press 1971

For Seymour Simckes

Copyright © 1971 by E.M. Beekman
All Rights Reserved

Library of Congress Catalog Card Number 79–150314

The translator is grateful to the National Translation
Center, Austin, Texas, for the support which enabled
him to complete the work. It is a serious loss to the
American literary world that this commendable institute
had to be closed for lack of funds.

The following texts have appeared in different form in
the periodicals indicated: "Convictions," "Anaïs," "Lines,"
"Small Forest," "The Sirens," "O Thou, My Splendid Solitude,"
in *The Massachusetts Review*; "Obsequies," in *Mundus Artium*;
"Aquarelle," in *The Chicago Review*; "Ika Loch's Brothel," in
*New Directions 21*; "Bankruptcy Jazz," in *TDR/The Drama Review*.

Printed in the United States of America
Designed by Richard Hendel

Life in fact's me.
              —Dudley

# Contents

# Introduction

This century is the fool of history. Never before has there been such an unrelenting succession of absurdities, ranging from the monstrous to the petty, with such dismaying acceleration. We have become so used to it that we live it as a quotidian reality in the home and have given it a corporate sanctity in society. We are stockholders in Folly, Inc. and the product has been packaged so well that, true to ideal mass production, the fearful and the horrible are indistinguishable from the startling and the amusing.

When a pertinaciously sensitive and sensible mind encounters such a world he is horrified and terror-stricken, horrified by the monstrous truth when Eichmann insists that he never killed anyone, by the sobriety of reports on "overkill" offering statistical evidence that an equivalent of fifteen tons of TNT per person on this globe is amassed in stockpiles, by the economical logic of destroying surplus foods in one nation while in another the majority is starving, by the dogmatic refusal of a church to sanction contraception on a globe choked by people. Detergents blight the waters of Lake Erie while in Japan a coin-operated machine retails oxygen. Causes of quality are deflated by quantity. Clamorous causes die in a deafening silence. Nothing is real, and that is reality. The self-immolation of a monk and the burning of a bra are both ceremonies of protesting freedom. When kept separated the emotional energies expended on these events are equal. But when forcibly conjoined a terrifying illumination sparks the mind to silence and rejuvenation.

In our time such a spark can be produced by art. For the pure and social sciences compound problems and conditions by excessively proving that they exist. Statistics do not cure. Thus encapsuled and verified, the problems are deposited within our general frame of reference and forgotten. Unfortunately much of modern art has given in to the insanity and confusion of our century and merely reflects the disorder. A garbage dump is constructed as an aesthetic comment on human waste. To try to torture intellectual justifications out of such a primitive equation is yet another neophiliac whim, as fugacious as no deposit/no return containers. Romantic escape is an impossibility.

Precisely because of its militancy, its innate desire for form, and covert idealism, satire appears to be the literary mode most appropriate for our times. The century has seen a flowering of satiric literature. If one recognizes satire's flexibility—ranging from savage to subtle militancy, from the fantastic to the bitingly rational—a great number of modern literary figures have served its cause. Mann, Joyce, Gide, Brecht, Beckett, Ionesco, Grass—the series would be very long indeed. Even the appelations attached to entire movements instantly recall a satiric lineage: Surrealism, Dadaism, Theatre of the Absurd, Black Humorists. With the last we have come to American literature. Some of the best fiction is being written by authors who are occasionally herded into this stockade. Joseph Heller, Bruce Jay Friedman, J.P. Donleavy, Donald Barthelme, Peter de Vries, Walker Percy, Thomas Pynchon, John Barth, Vladimir Nabokov, Kurt Vonnegut—all of them have turned a deaf ear to the critical jeremiads concerning fiction, and have armed their craft for battle.

This satiric attitude (for as a concept it is no longer a narrowly defined literary form) requires, ironically enough, a very sophisticated knowledge of form and an intimate awareness of language. To expose an ulcerous growth the surgeon must be dexterous with his scalpel. A hatchet job does little to relieve pathology. But control, skill, and a passionate immunity to suffering can chance to alleviate the pains of man. Confronted by an ailing society these authors dissect in order to heal. They are anatomists of folly. But these pupils of Menippus have joined battle with a far more insidious enemy than their Roman forebear ever knew. After two global wars and their attendant horrors unmatched in history, modern man despairs of being honestly optimistic. Hence most of their work shows man in bondage. Their fictions end in *culs-de-sac*, their conclusions are fearful. But there are two factors of liberation in their work. The first one is humor. Humor, specifically cerebral wit, confounds tragedy, collapses despair and, perhaps most importantly, insures distance. The technique and the attitude of humor are the highest forms of expression and of awareness. The second liberator is the very act of participation. He who entertains folly on her own stage knows her intimately and is immune to her attractions. Familiarity breeds contempt, and intimacy fosters knowledge. This is the level of the liberating paradox: in medicine the injection of the disease prevents the disease. From the distance of humor we are exposed to folly, suffer it, and will perhaps resist its dictatorial regime. These fictions are a homeopathy of the absurd. Cerebrality, humor, the skills of language and the satiric attitude, all make the writer of the modern grotesque, this anatomist of folly, kin to the ideal revolutionary: Lenin defined him as having a heart on ice and a mind on fire.

Paul van Ostaijen (1896–1928), the author of the tales which are presented here for the first time in English, should be counted among the foremost satirists of this age. Yet his career is a trial of errors, his posthumous fame lies primarily in his poetry, and he wrote in Dutch, that poor relation of Northern European languages. It is the last factor which has been the most decisive obstacle. Van Ostaijen's work is an indictment of the Monroe Doctrine in the world of literature.

The seventh and the Benjamin, he was the son of a well-to-do, retired plumber. As a formal student, Van Ostaijen was a disaster, excelling only in the history of religion. After he dropped out of school, he worked in the municipal administration of Antwerp, wrote his first essays on contemporary avant-garde art and his first collections of poems. With his fellow citizens he was a virtual prisoner in that Belgian harbor which, during the First World War, was surrounded by the German forces. Yet he managed to read a great many French and German contemporaries, and his first volume of verse, *Music Hall* (1916), was decidedly a literary success, followed by the second collection, *The Signal* (1918), which introduced humanitarian Expressionism into Flemish letters. One of the remarkable facets of Van Ostaijen's character was his ability to discover premature staleness in the arts and his uncompromising evaluation of his own work. When his literary confreres standardized the heretic movement into protracted respectability, Van Ostaijen disavowed not only the movement but also his own work which had been its prime mover. Later he condemned his very first work, *Music Hall*, as being adolescent and considered buying as many copies of the book as possible in order to burn them.

Shortly after the Armistice was signed and *The Signal* had been published, Van Ostaijen fled to Berlin. He had been something of a political activist in a situation very similar to that of Québec. Belgium is a bilingual nation. Split into a Dutch-speaking (the Flemings) and a French-speaking (the Walloons) sector, the Belgian nation seems to suffer at times from cultural schizophrenia. Neither side is powerful enough to demolish the other. Van Ostaijen's allegiance was clearly with the Flemings who, during his lifetime, were the underdogs. In several articles he had been an outspoken rebel, and he was further implicated in a demonstration against a Walloon cardinal. This earned him a three-month jail sentence, which was suspended by the Germans. Afraid that the authorities would arrest him when the war ended, Van Ostaijen went into voluntary exile. He had merely jumped out of the frying-pan into the fire.

Postwar Berlin, particularly during his stay there (1919–1921), was a bona fide madhouse. Political factions fought each other in the streets. The Communist revolutionaries Rosa Luxembourg and Karl Liebknecht were openly murdered by the authorities during the abortive Communist uprising of January 1919. Gustav Noske, a ruthless and efficient restorer of law and order, brutally suppressed the revolutionaries during fierce street fighting. A staggering unemployment rate, serious food shortages, and an almost comical inflation (by 1923 the German Mark had fallen to 4,200,000,000,000 to the dollar) compounded the political lunacy, producing a nation of despairing, frightened people. This mood and these events form the background of the film script *Bankruptcy Jazz*.

Van Ostaijen eked out a meager existence doing odd jobs and hustling loans from those better off and from friends at home. He also took drugs. The frightening hallucinations brought on by cocaine and his almost chronic disillusionment were voiced in a savage book of poems, *The Banquets of Fear and Pain* (written in 1921 but published posthumously). These poems chronicle his crisis in identity and the total erasure of his accustomed world. They indicate his desire to start anew, with a clean slate: "I want to be naked/ and begin."

Written during the Berlin years and published in 1921 in Antwerp with the financial support of his brother, Van Ostaijen's next volume of verse, *Occupied City*, is one of the most remarkable poetic documents of this century. The subject is his besieged home town, its desolation and folly when fear strips all conventional trappings from the human race and exposes its vulnerability. But it is the form of the poems which makes this book exceptional. Van Ostaijen had already studied the rhythmic and typographical innovations of Mallarmé and Apollinaire. But during his stay in Berlin he observed the Dadaists' explosion of the printed page. The Dada movement was in its heyday, and its assault on the conventional and traditional included everything from politics to poetry. The difference is that the Flemish poet used the technical innovations to create a new form intimately wedded to his subject. That is to say, not a free-for-all, but a disciplined fusion of form and content. Hence the striking oddities prove, on closer examination, to be profound and inevitable choices. Van Ostaijen shows himself a complete master of his medium.

The content of *Occupied City* shows a marked similarity in tone and theme to the tales presented here. Most of them were written during the same period. Like the tales, the poems are militant exposures of society. Their attitude is satirical, irreverent, accusing. As one announces, "The Great Circus of the Holy Ghost brings you tonight the world famous Trio: Religion, King, and Nation." But the poems betray suffering, an empathy with the victims of society's arrogant cynicism, which most of the tales lack. The idealist of humanitarian religion had made an about-face. No longer an activist, he now sadly admitted the futility of positivistic actions. As he reported in a letter from Berlin: "Wrote a novella in which I try to make monkeys of people. Positive criticism: baloney. Now I like novellas in which you can fool around so marvelously. People aren't worth criticizing. Only material for burlesque novellas."

In 1921 he dared to return to his beloved Antwerp. He was granted amnesty for his "crimes," promptly drafted and sent to serve with the allied occupation forces in Germany. Discharged in 1923, he was as usual faced with the difficult task of making a living. Despite very cool relations with his father (who thought his son a failure), he lived at home and tried to earn his bread in a variety of occupations. He worked as a bookseller, art dealer, and journalist. Slowly his reputation began to spread among a larger circle of discerning people. His essays, critiques, and theoretical expostulations explained the daring alchemy of the poems he was then writing. After the explosions of *The Banquets of Fear and Pain* and *Occupied City*, his later work is an implosion—meditations on eternality. Poetry is no longer "thought, spirit, well-turned phrases, it is neither doctoral nor Dada. It is simply a game of words anchored in the metaphysical." And the poems he wanted to collect in his first "definitive" volume were distillations of astonishing purity and simplicity. Yet these apparently artless lyrics resonate with profundity. Van Ostaijen had reached the limit of poetry: the maximum contraction of language to express the maximum of meaning. And that final message reflects the paradox of man, who lives the finality of the flesh suspended in the awareness of infinity. Perfection is always just beyond the reach of his hands. And so these lyrics ache with the realization of the insufficiency of expression, the failure of aspirations, since "a poem is never as perfect as a mammal with a finally severed umbilical cord." The grandeur lies in the attempt.

Just when his circumstances were improving, Van Ostaijen's precarious health suffered a sudden decline during the spring of 1927. In September of that year he entered a private sanatorium in Miavoye-Anthée, a tiny hamlet in the Belgian Ardennes. Despite his failing strength he kept on working. In a life full of ironies it seems appropriate that he received a government grant just before he died on March 18, 1928. For four years his grave was unnoticed and forgotten. But in 1932 his remains were transported to a more dignified cemetery in Antwerp, only to be disturbed once more when he was officially interred in a section of the municipal cemetery reserved for national luminaries in a grave graced with a headstone.

The following tales, which he called "grotesques," show that Van Ostaijen had his posthumous revenge on Folly, Inc. All of the major concerns of our society are deflated by his savage wit: politics, nationalism, warfare, sex, prison, and sundry matters. Yet these topics are reflections of a unity: all the tales postulate a grotesque and vicious disorder as the norm and proceed to argue it logically into antithetical truth. Van Ostaijen is not so much interested in conventional plotting or the narrative line as he is in the peccant nature of logic. We have so much faith in the logic of official arguments that more often than not we fail to examine their premises. It is relatively easy for the satirist to undermine our faith in progressive arguments. With a straight face he legislates a premise, then with a slight shift of perspective follows a logical course of argument until he has reached its inevitable conclusion. That he ends up in a fearful realm of absurdity is the fault of a world out of joint, not his doing. Swift's "Modest Proposal" is the classic example of such a technique, but we have to add Van Ostaijen's work to the short list of masterpieces. In "The Lost House Key" a city suffers an epidemic of syphilis. Instead of combating it the citizens elevate it to a norm. Pursued with relentless inevitability, syphilis becomes the "accepted" mode of life and its opposite, the reader's "healthy norm," is considered an evil and antisocial condition. It is a matter of moral focus, a matter of fundamental hypothesis.

The satiric mind understands this perversity. He has no quarrel with what is essentially a social contract based on mutual agreement. But when he finds such an *understanding* worshipped as an absolute to which lives are offered and for which sufferings are excused, his anger is aroused. He proceeds to show that language is neutral, that it is men who charge it with emotion. The cry of passion is sweet to the lover but an expression of pain to an outsider. We create and live a paradox. He also demonstrates that language destroys as it creates. Positivistic logic can be detrimental, religion can be demeaning, mores can kill. In "The City of Builders" Van Ostaijen shows that progressive actions can turn regressive, by pursuing logically the circumstance that building implies tearing down. The consequence of ignoring the latter is reminiscent of Five-year Plans, Cultural Revolutions, and Great Societies. "Ika Loch's Brothel" presents the whore logic. In Dutch *logika* is logic, and the name of the madam is an anagram. She has no experience or knowledge of sex, yet she has sublime confidence in the logic of her arguments concerning her clients' desires.

A variation is to accept an existing condition or belief, embrace it passionately, and live it absolutely. Idealists of this sort are very disturbing to the powers that be and repugnant to the originators of ideas. Idealists are literalists, and the devout disciples of Freud will see a phallus in a toothpick. Or witness the embarrassment when a minority applies the dictum that "all men are created equal." Hence no. 200, the hero of "The Prison in Heaven, "stops being an asset to the state when he simply insists on his right to be imprisoned—even when he has to murder. Conversely, in "Patriotism, Inc." the governments of Fochany (=France) and Teutonia (=Germany) exploit nationalism which, by definition, is a partisan virtue, and turn it into an *inter*national corporate venture. Their logic is the logic of the military-industrial complex, universalized. "Patriotism, Inc." would have no use for that other idealist, Ricardo Gomès. In "The General" this astute philosopher admits that antimilitarism is a virtue, not because it is morally sound, but because no one knows how to wage war correctly.

The grotesque world is not a laughing matter. The unmitigated incongruity is fearful. Its modest proposals admit one to the nightmare of reality. What is so frightening is that none of these stories is implausible. The satiric mind has no use for fairy tales. Its basis is realistic and its lunacy is all too familiar. Furthermore, in these cerebral grotesques one is caught in the ratiocination, obliged to follow an argument, whereas pure fancy can be left at any point. It is therefore easier to admit the gentler madness of the film script, *Bankruptcy Jazz*. We can entertain the thought of Charlie Chaplin as our head of state, but we know that it is a fiction. A careful reading of this Dada scenario will reward the student with the discovery that Van Ostaijen anticipated, as he did so often, recent film techniques, to my knowledge, by more than forty years.

From a technical point of view, the peculiarity of the style of these grotesques is due to Van Ostaijen's use of what may be called a metonymic style. A metonymy is a rhetorical figure whereby an attribute is substituted for the thing meant: for example, "Washington" for the "United States Government." A metonymic style develops by contiguity, that is to say, unlike a metaphoric style which progresses via similarity, a contiguous style develops via proximity, a series of phenomena are linked to each other in terms of specific images. For example, in "Hierarchy," the first paragraph posits that soldiers are virile. The second paragraph states the problem: the soldiers can find no women in Cattaro. This problem is solved by finding four female wrecks. Here the story would normally conclude, but in this case it is the beginning, for this situation calls up the notion of hierarchy, with its attendant problems of discipline. By now the original worry about the sexual frustrations of the soldiers is irrelevant—only military hierarchy is important. Like the other stories, "Hierarchy" develops by association from an original premise. "Between Fire and Water" is an astonishing description of this process. A cross between a narrative and an essay, this fictional hybrid successfully communicates that peculiar state of awareness when we are neither quite asleep nor quite awake. Released from ordinary constraints, the mind associates freely, though it is still subject to intruders from reality. But these are reinterpreted according to the train of thought or "arabesque," as Van Ostaijen calls it, and no longer have the obstinate immutability of concrete events. Yet the process of free association (also basic to Van Ostaijen's poetry) has its own laws. It is not random confusion. Nothing, it would seem, is irrational by nature but man makes it so. If we shed atrophied preconceptions we can understand the logic of dreams, of the subconscious, of the most outlandish occurrences. Anything that we have stored in our mental larders can be released in sequential order, though not necessarily in a commonly accepted series. In that state of mind which is neither here nor there, conscious nor unconscious (that is, not readily indexed) we allow ourselves to register the riches of our minds. It will be a contiguous series with its own harmony, and when we are gifted it will produce poetry. This, incidentally, is also an explanation for Van Ostaijen's curious use of time. Contiguity is progression by proximity, hence it allows the writer to experience time in several tenses. When the bondage of similarity and its military sense of order have been discarded, we can again know the contiguous flow of time. In the present, we can remember a past, and at the same time without disturbing the other tenses project a future. Past, present, and to come are often experienced *simultaneously*.

Furthermore, these tales destroy or mock traditional standards of fiction. The characterization is deliberately cut to one-dimensional etchings. We learn very little about the heroes. Action is kept to a minimum, introduced only as a device to make a point. In "Ika Loch's Brothel," a stranger murders Promethea, apparently to show that Ika Loch's abstract conceptions of sexual relations cannot be shaken even by the reality of a *crime passionale*. So these tales destroy the preconceptions of popular fiction in terms of expected character-ization, narrative development and narrative content. Another feature, which according to Northrop Frye is "endemic in the narrative tech-nique of satire," is Van Ostaijen's use of the digression. His violations of the narrative norm serve to underscore the freedom of the satirist, his disdain for conventions, his consequent objectivity. For the satiric writer, and Van Ostaijen in particular, strives towards disindividual-ization, a type of indirect communication. Objectivity in this instance only strengthens the illusion of authority; the detachment under-scores the essential morbidity of the world represented and does not allow the reader to avoid it by attacking the author.

In one tale, "The Kept Hotel Key," Van Ostaijen neglected this esthetic and ethical distance. The icy relentlessness of the other tales is absent in this "grotesque with a tear," this grudging nod to tragedy. And when Van Ostaijen allowed himself proximity, his hero pays with an all too human suffering none of the other stately marion-ettes' experience. The almost unbearable frustration, the seething hatred, the demonic presence of violence—we know this all too well. It is probably Van Ostaijen's most personal fiction.

But despite the horrible verisimiltude of the tales of Van Ostaijen, there is an implied freedom. Satire assumes a standard of excellence which is abrogated by present usage. Why else would Swift bother to spend a lifetime's energy in rebellious prose. In the end satire is not nihilistic. Its intention is to cut the reader into awareness. To follow a *reductio ad absurdum* to its bitter end is a liberating process. When we have completed it, we should be unable to subscribe to a similar folly ever again. Satire shows us the relativity of intellectual and moral positions, and thinking a paradox through sets us free, immunizes us against the disease of calcified singlemindedness.

Van Ostaijen the poet is also present in these tales. His extraordinary perception of nuances and his skill in verbalizing them are particularly evident in two passages. The description of Promethea in "Ika Loch's Brothel" is like a fragile poem, while the scene in "The General," where the narrator and the General walk in the park during the early hours of the morning, is so poignant and melancholy that it rivals the best in descriptive fiction. The ten prose poems in this volume also give the reader a sense of what Van Ostaijen's lyrics are like. Contrary to the ambling discursive grotesques, they are terse and compact. The longer prose works are finally distilled into the essence, like a prolixity of flowers reduced to a quintessence of scent. All of these prose poems illustrate that to see is to know, for, if anything, they are distinguished by an acuity of perception. There is a line of progression in these pieces. While most of them convey the inexorable sadness of human futility, there is an increasing acceptance of the inevitability of defeat and of death which, in "Obsequies," becomes a transcendental revelation. As in his final lyrics, these prose poems show Van Ostaijen turning away from the world as from a circus to occupy himself with the mystery of being. He knew that "the lyrical emotion is a negation of a pessimistic view of life." And his final serenity is not optimism but the tranquillity of wisdom.

## Textual note

These translations were rendered from the revised second edition of the collected works of Paul van Ostaijen: *Verzameld Werk. Proza I*, ed. Gerrit Borgers, 2nd ed. (The Hague: Bert Bakker/Daamen N.V., 1966). The editing was guided by the simple rule that passages which would be incomprehensible to an English audience unfamiliar with Belgian or Dutch literature and culture, without an amount of explanation incommensurate with their importance, should be abridged. Annotations are provided for those references which one cannot expect a contemporary audience to know. (For a detailed study of the texts presented in this volume, see my book *Homeopathy of the Absurd: The Grotesques in Paul van Ostaijen's Creative Prose* [Amsterdam: Martinus Nijhoff, 1970].) When translating I juggled with two principles which sometimes were mutually exclusive. I attempted to render the original as faithfully as possible while at the same time producing intelligible English. Contrary to many other practitioners of this thankless art, I felt no inclination to improve on the original text. Van Ostaijen was well aware that his style was peculiar, and intended it to be so. One cannot satirize philosophic argumentation by using a style fit only for pulp magazines. Often he chose not to be understood. If this offends, so do Hegel and Marx. Wherever possible, original turns of phrases, unusual syncopations, and unorthodox grammatical usages are rendered into English. I have tried to present the original in all its eccentric brilliance, not what I thought it should have been or what would be kosher in our sober tongue. Any other way would have been presumptuous.

# Patriotism, Inc.

## and Other Tales

# Between Fire & Water

**A**round ten p.m., after we have been travelling for three hours, we arrive at a railroad junction. Two gentlemen get out. A lady gets in. She sits down diagonally across from me, then next to me.

I sit with my book, which sometimes I read, sometimes I don't. Yet such travel literature leaves a strong impression. The others talk. A general conversation that is dropped and then started again between two people.

The lady presses my foot. That is a mistake, of course. But on a train you try your best to believe in adventures. That's why I don't believe it to be a mistake. Though I am positive it is. Everything is strange in a railway car. You ride and yet you can throw the ashes of your cigar in an ashtray. Like home. That is marvelous, because it is so complex and so simple. That is indeed a beautiful complex: simple and complex.

Around eleven a gentleman asks if he may put out the lights. Of course, why not? If I am reading? Not really, I can sleep just as well. Everyone makes an imperative gesture, let us sleep! Everyone squirms in corners. Where there is no corner you try to make one. It doesn't work of course. It is a mathematical attempt.

I don't sleep. I definitely don't sleep. I am still, though not sensually clear—my eyes are closed, too—quite conscious of space. That is to say, a gentleman is sitting across from me, there is an unlit lamp. Only where the lady is sitting does this sense of consciousness become rather opaque. Yet I hear very clearly the movements of anyone who stirs, etc. I do not make the effort to bring isolated observations to a general conception. I become aware where the noise comes from, so it can be assumed that I am still quite alert. Yet I know that I am neither asleep nor awake. If you are awake, all objects of the reality you perceive appear finally in a general harmony or disharmony. What I am presently aware of must be separate occurrences. But it is remarkable that I no longer try to unite them in an absolute image. And as far as I can remember, one must ascribe this to a lack of energy for ordering things, described in a naïve physiological manner as a superior brain authority. I am still clearly conscious of this: with a small plus it is different. But I no longer assess a plus. Indeed, my energy to order things doesn't exert itself that much. This energy is precisely more than this plus which would change everything, and therefore I cannot determine it any further. Obviously a function has been cancelled, probably between an observation which in itself cannot properly be called sensual any longer, and a superior authority for generalization. The occurrences in the compartment are such that they appear to me in reality to be commonplace and at the same time fantastic, hence again the cancellation of the attempt to establish a more exact knowledge of the relationships. These occurrences are taking place, I perceive them, and since I am not asleep I register this perception, and since I am not awake there follows no further physiological-psychological induction. The best way to put it is that it is like a stone which falls into water without creating circles. Only what follows proceeds from this intelligible situation: just now I am meditating about this curious situation. For a moment I want to pin down what it is, for a moment I want to create clarity for myself. Then I have this sensation of a candle which does not need to be blown out in order not to give light any longer, but which suddenly simply goes out for no reason and without awakening in me the desire to exact a reason. In like manner I do not pursue my reflections about my situation any longer. Where and how did this thread break? And surely another motif follows this meditation, just as in a waking state when thought draws the most arbitrary arabesques about perception, the past, and desire, a situation which Poe masterfully objectified in his *Murders in the Rue Morgue*.

And here I have to clarify again my state of mind in relation to sleeping and waking. When you are alone and left to your own thoughts, then this process which we shall call "mind," for short, follows often an equally apparent chance direction, the arabesques which proceed across memory, perception and desire appear equally improvised. This is independent from an *immediate* mental orientation, which can be proved by the fact that a sudden observation is worked out by this arabesque. For example: I think of a dead friend, but suddenly my stroll brings me past a beautiful house and from this house my thought-arabesque rolls over houses, architecture and gothic, when it seems suddenly and without apparent reason to be broken because I was mumbling something about Plato. Several days ago I read a sentence somewhere which went as follows: the Gothic is the predication of spirit over nature. Hence Plato is a gothic man. Intelligent psychoanalysts, however, can follow this arabesque for quite awhile and suddenly throw the thinking man the result of their pursuit, which coincides with his meditation at that moment. Poe pointed this out long before the psychoanalytic method. He described such a case so precisely that you wonder whether science is really so fantastic, or whether fantasy is so scientific. Is this a possibility, that this arabesque which I cautiously said was apparently accidental and which can be followed quite precisely by a second one, is a conclusive proof for a casual relationship—especially since the second one, as in Poe, does not have any pretentions of being telepathy or even intuition, but develops it as a very cerebral function? If so, we can only speak of an individually determined being, i.e., an artist passes a house, and it is individually and deterministically concluded that he will retain this observation in his thought process. An officer who passes the same house, his head full of strategy, does perceive the house, but it does not penetrate his knowledge, the way Socrates distinguishes between knowledge and perception. The arabesque of the artist is influenced by this perception which with him has to become knowledge. The arabesque of the officer is not influenced. He who pursues the train of thought of this person has to take refuge in psychoanalytic methods, to take the *individual* personality as center and to proceed from this deductively. This psychologist first has to separate the observations which lie fallow from those which become knowledge, and secondly to compare the observations which have become knowledge once more with the individuality, to arrive at the sum of categorical influence. This is the same process the telepathic object or spiritual medium follows according to the unclear-clear law of a psycho-rhythm. Of both the methodologist and medium compassionate participation is demanded; of the first only analytic-objective, hence a minimum; of the second a maximum, synthetic and subjective. There is here only a difference of degree, of a lower and higher degree, really a large difference, but not a gap. The one is contemplation, the other boundless participation. Boundlessness has here not an anarchistic, but a cosmic, very ordered meaning. The causal chain, however, which excludes chance within its total hegemony, also has its limits. That is to say, how a house shall be interpreted lies causally determined in the individual, but then the house must first be included in the train of thought, and this takes place by means of an apparently casual stroll which cannot be further dissected into elements.

Between this situation and others such as reading a book or writing a letter, there is a difference in details, and this difference points to an inclusion of an apparent chance component in the first case. Here we can deduce the development of the thought process from the first object, by viewing the chance components as a sudden occurrence. In the second situation you return, no matter how much details may distract, to the first object. In the first case completely divergent, in the second case convergent. In the first case the thought is completely self-sufficient, in the second it has always a shadow of a utilitarian purpose, albeit clarity of the thought itself. On the one hand it follows the train of thought, on the other a preconceived goal.

We now come to a special consideration: the difference between this arabesque and a dream. This arabesque has three temporal possibilities, past, present, and future in its reach, but it can never place them on one level. *Everything occurs in sequence.* You think of a friend, suddenly you see a house, you create an image of an architecture of the future. Everything appears sequentially tied together by transitions which have, so to speak, causal fortuity and fortuitous causality. This arabesque never arrives at a grotesque confusion of temporal possibilities. Only the qualitative difference between them is cancelled out: the past is not a perspective and the future is to be understood as an observation of reality which has become knowledge. It is a true arabesque, without depths, pure flat ornament. It is never a history or an episode, it lacks the linking object which gives occurrences relationship.

It is clear that this arabesque differs from that which usually is called thinking, be it thinking about a single local occurrence or thinking in the philosophical sense. This difference is so clear that in popular speech the arabesque is designated as "dreaming." Someone who thinks this arabesque is interrupted by the question, what is he dreaming about? Popular speech knows very well that the word is used figuratively here, but in this way it expresses quite clearly that this arabesque is a step on the road from thinking to dreaming itself.

With one haul, however, the dream stands much closer to concrete thinking than to the arabesque. The dream too is a systematically insisted history. The dream stands in a directly ambivalent relationship to concrete thinking. The arabesque has no point of view regarding thought. The dream remains hostile to it. The dream is a wish-fulfillment, says Freud. You can go further and say that the dream is an unconscious reaction against the historic, material, conscious aspect of our normal thinking. The dream is the experiencing of the subconscious in such a grotesque manner that it becomes a critique of normal thinking. The arabesque passes over time-nuances with complete indifference. Being now in the past it is suddenly in the future. Yet this needs to be mentioned: the arabesque is always complete in one of these nuances, it is never grotesque and does not melt them into one time. It moves indifferently from the one into the other. The dream is hostile to these classifications which belong to the system of conscious thought and reduces them—sadistic burlesque—to one plan. The dream is a wish-fulfillment and therefore realizes the wishes of the subconscious, nonetheless real, state of mind. You could call this the positive side. The thought of interpreting a precise dream as only physically determined by the position of the body touches upon the reason, not the cause. The interpretation which the dream affords to these physiological emotions remains for a moment still untouched. This interpretation is determined by its ambivalent character in relation to conscious thought. The dream constructs a complete history on what conscious thought would call totally unhistoric grounds. The dream plays everywhere in an ambivalent manner with perceptions and epistemology. A falling feather makes us cry, a meteor which smashes our legs makes us laugh, we encounter a friend in the year 2000 who was dead long before the dream took place. And the dream fights with its own weapons. Just as conscious thought created logic, the dream replies as an ambivalent consequence with the absurd and the burlesque which therefore, absolutely speaking, are no longer absurd or burlesque. I say therefore that the dream has a system which is exactly contrary to conscious existence, the episode in the dream is epistemologically absurd because it strives to be epistemologically exact in conscious thought. But there is an episode, a generally linking object wherein the anachronisms are but reversed synchronisms. There is indeed one plan.

The arabesque has no plan but her own improvisation. The arabesque is situated on a bypath of ordered thought. The dream is its opposite pole. The arabesque is situated on a bypath and naturally on the road towards the dream. There is however a fourth situation, mine in the railway compartment, which is neither dreaming nor waking. It is situated much deeper in the subconscious and therefore nearer to the dream than the conscious arabesque. It is a bypath from the dream to conscious thought. It has a lesser relationship with the arabesque—something like that of a satellite. If we assign to concrete thought the number 1, then the dream is 4, the arabesque 2, and the aforementioned situation 3. This is their proportional scale.

I can make the situation clearer with a few antitheses. When the sleeping person is awakened he transposes himself slowly from the one world, of sleep, into the other, the so-called outside world—but only *gradually*, no matter how much practice may simplify the process—we wake up at least once daily. It may happen that he is still blabbering words which have a relationship to his dream, and so on. The way I was in the compartment does not allow me to be what is called awakened, only to be disturbed. If I am being disturbed I clearly have the feeling of normal thoughts which are dispersed because of it. If anyone were to ask me for the subject, I would not be able to comply. "That's true," someone counters me on this topic, "the dream also has a solid belief—though not conscious—in the concreteness of its thought." True, but I have a conscious belief and control over it, however. If I accidentally, after a disturbance, retain a thought, the result is, "The lamp doesn't shine too well—what's that—is that strange person, etc."

Neither do I think an arabesque, since in this thinking everything is marvelously clear. It is an arabesque but completely veiled. My situation is not a dream because everything happens sequentially, and the periods of this sequence are mostly cut off by perceptions of the outside world. I already hear the ticket-collector in the corridor, and I am still lucid enough to conclude, "Someone who walks like that has to be the ticket-collector." But it is really less mental lucidity than the proof that my senses, trained for observation, have still maintained this ability to come quickly to a conclusion. My situation is an arabesque behind a veil, and at the same time an unconscious wish-fulfillment, simultaneous with these realistic observations. The first one wants to prove that I am in an intermediary situation, the second that I really am dreaming, the third that I am simply awake. And all this moves at the same time. While I perceive things from the outside world, businesslike, I weave my arabesque more unconsciously than the one described above, and I transform a wish into its fulfillment.

The woman who is sitting next to me has certainly not been indifferent to me. I feel how she has, while asleep, let her head sink on my shoulder. I do not look up to verify this. I press my eyes shut and also try to sleep. And so I think and follow my veiled arabesque.

Now I suddenly feel that the woman is making a movement and something like a sigh. Then she gets closer . . . .

And my head is stroked by her hand. Ever stroked. *Her fingers which I perceive as being separate*, wander through my hair. And it starts again, ever anew, rhythmic with the jerking of the train, I think quite businesslike. And I think something else in a businesslike fashion: her head rests on my shoulder; because she is sitting to my left, her right arm is pressed between her body and mine; hence she cannot possibly stroke me with it. Her left arm, however, would have to describe too large a circle to reach my head. How does she reach my head?

But she is good. She doesn't let herself be disturbed and keeps on stroking, probably thinking that I will wake up and stroke her in turn or speak to her. I do not move, for if I were to move I might frighten her, might make her suppose that it is unpleasant to me. I remain seated without moving. But I feel the pressure of her hand becoming stronger and her stroking more loving. Naturally in the meantime I think my arabesque ever further and note sounds in the corridor.

I do not question for a moment that it is she who strokes me. *Her hand is wonderfully soft*. And even big, I seem to feel. But a big female hand is unpleasant, and that's why I probably do not pursue that thought. I allow everything to happen, waiting until she herself will provide the opportunity for the resolution, for she must have had a plan when she began. Surely she is developing her plan. She draws my head closer into the reach of her hands.

How will this adventure end, I think. There are so many people on this train, and we definitely will never be alone in our compartment. Yet it is clear that this can only be a train adventure, and once our destination is reached it will no longer be binding. She probably has a lover and no time. She only wants to make use of her journey to have an adventure also. A travelling adventure. I look for ways to bring this adventure to a good end. Not so easy in such a chock-full train. Perhaps the dining car affords possibilities. Yes, that's it. I feel content with the result. Let's get to it! I put my head deeper in her hands. She notices the movement and strokes even harder. Yet strangely enough, she does not attempt the least proximity with her feet.

This is very strange—I have the feeling that I cannot open my eyes because everything would be finished then.

I open my eyes. I see a motionless lump next to me. A won-lost sleeping woman. I look immediately at her left hand, which hangs limp and motionless. I don't have a moment's anger over my misleading dream. Disillusionment, because I imagined things other than they were. More of a quiet wrath for the carelessness of my perception which allowed itself to be deceived.

Deceived! By what? Of course, it was the knob of the heat regulator against which I was perpetually being thrown by the rhythm of the train. There is still a secret hope that I might have made a mistake, and that it wasn't the knob after all. But time rushes by and the woman sleeps on. How can one be that unadventurous?

It is day in the compartment.

I reflect on what has happened during the night. Everything presents itself again as being so natural and—if we can use such a word for a memory—as so completely conceivable to me. Even if I had forgotten the dream I could still rescue some fragments with great difficulty. And I come to the conclusion that it is really wonderful to sit under such a knob. If the subconscious were not a major factor here, you could sit every journey under a knob and enjoy this situation quite happily, which is more than a dream because it is enjoyed in such an extraordinary, conscious manner, i.e., this enjoyment persists also into memory, lively and sensual.

So I think. Then . . . I discover that the heat regulator is not above my head at all! Only if I stretch my hand out can I reach it.

Above my head seesaws the umbrella of the lady. Quite probably it came slowly into this position during the night.

That I felt the five fingers remains quite incomprehensible to me . . . . And this copper knob is not quite so wonderfully soft either.

The lady wishes to smoke a cigarette. She asks me for a light.
What is a light?
I strike a match into flame.

# The Kept Hotel Key

## or the small, stupid deed

I knew Mr. Josef La Tour very well. After the fifteenth glass of Pilsner he usually declared that he was an Epicurean. Which he explained: a nice glass of beer, a shot of brandy once in a while, a glass of port in the morning, a good looking woman in bed, and there you've got my philosophy of life's joys. He thought that I was a decadent person. If I asserted that Epicurus was not quite so simplistic, I was intellectualizing. We were never friends. According to Josef La Tour I drank too much coffee and tea for that. More than once he would argue, "I have as much coffee as I want, at home with my wife. I only go into a café with the understanding that I will taste the imported beers. A café is nothing to me without Pilsner or Christmas.[1] Maybe you find this bourgeois. But I assume you are educated enough not to a priori reject the bourgeois. I say that the bourgeois has many good qualities. I could prove to you that if art still exists, you have to thank the bourgeois for that. The bourgeois rejects all art. This is a great service, however, insofar as he breaks the necks of all dilettantes at the same time. Ultimately speaking, you can only reject what can be discarded. I imagine the bourgeois to be a kind of security policeman for art. His work is only negative. Without that negative element we can't get any further." I was never able to convince him that beer was only a pleasure for me occasionally. He was always afraid that I disapproved of beer because of a fundamental estheticism. And he was really skeptical when I declared that I considered coffee a pleasant beverage. I must have had that opinion from Edgar Allan Poe, Charles Baudelaire, or De Lautréamont. Josef La Tour was always talking about "Edgar Allan Poe." I do not recall ever hearing "Poe" coming from his mouth. If I am mistaken on this subject, it is only a case of an exception which proves the rule. When Josef talked about literature, he was a sort of walking handbook of literature. He had certain classical airs, a little of the prototype of the classical bourgeois of our century. I jokingly called him "the classical bourgeois." He himself often joked, "I don't know what I positively am. But I am surely an abortion. I am a cross between an object of Molière and a victim of black magic." He usually said things like that after his twentieth glass of Müncher, when melancholy began to overpower him.

He was often bitter about my conduct. It was fine for me to say that coffee had positively the same effect on my system as beer had on his, it didn't make any difference. I said, "I am as drunk as you are, I can just as easily fall from the warmest joy into melancholy, and vice versa." Once I even said, "Coffee makes me primitive and leads me to live my subconscious life. Beer makes you simply wildly happy or wildly melancholy." I was right. It's no use being right. Hardly had I said this when Josef La Tour burst into tears. I heard the waiter mutter, understandable that a lush weeps, and confirm this with a popular aphorism. I myself was obliged to convince Josef that I hadn't meant it that way.

"Come on, Jef, it's just the philosophy of a fool. Let's go to the Salvador-keller."[2]

Jef's eyes. He laughed, such a good kid.

"Yes," he said, "but you've got to drink a glass of beer with me." I promised. I saw how Josef suffered because he thought I was lying to him. I never let myself go. Even when I was dead drunk. And I always remained an esthete. Full of literature. As if I could really mean it that I liked coffee on other occasions than breakfast.

Josef hated five o'clock tea. "I find five o'clock much too early to find a whore."

Such was Josef's fate. He was completely this way. He saw action in everything. That anyone could act passively lay outside his train of thought. He saw the need to intervene everywhere. That's why the theme of incubus and succubus was very dear to him. "There is a devil who persecutes me and every woman is this devil. He doesn't let go of me. I am always forced towards intoxication."

He also said, "Intoxication is unity for me. The only possibility of escaping stupor. I accept the succubus. I no longer wrestle. I am ridiculous when I wrestle."

A few times I have told him my opinion. "It is quite unclear to me that you can like beer that much, Josef."

"Your succubus is intellectualized," he said. "It is a cognac-and-coffee whore. My succubus is from a more ancient time. She has Breughelean airs. But my beer-guzzling is really endlessly great. That you can't understand."

Often there was silence between us. And then Josef drank.

"My life is determined by the stronger will of a mean punk of a devil."

Josef was married. His wife was a good soul. She was content if he came home normally drunk. But she loved Josef very much. She complained bitterly, "If Josef didn't drink like that, it wouldn't be so bad."

She didn't react very strongly. She had soothed herself with the atavistic fable that Josef had a dry liver like his father. There was more. Deep down she was content with Josef. She was jealous. Better that he drink than go to whores. And she was absolutely convinced that Josef didn't do that. He only drank beer. He went out to have some fun. There was nothing bad in that. Everyone has faults. She was content that Josef's fault was not a lack of love for her. And her bickering was therefore quite feeble since she feared that Josef would leave his quart to go to a woman. And *she* wasn't the woman.

Josef's life was simple to be sure, but not as his wife imagined it. He drank beer in order to go to the streetwalkers and when he came from the streetwalkers, beer to forget the streetwalkers. Nothing is so full of temptation as meanness, according to Josef. But as far as this was concerned, he had a holy terror regarding his wife. Both practically and theoretically. Practically, his wife was a good egg in her ignorance, her childlike trust that she possessed Josef just for herself. To destroy this would be incredible stupidity. Theoretically, if his wife knew of his adultery, it would no longer be adultery. His adultery was only conceivable as the pleasure of measureless cowardice: to deliberately betray that good egg who, believing in Josef's fidelity, had fallen asleep with the limp feeling of being a wreck and enduring the future. That was what he needed. The meaner the streetwalker, the better. To put it somewhat mystically, the stronger the sacrifice of good to evil.

Josef La Tour's life wasn't quite so simple as one would think after remarks such as, "a nice glass of beer and a good-looking woman." Josef saw himself much too clearly not to see the laughable aspect of this bourgeois-mystical marriage. At one point he would exaggerate his being a bourgeois, and then his mysticism. But in both cases he held on to the philosophy of beer. Until this ridiculous story put an end to it.

But that again wasn't the way it really was. Anatomists can prove that Josef La Tour was completely saturated with booze. The end was near. But the question still remains, was he completely saturated with booze because the end had to come *now*—or did the end come because he was totally saturated. This dilemma cannot be cleared up by an examination of Josef's rotten liver. What is certain is that Josef had reached the end. So much so that he had to cave in without bruise or crack. He became more and more dopey. I have to admit that I avoided his company. His dopiness became unbearable and incoherent. He raved against the bourgeois, his wife, etc., who thought that he drank because he had a dry liver. The causes lay somewhere else. He pointed at the old woman selling newspapers and said, "There is the devil's whore. I get plastered for her sake. She spurs me on to be nasty. Her pleasure and her satanic instruction is that I dirty myself on the stage of the world. In order to please her I am the most trivial bastard." Then he would rave again against the esthetes who saw eroticism everywhere, the idiots. He got soused in order to get plastered, and that was all. Beer and more beer was the only thing he looked for.

It came to a point where he couldn't untangle this duality. Soon he was mistaken more than once in his plea. So that a speech which started out being against the bourgeois ended with his views against the esthetes. Naturally, he never said that he chose the middle of the road. He was against one or the other, but got confused. When he noticed this in a moment of lucidity, he became infuriated and destroyed whatever came into his hands. He had beaten up the daughter of the boss of the Holy House who knew how to get along with the customers—at least that's what the boss said. She had kept on agreeing with Mr. La Tour, until he suddenly noticed his own drunken babbling and asked why she always agreed when, with two succeeding opinions, he had defended direct oppositions. The daughter had laughed about it and had even flattered Josef. "Well, you see Mr. La Tour, I don't know all those things as well as you do."

That had been too much for Josef. He had been debating the most incoherent drunkard's nonsense, and this lost whore, an hour too long out of the water, came, after having made him drunk as a skunk, to tell him that he was a clever one, all right. He got up slowly. Suspicious and quiet. Then, quick as lightning, he grabbed his chair and beat the girl over her head. He slammed her on a bench, smashed his fist in her nose. The blood streamed bumpily with irregular pauses in between. This had all been very quick. He solemnly wiped his hands clean on her little, very white panties and left. He gave the father money so he would let things be.

It rained, Josef came home. His wife had been in bed for a long time already. She opened her eyes and smiled drowsily in a good-natured way.

"Marianne, I love you so much. O Marianne, you don't know it. But I can't do anything, I am a dog and a slob."

"Get into bed quickly, husband." Marianne was radiant. "Why do you drink so much. It is so unhealthy."

He coughed. He looked into his handkerchief. He didn't know whether it was blood from the Holy House or a flake of blood from his own body.

He travelled to Brussels. A bracing feeling of criminality clung to him when he, poor Harlequin, let himself be dragged through the thick circular march along the Nieuwstraat and the Anspachlaan.[3] Sometimes he loved this city. Love which grew from the depth of the other pole. In the eye of God who does not know impurity, this city is a floating wreck of sin. It was a pleasure for Josef to feel that, with each step, he trod God under foot. With the same feet he had received from God. That's how he used a gift of God. He thought, "For twenty years I have served God in a retreat in the midst of mountains. And now I am destroying all the work. I chopped down the mighty Christ who stood in front of my retreat, and now I follow sin."

He went to the bars. He allowed himself the luxury of getting drunk on whiskey.[4] Women pranced by to show the beauty of their legs. They sang along with the songs or hummed. Their lives lay like an erotic ball. They measured each man by an erotic yardstick. Every man represented for them the possibility of either a dude or a pimp. They squeezed the dude dry and let themselves be squeezed dry by the pimps. "No béguine[5] anymore," they thought. A pimp danced. They would be caught until he threw them away like a squeezed-out lemon. The world turns around sex. That was the simplest formula for their concentration. The day was divided according to the erotic possibilities it offered. Josef sat like an astonished child in front of a box of toys.[6] He enjoyed himself by sharpening the contrasts. "Here they know how to live. I myself am drunk as a skunk. My mysticism has no other cause. These people know how to live, and I don't. I'll never be able to have both feet in one place. One foot is in Jerusalem and the other in Babel. Even more stupid—Jerusalem and Babel are the most idiotic sublimations of my fear and desire. I'll never be able to desire in a simple way. I sublimate the simple desire of these people. All my mystical dopiness is—let me tell it to myself clearly for a change—only pouring oil on the fire. These people are too strong for me. They can live without being troubled, desiring the only life there is."

While they were dancing the women lay like toys in the arms of pimps. The pimp pressed a button, movement. They wished to be nothing more. To be a toy in the hands of the pimp, that was to satisfy every desire. That's how they danced. They danced erotically, completely satisfied. They looked shyly at the pimp to see if he desired anything more. He laughed, Toreador. When he pushed a button, she left him. She looked for a dude.

She went up to Josef. It wasn't fun. But she had to work, after all. She sauntered past his table. She smiled innocently. If that guy would just say, here are a hundred francs. That's what it boiled down to, after all. The whole comedy which came before was such a drag. Now she had to ask for a cigarette again. And say, "Well, all alone tonight?"

It was a damned piece of shit.

Jef's face relaxed with lively greediness. She crossed one leg over the other, so the form lay ripe and naked. This leg played like a pendulum. How would she have to deal with him? There are those who want to hit, and others want to be hit. Jef waited. To be treated like a dude. Finally she would steal his last penny and flee to her pimp. She had to take everything from him, the golden wedding ring, too. When she had taken everything, she wasn't allowed to stay a second longer. Then she was supposed to say, "I am going to find my boyfriend." That's what Josef was thinking in his inverted greediness.

She became afraid. Josef put his watch on the table and said, "That's for your pimp." She laughed and giggled, but in a stupid way. She said, "I don't have a pimp. I'll give it to my father."

"So your father is a pimp," Josef grasped at the new possibility he wanted.

The whore remonstrated. Her father wasn't to know anything.

Josef kept on pushing for his flagellation, which wouldn't come.

"Why don't you tell me what the name of your pimp is?"

She evaded the answer. Maybe it was somebody from the police. They act in such a stupid way. And when they know everything, then they show their card, the bastards.

The conversation became dull. The whore dared not flee. The dance turned monotonously.

Jef pressed his eyes shut. When he opened them again, he laughed at his stupidity. This whore was the most middle-class tea time. Whores, pimps, and customers played together in a jovial convention. The boss was the most active at the convention. People understood each other marvelously here. The women stank of the bourgeoisie. He conjured up for himself the most stupid illusions. That these women would have an idea of the demonic. He crawled for a woman, and she became afraid of his crawling. The height of her demonism was to get into bed and collect 100 francs.

The woman was afraid when she saw him calm like that. She put the watch back on the table. Josef had only said that as a joke. Josef took it back. Of course he had meant it that way. To fill the evening. If she wouldn't hit, then she would be hit.

Then the whore saw Josef the silly bourgeois. But in her delusion she turned her stupidity around. "He's really stupid," she grumbled when she left.

"You love me, you love me, that's it." Josef realized the demonism he had sought fruitlessly in others.

"Idiot." The whore testily looked for another customer.

No one understood him.

He stretched out on the ground, put a whip in the whore's hand and begged. She didn't hit. Let the whip drop. Helped him up.

He took a woman and begged, betray me. She put her Madonna head in his lap.

His entire life was like this. He was sick of it. Rue St. Laurent used to satisfy him. At that time he had found a simple pleasure in being brutally exploited. He had put his briefcase on the nightstand. Such easy fetishism didn't help him anymore.

He stopped. Above him two arc-lamps. Next to him smiled a Negro in red.

Hey, Madrid. Have fun, dance, people are gay.

He went. There was a feast inside. Girls from fourteen to twenty, gigolos up to twenty-five. A cloud of cheap perfume. When it was time for the tango, the girls were more than naked, and their legs stood ready to break around the slim ankles. Billows swayed between puberty and desire. The girls hung like the beauty of broken flowers in the arms of the God-gigolo. Their arms over the back of the man hung light and pressing in the space, so cool and promising. There was an urge for complete destruction. One forgot that the place stank of cheap liquors, patchouli, and women. Josef sank down on a couch, happy. Here was the final goal. He was sitting next to a gigolo and his girl. Seventeen and fifteen. He paid for champagne. The gigolo moved over in order not to disturb things. Nothing happened. "He is a stupid cluck," said the girl. The gigolo had only condemnation for her. She was much too young, a silly goose.

But Josef said: "Sir, I want to buy your woman for this night. How much? Do you love each other?"

Then they had to embrace each other. She nestled, a small warm animal, in the arms of a pimp. He kissed her on the lips. She said, "We're going home, come. I want to stay with you today."

They danced.

When she was completely knocked out, the pimp threw her in Josef's arms.

"Thank you, thank you," murmured Josef gratefully.

He disappeared with the little Angèle, stuttering his thanks once more for his beautiful Christmas present.

He shoved Angèle into a carriage. "Now, I've got you." He spoke with difficulty. Hatred was so heavy in him that he had difficulty in finding his tongue. He wanted to say a lot at once. He had her now. He had paid her. He had even given his watch to the pimp.

"Angèle, Angèle."

He didn't know what was what. Then he hit her with both his fists in her face. She bled. He said: "Did I do that, my little darling," and broke into tears.

"Poor child." He kissed her blood away.

But in the hotel he was the first one again and swore at his sentimentality. "The whores have Van Eyck snouts[7] here." The little girl found the way. She laughed. "You piss me off. I love my man. You sure cough up the dough, though." "Say that again," begged Josef.

He went to sleep in the other bed. "I will not touch you, my little holy whore."

He didn't sleep. She slept quietly. That bothered him. Flat daylight was already coming into the room. He got up. He was an idiot. He had paid her, and he was leaving her alone. In her interrupted sleep she withstood him. It seemed to him as if he were raping a young girl. And with it the assurance of his victory, which he had bought. The tumbling morning had a smell of hay. The room was one piece of a broken man.

Around twelve Josef swayed across Brouckère Square. On the second floor of the Hulskamp he found a good place. He drank coffee and had a shot of brandy. It was a dog's life. Josef couldn't stand the sight of another beer. Activity in the city was tame. The trams clanged incessantly, that was all.

When he was outside again, Josef felt something in his pocket. It was the key of the hotel. When he passed the hotel, he would go inside for a minute. But Josef thought at the same time, if I don't go now, I won't go at all. That was clear to him. That was the small, stupid deed. He kept the key. Later on he even passed the hotel, didn't leave the key. He consoled himself, he would send it by mail.

He knew he would keep the key. His stupid deed cannot be explained. It was a beginning, it was the end, it was the beginning of the end. It was something of little importance which suddenly became enormous. It was the constant negation of himself. It became a grotesque with a tear, and it had at the same time a ridiculously tragic quality.

He hated Brussels. He was sick of Brussels. Patchouli city. Last night he had conquered his eroticism and broken himself. He didn't care anymore about the opposition between Madonnas and whores. Whores laughed goodnaturedly like Madonnas, and the latter answered completely to the famous Italian curse. All these contradictions, the content of his eroticism, were simply lies. Life was the most common banality.

But a sudden flash illumined a new contrast, where he gathered again the entire emptiness, the beginning of the end, that he didn't deserve the love of his wife. Everything could have been so good. Not any more. It was too late. He also hated his wife. She persecuted him with tenderness. Someday he was going to commit suicide to escape the persecution of that sugary voice.

In the train he felt an object between himself and the bench. It was the key. He thought, "As soon as I arrive I'll go to the post office." Which he didn't do.

His wife noticed the absence of his watch. Josef wanted to answer,

"My watch disappeared, but I've got the key to my infidelity in its place." The watch was a present from Marianne.

Marianne was full of love and devotion. Had he slept well and hadn't he drunk too much. And wasn't he very hungry now. He looked so tired.

Jef spoke. "Marianne, I have been unfaithful and how. With the most vulgar little whore from the Noordlaan,[8] and nice, nice. . . ."

Marianne laughed timidly. Jef laughed fearfully and said, "Come on Marianne, that was all bull."

"You sot." Marianne was radiant. She served him, and had he had enough.

If she found the key everything would be discovered. He wouldn't be able to lie. Furthermore, he would be tempted to tell her the plain truth. That he saw clearly. He would destroy her quiet dozing. Tomorrow he had to rid himself of the key. He would leave his wife at least her peace of mind.

He couldn't get rid of the key. I advised him simply to throw the key away. I knew he wouldn't do it. I received a note. Josef wrote me, "You advise me to throw the key away. I didn't think you were that foolish. It is after all as clear as glass that I can't do any such thing. Not able, you understand. I even tried it yesterday. I tell you, it was as if a strange hand held mine back. Half an hour later I threw the key away. I went back to find it. Thank God, I found it. I can do anything now. But if I throw this key away, I don't throw my remose away, I get myself into a new remorse. That I paid no attention to the godly powers and the Christian duality of body and soul. I can throw the body of the remorse away, but the soul (the Platonic idea of the remorse, if you want) I cannot get rid of. Even if I throw the key away my primitive remorse remains, and with it comes a second one, which is to have thrown away the object of my remorse, the recollection of my guilt. When one has sinned, it is not enough to say, I haven't sinned. To throw my key away is not a solution. I have to have the courage to carry this adulterous body further along in my marital life. But this isn't purification either. Purification occurs only through searching purposely for suffering. I hide the key from my wife. I am only afraid that she will find it. Penance is now breaking the final illusion of life, that is, Marianne's. That I don't dare. That is my fate in life. I would gladly hang myself. With best wishes, your Josef."

I received many notes. Writing is a calming thing for me, said Josef. He also wrote me:

*The only thing I have left to do in this life, is to destroy the happiness of my wife. Everybody knows I am a bastard. Only Marianne doesn't know it. I have to make this clear to her once and for all. My life on this earth makes no sense any longer. It does so only for Marianne. Because she lives with the hypostasis of me. I must say, "Marianne, I am not a good husband. I have slept with whores, and I have placed your portrait in the bed of adultery. I gave the prayer book belonging to your beloved mother to a whore in the Vesting Street." Marianne would not hate me. But I would become indifferent to her. She would look on life as being colorless and accept the days as a small burden which God gave her and which one has to bear until the end. I want to leave life. But I cannot do this as long as someone loves me. Not because I put value on this love. I only realize that I cannot burden my conscience with this new deceit. I have to disappear unnoticed. My death must be a matter of indifference to everybody.*

*As long as anyone loves me, I cannot leave life. She would be sad about my death. This would be the final deceit on my part. That I don't want. Everyone has to know that something useless has disappeared with me.*

*I want to disappear. As quickly as possible. That's why I have to break Marianne as quickly as possible. And again, for that I don't have the courage.*

*Drinking is nothing anymore. I no longer get drunk. The remorse is always there, the remorse for what is past. Josef, what has become of you. And then always this feeling, why don't you make an end of it. And yet I don't make an end of it.*

*I still have compassion for Marianne. And so many feelings which I can't describe. I am afraid that Marianne will find the hotel key. I hide it. I get up at night. I want to see whether Marianne really hasn't found it yet. I run through the rooms. Marianne asks what is going on. I want to beat her and don't do it.*

*I find that all cities are terribly ugly. I have been outside. Trees are terribly stupid things. They're only useful because I can eventually hang myself from one of those things.*

*I am sure I am going crazy. Imagine, I went to a doctor. This young man asserted that I had a liver illness. That isn't impossible. But it doesn't matter. I know what I have. I don't need to tell him. I have a very great remorse for my indifferent life and a very great indifference for my remorse. I really don't know why I feel remorse. Yet I do want to make an end of it. And in this way once and for all. If I wanted to, I could stop feeling remorse. I wouldn't have any. But why want something so stupid.*

*I say, I want to wreck Marianne's life before undertaking the great journey. Because I don't want anybody to think of me with pity. It's all the same to me, except this, that I don't want to be loved. This sad comedy has to have an end.*

*Why does Marianne love me. This feminine idiocy.  Jef.*

Some time later I met Marianne. She looked sickly. She told me, Jef had become so strange lately. He got up during the night. As if he were a sleepwalker. And he didn't go out anymore. What did all this mean. Jef was definitely ill. Once he had forced her to drink champagne because he had to tell a big secret. Then he said that he wouldn't tell it, he would rather take it to his grave. And that she, Marianne, had to square it with herself if she kept on thinking tenderly of him.

"He shouts constantly, 'Whoregoat.' He asks if I see horns. Once he grabbed me. He yelled, 'You know where the key is.' He is very sick, sir. You should visit him sometime."

Marianne had visited the grave of her child on a Sunday afternoon. It had died, two years old. She came home. A silent smile of contentment that she had planted flowers on the grave.

Josef was gruff. He said: "Sit down, Marianne."

Then he spoke:

"I know you found the key. I had it hidden in the mattress. It's all the same to me. This key is from Brussels. I slept there with a little whore and made her a present of my watch. Oh, Marianne, I have been unfaithful so many times. A huge notebook is not big enough to keep it all. I have slept with your niece, Marianne, that fourteen-year-old thing. There isn't a whore on the Keyserlei I haven't slept with. I don't feel sorry at all for having done so. But I feel remorse. Why, I don't know. I can't stand your being so full of pity. I gave your mother's prayer book to a streetwalker as a present. Her pimp sold it."

Marianne looked dumbfounded.

"Come, Marianne, let us drink champagne again tonight. Tomorrow I'll shoot myself. I am not myself. Impure devils play around my body."

"Husband, my sweet man, you are sick, you are sick."

The door slammed shut behind Josef. He heard Marianne call, "Please stay here, Josef." But he walked away quickly because he knew she would come after him.

The docks were very quiet. Here and there an electrical instrument played from a sailors' dive. Josef gave the key of the hotel to a trimmer. "That is a talisman."

He saw how the water played around the little boats. A secret and contented sound. A contentment full of darkness. In a dive on the Rouen quay he polished off a few. "That gives courage." The barmaid asked if he was going to stage a holdup, and if it came off would he buy her some underwear.

The wind from the river slapped the light up and down the gaslights. It took a long time before he found what he was looking for. There is really not much space on the docks. Not even there.

The next day boatsmen on board the *Vier Heemskinderen*[9] picked up the corpse of the aforementioned La Tour, Josef-Jan.

---

1. A brand name for a beer.
2. This drinking place and others mentioned in the story are or were dives in Brussels and in Antwerp. Van Ostaijen frequented some of them. De Hulstkamp, however, is a respectable café on the main boulevard (De Keyserlei) in Antwerp, where artists used to congregate, including Van Ostaijen and his friends. In this story, to cover his tracks, he places the café in Brussels.
3. These streets, with rue St. Laurent, form the very busy shopping center of Brussels. There is no worse place to be lonely than among shopping crowds.
4.Whiskey is an imported beverage in Europe, and therefore very expensive.
5. *Béguine* means a member of the religious organization of Beguines, generally a nun; and, in slang, a bigoted person.
6. In Dutch, *speeldoos*, which means either a box for toys or a music box, and, in slang, a safe.
7. A bitter irony. Jan van Eyck (?–1441), a Flemish painter, is famous for his impassive and serene portraits and for the triptych, "The Adoration of the Mystic Lamb." The juxtaposition of the devotionally sublime and the realistically disgusting is the basic theme of this story.
8.With Vestingstraat and Rouaanse Kaai, representative of the lower depths of Antwerp. Whore districts, dives and crime.
9. The name of the ship was deliberately chosen. It refers to a legend put into verse in the twelfth century, dealing with four brothers who have to flee after one of them, Reinout, kills the son of Charlemagne in a duel. A long feud ensues wherein the brothers are helped by a magician and by their enormous horse, which carries

all four of them into battle. They are betrayed by Reinout's father-in-law and disinherited by their own father, and wander as outcasts throughout the world. A reconciliation is finally brought about, but the sacrifice is the drowning of their horse in the Oise river. After having lived as a hermit and as a crusader in Palestine, Reinout returns to the Lowlands to become a simple workman, helping to build the St. Peter Cathedral in Cologne. His fellow workers murder him out of jealousy, but immediately after his death miracles occur around the corpse, and he is finally honored as a saint.

# Ika Loch's Brothel

After an effort as brief and easy as any other routine that gets established in a natural way, Madam Ika Loch became the head of a first-class brothel, a business which was soon operating on an awesome profit margin. This success, however, did not surprise Ika Loch in the least. She considered it so obvious that a business which she directed should flourish that, locked in her obviousness, she forgot to pay the dividends to her capitalistic cronies at the end of the fiscal year. Reminded of it, Ika Loch said, "Oh yes, of course." And while saying this she made such an artless gesture indicating the unimportance of her forgetfulness that her cronies found fault with themselves for having reminded the directress, rather brutally, of certain obligations.

Ika Loch had no fear of those laws which, in her function as directress, she had to subject herself to, but only a purely intellectual respect. It would never have occurred to her, for example, to violate the eight-hour work day of her personnel by imposing a personal schedule. She attached the greatest value to strict observance of mutual obligations. Since she was used to speaking in platitudes, she clarified her position with such comments as, "Render unto Caesar," "To each his own," and especially, "One must have law and order." By which she did not mean that she approved of the eight-hour work day from a sociopolitical point of view. No. She only meant that, as long as this law existed, it definitely had to be honored, or otherwise the transgression of the cause would determine the transgression of the effect and thus go miserably on *ad infinitum*, up to the decisive destruction of the essence and even the concept of right order. She might have said, "Right or wrong, it's my law."

This stated, I can now point out that the behavior of Ika Loch in her establishment was amazingly authoritarian. Now if anyone thinks this is only natural, it is probably because he associates this trait with the wrong object. Let me explain, therefore: the authoritarian behavior of Ika Loch was in the first place toward her clients—you might say, exclusively toward them. She was no more authoritarian with her staff than is commonly the case between employer and employee. But she was authoritarian with her clients, and since this certainly meant a break with the previously honored tradition of madams, whose sub-missiveness before their clients is proverbial, I can call this character-istic amazing indeed. By formulating this characteristic we touch the heart of the matter, Ika Loch's quick success. For that is precisely the strange consequence of the practical application of this characteristic. Instead of antagonizing and estranging the clients by her authoritar-ianism, the clever madam succeeded in having this strange character-istic (for her profession) appreciated as a rare quality.

From the moment she opened her establishment her behavior was authoritarian. Client enters the salon. Immediately Ika Loch appears and inspects the client—strange behavior for a madam, especially since Ika quizzes him about what he wants. She is finished with this examination in a jiffy. She declares, "I already know what you desire, Sir." If, despite this assurance, the gentleman tries to give her more precise specifications, she showers him—with words, naturally, Ika Loch is a madam—"Enough, sir, I know it. Do you think that I am without expertise and experience? Trust me: I know what the gentleman wants. What?—No, now make yourself comfortable and wait." And to the chambermaid, "Notify Mme. Anaïs." If Mme. Anaïs is there, Ika Loch does not give him enough time to make a decision. "Anaïs is darling, isn't she?" And then, in relation to her judgment of the client's taste, "She is slender—she is a beautiful woman—she is not beautiful, but she is interesting—she is perverse—she has small feet." When, following this plan, she has praised first the general virtues of the object, and then determined their specific compatability with the client, she concludes—she has been using this phrase for many years—"Elle est bien ce qu'il vous faut." With that the matter is, as far as she's concerned, finished. Then she bustles about while she gives orders, practical executions. "Room no. 10 for Mr. X and for Mr. Z, 27. For room no. 10, Burgundy, the real stuff. For 27, champ-agne, 2e zône." She spurs the indecisive personnel on, "Come on, Mme. Anaïs, you can certainly see what the gentleman wants," and she resolutely herds the couple to the stairs. If there is a momentary lull, Ika Loch takes advantage of it to congratulate herself quietly on her glibness.

At first the clients were not exactly pleased with this behavior of Ika Loch. They defended themselves. Some grumbled, others let it be known in an insulting way that the lady in question was not for them at all. More than once a gentleman left the establishment with threats, despite Ika Loch's attempts to stop him by holding on to his coattails. But she paid no attention to this and sincerely bemoaned those stupid clients who still, against their own best interests, stubbornly thought they knew.

This does not, however, exhaust the possible reactions. It also sometimes happened that Mr. X would be pleased with Ika Loch's recommendations and would disappear with some Anaïs or another. But when they were alone, he would discover that he was the one who had been fooled. Anaïs was not . . . *ce qu'il lui fallait*. And no matter what this good soul of an Anaïs might do to help Mr. X out of his gloomy sense of being victimized, it was all to no avail. Mr. X would complain bitterly to Ika Loch. But the Madam would stick to her guns. According to her the gentleman was too nervous today, he would do better to go home, since she would guarantee, naturally, that Mme. Anaïs, under ordinary circumstances, would definitely be something to the gentleman's liking. And in private to Anaïs, "My child, it's certain that you please this strange gentleman. If he seems dissatisfied it can only be ascribed to your feeble efforts to please him. I demand that you pay attention, so I won't have to spell this out again for you."

Soon Ika Loch had drawn up a diagram based on recurrent episodes, to identify the tastes of the most varied guests. This diagram was not subject to nuances, which was right up Ika Loch's authoritarian alley. Nevertheless, she did not construct her game of matchmaking so much on the popular principle that birds of a feather flock together, but on that of contradictions. And it often happened that she was not mistaken. This diagram, based on bare fact, led to the practical result that Ika Loch's success in identification barely exceeded the level of happy coincidence.

For instance, Ika Loch was convinced that a corpulent gentleman would find pleasure in a slender woman. And young girls, who had been in this occupation only a short time and who had not mastered it yet, were, according to her, cut to measure for elderly connoisseurs. She sent the heaviest women of her establishment to youthful clientelle. This had to be, she felt, correct. It had caused her much more trouble identifying the taste of slender gentlemen who, clean-shaven, secretively hid their age somewhere between twenty-five and forty-five. But she had quickly extricated herself from the dilemma by means of dictatorial decisions, partly by accepting the now- (for want of others) welcome popular wisdom of color contrast (blond and black), and partly by seeking the aid of psychic-cerebral-value-patterns, the latter on Ika Loch's axiom elevated to an hypothesis, that clean-shaven men, when not perverse, are at least refined. When I add to this that, according to Ika Loch's simplistic diagram, $P$ (perversion)$=R^3$ (refinement), it becomes understandable that, regarding perversity and refinement as a mere difference of degree, she thought she could fulfill the needs of her clients by means of prescribed subtleties which varied only slightly. It must be said, however, that Ika Loch, in order to arrive at this final conclusion, needed much less time than we do to reproduce this train of thought. With her everything went one-two-three-go, and actually three was a completely superfluous measure, so precise and definite appeared one and two to be. One and two represented, so to speak, the wise exercise of the school master in which all the boys, including the most stupid one, have to chime in with a spontaneously blurted out "three," to demonstrate the teaching ability of the schoolmaster. Polka was for Ika Loch the most beautiful dance.

Svelte women for corpulent gentlemen; ephebes, heavy women; girls just slipping from the shell for epicurean old gentlemen; and for the rest of the clients, that mass of men floating between twenty-five and forty-five, the erotic-cerebrally interesting ladies—this, in broad outline, was Madam Ika Loch's diagram—her work chart. Too bad that, to put it plainly, the objects to which the diagram was applied were not very pleased with it. Sometimes, in that fine brothel, no. 33, things degenerated into rough scenes of swearing and insults. Such as when a fat fellow once rejected the woman—"meted out" to him, if I may put it that way—his excuse being that in his capacity as bone merchant he had gorged himself to the point of being sick of seeing skeletons. Yet even ephebes showed themselves so rebellious that they maintained they preferred four hours of arrest to the company of the ladies screened by Ika Loch. One day a small revolution apparently took place among the clients of house no. 33. No one was satisfied. An old gentleman wanted the lady of an ephebe and the ephebe wanted the one of a fat sailor who, in turn, was madly in love with a lady with mahogany-red, short-cut hair, delegated by Ika Loch to a clean-shaven gentleman who, according to her diagram, she held to be refined, but who in reality was an instinctual elementary high-school teacher. Everybody left the brothel, furious.

By the next morning Ika Loch had already gotten over her dejection and was ready with a new scheme, almost an inversion of her former one, in which she had elevated to a standard norm her experience that a sailor had once shown himself more refined than a professor. Without any feelings of guilt she renounced her former scheme, with the confidence that she now possessed the philospher's stone of wise madams.

One day Ika Loch announced in a festive mood, "Promethea." This delicacy was intended for a sea captain deeply ensconced in an armchair, who, dead drunk but apparently still good-looking, stank of liquor seven miles to windward. Promethea! Barely and briefly her fingers touched the veil, lightly pushing it aside. That was all that was necessary. She was standing in front of the veil. She moved her body as if independent of it—a servant had put Promethea there and this servant was she herself. She stood in front of the veil of dull black silk, her body outwardly motionlessly, tensed in orange silk. Only the belly, up to just below the navel, was bare, but so flat was this belly that, tracing it, a thin pencil line could have marked its shadow. She betrayed no young girl's bashfulness, and no use of the science of courtesans. Her pink nails did not evoke any memory of nail polish. They were pink. The only jewelry she wore was a necklace of insignificant aquamarine—beautiful as a chance beetle on a leaf is beautiful—a harmony of barely shown things, the thin blue of the necklace on the pale amber of her throat. Sharp and exact weighed the necklace, throat against body. Her hair was ash blond, without a trace of the hair stylist. Her mouth was not wound sharp and it barely wore an indeterminable promise. It closed around a mystery of wordless concupiscence. Her slightly curved lines faded into the thin capacity of her thin bow legs. The burden of the small body was almost too heavy for them. The air around them too heavily charged, it seemed as if the legs, in a last effort, were for a moment still perfectly beautiful, before they sprung under the weight of these opposing energies. Only in her legs was effort visible, so sharp was the sicklecurve. But her body and her countenance were at ease, in perfect peace—Prometheus had removed her brains to form her completely perfect beauty. A supreme classicism, of the type which creates its idol from itself. So self-contained and mute was her beauty that motherhood did not touch her scant hips. From the point of view of fertility, already sexless. An end was she.

That Promethea was very beautiful, Ika Loch understood, but she lacked the sensuality to understand the superlative. An artist had dressed Promethea. A few times Ika Loch had wanted to indicate slight changes—she even wished to go over Promethea's lips with a lipstick. (Naturally she meant well but Ika Loch did not comprehend the relative value of lipstick. She never comprehended the relative value of anything. Whatever she had once decreed was in fact axiomatic, yet seemed to her true, as if proven.) Finally Ika Loch showed herself very pleased with Promethea. To be able to wear the dull black and the brilliant orange well was, according to her, Promethea's most outstanding feature.

Promethea's beauty could do nothing against the sea captain's limitations. He sat behind a thick wall of liquor, a priori determined to swear. Which he did as soon as Promethea had pushed the veil to one side. Her immobility, broken only by a forced laugh which escaped her, gave him an opportunity for easy criticism. She was stupid and affected, thought the sea captain. Ika Loch made Promethea turn on her toes, like a detached model. Just at this moment—her back was in profile, half turned toward the door, and the sea captain had trouble concentrating on a new series of swear words—someone threw the door of the salon open. A gentleman in a black coat entered, stood motionless for a moment as he and Promethea looked at each other, then conquered his hesitation with an heroic effort— already Promethea had fallen into his arms with a short cry of happiness. He fled with her up the stairs. The sea captain remained for a moment lost in his stifled rage. Perhaps the incident had moved him. Did he now see Promethea in her peerless, soulless beauty? Quickly he had Ika Loch by the throat. He would have strangled her if the unassigned personnel had not hastened to free her.

Ika Loch did not comprehend the connection very well. How come? Naturally it did not occur to her that she might have been mistaken. She found the happy way out by ascribing everything to the liquor. And as for the gentleman who had so masterfully carried Promethea off, he was probably a jockey. "It is a jockey," she said. She had thought "probably" a jockey, but while her words followed her thoughts, she took hold of herself again, realizing that the adverb damaged her rigorous system and said, therefore, "It is a jockey."

When three hours after this occurrence there was still no news from the jockey, Ika Loch decided to force the door, which had been locked from the inside.

Promethea's immobility in death was equal to her contained peace in life. The triangular wound rose through the abundant red as dark violet, matted and deep against the pale body and the sharp orange. The jockey must have disappeared long ago. Moreover, whether or not he was a jockey no one has ever been able to establish. He was a sex murderer, to be sure, but that is not a matter of social standing. The murder, however, was more than enough to shock Ika Loch. One certainly did not come to a brothel to commit murder, one came, as they put it, to amuse oneself. And what the police kept on referring to as a "sex" murder remained incomprehensible to her. She saw no connection between sex and murder. It took a long time before she understood. And even then her understanding was merely an admission of the term. The fact remained foreign to her. But later on she would use the term to designate what was foreign to her.

This masterly sex murder, defined purely negatively by Ika Loch, was wonderful advertising for brothel no. 33, which up until that time had been, if not disreputable, at least of dubious repute. In one day the opinion of the brothel's clients changed very much in favor of Ika Loch's knowledgeably directed bawdyhouse.

The change of opinion came about by a quite simple process. At first the brothel regulars had agreed that Ika Loch paid no attention to their desires and that the authoritarian behavior of the madam was intolerable. Since it appeared, on the other hand, that this behavior could not be crushed, the clients had gradually cut down on their visits to the establishment. Yet—and this gives us the first link to the inversely determined success of Ika Loch—not all of them had been very firm in their conviction. Therefore the brothel visitors soon let themselves be divided into two categories: those who flatly rejected the behavior of the authoritarian madam and those who began to believe that they, and not Ika Loch, were mistaken. The latter concluded that Ika Loch always seemed to make a mistake in their desires with such utter conviction that she must have very good reasons indeed. This was probably the case, yes, really already proven *ad absurdum* to be so, for if it was not the case, then the authoritarian behavior would be, from Ika Loch's point of view, simply suicide—

something which is contradictory to the nature of a madam. And finally, what did they, mere mortals, know about the mysterious flow of their sexual desires? What did they know about their subconscious, which—as has been known since the memorable discovery of psychoanalysis—manifests itself primarily in sleep and dreams. Had they ever controlled their dreams in order to unveil the essence of their subconscious? What did they really know about determining factors during their puberty? Ika Loch had definitely studied psychoanalysis. No one could question the fact that she had mastered Freud from *A* to *Z*. As a matter of fact, this was the reason for the authoritarian behavior and understandable feeling of superiorty on the part of the perfect student of Freud. Yes, even those who belonged to this second category were soon convinced that all madams should diligently study psychoanalysis, and they would not have been surprised to receive visiting cards announcing: "No. 33 has the most beautiful women. Directress: Ika Loch, Ph.D. and M.D."

Yet at first their enthusiasm remained purely theoretical. Energy— or pure accident as a surrogate—is always required to transform the theoretically gained point into practice. Being under pressure especially from those in the first category, they did not quite dare to return to house no. 33. But their viewpoint gained ground. No day passed without the first category losing a follower who admitted he was indeed not on sure footing in his subconscious and that Ika Loch's authoritarian behavior proved her expertise.

Then the sex murder occurred. Those who had gradually admitted their stupidity rejoiced at this unexpected proof. Indeed, refined people knew how to find Ika Loch's brothel. Even the sea captain became one of her noisiest defenders: Promethea had torn the gray web from his intoxication revealing the contrast of sharply glittering orange silk and her navel, painfully still with apparent peace. Already numerous, those who had subscribed to the second opinion found their way again to house no. 33. Through no fault of her own, Ika Loch now acted according to the principle of calculated tactics. She remained authoritarian, just because she happened to be that way. Only now with the result that her authoritarian behavior was immediately seen as superior knowledge. The clients had found their way again to no. 33, not hoping to feel at home immediately in such an orderly brothel where, with scientific knowledge, a choice was made, no, but as if they were undertaking a pilgrimage. They were quite satisfied when Ika Loch appeared not to be angry about their desertion, so they enjoyed her complete authority, and persisted—once alone with their designated lady—in seeking for their essential subconscious according to this problem: given the partner designated by Ika Loch, $X$, determine the value of $Z$. Ika Loch's authority guaranteed that the relation $X/Z$ was not based on a mistake, not even on an *erreur sentimentale*. But these gentlemen were clever enough not to give exact information to sceptics, who were becoming more and more rare. Perhaps they were already so convinced of the charms of the new life Ika Loch had unveiled for them—and this new life they proudly called the sexual-cerebral sex life—that with complete conviction and (correlative) wholeheartedness, they profited from this discovery. Ika Loch was right and they were wrong. There did remain a grain of scepticism in them, but she had made the visitors shy about confessing their scepticism, and when they did enter the house overcome with such scepticism, Ika Loch's authoritarian behavior was sufficient to disarm them.

What was the outcome of this turn of events? Now, as before, Ika Loch continued to not give the clients what they desired. But the clients had become wiser and called their own wishes superficial. They no longer attempted to practice their sexual preferences objectively. Let Ika Loch have her way—didn't she possess the key to the most secret of secrets? She kept on giving the ephebe a woman whom he never in his wildest fantasies would have sought out for sexual relations, and Anaïs remained reserved for the gentleman $X$. In other words, Ika Loch had managed to bring off this masterpiece; to eliminate the existing wish to smother passion in sex, and on the other hand to force upon them a wish which was not even superficial, but nonexistent. (It may be noted that various clients had no problems in being pleased with all of this, since they were already, so to speak, in a succubine relationship with women.) In short, even though no one could get around the fact that what he enjoyed—with Ika Loch as intermediary—did not by any means answer to the pleasure-image he retained from the past, he was forced to admit rationally that this madam offered the best one could humanly hope for and, furthermore as a result of this, to dismiss his former image of pleasure as an illusion of puberty.

Soon this brothel was considered to be a municipal curiosity. The scientifically correct brothel of Ika Loch.

It is clear to me from the above that Ika Loch's brothel has been defined only externally—in terms of reaction rather than action. This observation, which I hereby admit to, is valid. As an excuse, I dare to admit—which in any other case would be an unconditional admission of weakness—that, literally, it requires a superhuman strength to present Ika Loch in psychologically exact terms, that is to say, esoterically, known only and immediately by her own specificity, rather than by the indirect path in terms of the reactions of the out-side world. An apology may also be my intention—this tale had no other purpose but this one, to record a few naturalistic data. But I would nevertheless almost dare to declare that Ika Loch's essence can only be approached indirectly. Outside her realm of authority, she is so seldom in the foreground that, if the reaction did not exist as evidence of action, it could be assumed that she was only an illusion—as a madam, a sexual delusion.

That her essence was entirely cerebral could have had its cause in her youth. When Ika Loch was still very young (but no longer a virgin—her only sexual experience had been a passing joy behind a circus tent) she had had to submit to an operation of the genitalia: her ovaries had been removed. From this circumstance followed the present state of affairs, that she, a madam, did not have the slightest notion of sex—indeed, she simply could not understand the urge. Her knowledge was purely professional, she could not build a bridge from her personal experience to this purely professional knowledge. But since she could ascertain the existence of this urge in others, even in some objects which belonged to her establishment, she lived with it as a factor which you had to admit to in passing. The fact, however, that most of the whores were as crippled as she was made her strongly believe that the other ones were defective.

She was also nearsighted—rather detrimental to her profession. The human figure as a totality could not be concentrically a stimulus to her. She was forced, therefore, to record details one by one, collate them, and from her collation project an eccentric image. When inspecting women who offered themselves this could be very damag-ing, especially in the beginning. Ika Loch did the best she could. She forced her other senses to a fierce first aid. Her tactual sense served as a third eye. No matter how true it is that practice makes perfect, she could not master this deficiency. A head and a neck, as a totality, are still not the same thing as the sum of the two parts. Hence her authoritarian behavior was required to force some of her boarders on her clientele. For that matter, chance was always kind to Ika Loch. She had made unlucky chance into a chanceless norm.

Concerning questions of actual business management one can only say that Ika Loch possessed a real talent for organization. The furnishings of her brothel were smart, without extravagance. The rooms on the first floor were properly bourgeois. Those on the second floor were furnished more sparsely, though they were no less spic and span. Ika Loch would not allow her boarders to pin postcards on the wall indiscriminately. The distinction between the first and second floor was continued in every detail. The washstand in a room on the first floor was of porcelain, and on the second of enamel, usually white with not too garish little flowers. There was also a deluxe room, in light, expensive wood with dark intaglios, late Biedermeier, I believe. The washstand of this room was most certainly of exquisite quality, the earliest Marcolini-Meissen. A nightvase with a deep red rose. This room was reserved for important guests.

# The Lost House Key

**how it happens or didn't I tell you**

*The striving of the human spirit to perceive
everything coherently is so great that, when
one remembers a disconnected dream, the
incoherency is instinctively corrected.*
  —Jessen: *Versuch einer wissenschaftlichen
    Begründung der Psychologie.* Berlin, 1856.


**M**r. Hasdrubal[1] Paaltjes* was an inspector in the Department of
Bridges and Roads. Furthermore, he was widely esteemed as a
man. He lived in a city of half a million inhabitants. Which was why he
had the airs of a big city man, without his fame disappearing in the
struggling antheap of a city of a million. Men, and women without the
flame of love, worshipped Mr. Hasdrubal Paaltjes, because he was a
serious official with prospective retirement benefits. And also because he was a lovely person and because, without youthful passion,
he could still warmly participate in any discussion on politics, world
war, earthquakes, Turkish immorality, and art. But women who still
possessed the fire of love saw in Hasdrubal a robust man of forty and
did not doubt his powers of achievement. Many a young woman had
Hasdrubal's portrait directly over her bed or on her night stand.
Other women who had experienced bitter disillusionments in their
marriage managed to get their husbands to invite Mr. Paaltjes over.
That's how they too obtained an autographed photograph. During the
hours of the most bitter despair this photograph proved to be an
acceptable substitute. The husbands knew this. They felt, as long as it
stops with a photograph. Of course they didn't know whether it did
stop with a photograph. It was simply the pleasant interpretation of
something unpleasant. Only the woman knew how it stood with her
and Hasdrubal. Incubated reality, or merely an idyllic dream. The
women were not mistaken. They are indeed the x-rays discerning
masculine powers of achievement. Scientifically probably more correct. A woman is never wrong. And if she does make a mistake, she

---

*Some chronicles also speak of an Asdrubal Paaltjes. This Asdrubal Paaltjes is most
certainly identical with Hasdrubal Paaltjes. Most of the chroniclers, however, refer
to him as Hasdrubal. We deem it advisable to follow their orthography. What
probably happened was that a French typist who could not comprehend the difference between *A* and *H* made this faulty spelling current, as far as one can speak of
being current. (Author's note.)

says, how is it possible that I was mistaken! In this manner she combines both her disillusionments. And she says this of course in such a way that one can only think there is a defect in the psychophysical x-ray instrument. But in her heart is a deeper sadness.

No one in the city noticed that Hasdrubal Paaltjes became the pulse, the motor of the city. If only someone had noticed it then! How many evils would have been prevented! But such things are only noticed in the inevitable effect. And so someone writes later on: those misfortunes came to City X because Hasdrubal Paaltjes, that monster in human form, had become the motor, the pulse of that city. Ascertaining is a special joy, a kind of spiritual staining of oneself. From the rest of this tale it will become clear that what was involved here was no less a catastrophe than that of Babel or of Sodom.

The story goes as follows: Mr. Hasdrubal Paaltjes had been whooping it up with some friends. When he was soused and, with the help of a cabdriver, he finally had found his house, he couldn't find his house key anywhere. Inebriation is a sober condition. It is the condition of the sober balance. Yes and no keep on destroying themselves. Whether he really did lose his house key, no one has been able to prove either logically or mathematically. There are those who maintain that he didn't lose his house key, that he probably held this key in his hand, but that this small detail escaped him.* But most people find this a bottomless hypothesis. Those who hold the first opinion belong to the movement which they have called neopsychologism. Those who belong to the second movement deny the first the right to any scientific title whatsoever and call them mockingly the hyperbole-hypothesists, while they claim for themselves the name of ratio-realists. Some foolish readers, dying to hear the Paaltjes story, probably have little use for these digressions, which they may disparagingly call details. For their benefit we will point out that these two opinions have already provided the basis for an all-encompassing

---

*The accusation will be made against me: if the matter of whether or not Hasdrubal Paaltjes had lost his house key was never cleared up, why did I choose the title, "The Lost House Key"? The answer is that the opinion of the ratiorealists is the one which is generally accepted. It is approved by religion, state and society. The psychologists are considered to be tasteless eccentrics, cerebral knock-abouts, and unscientific fanatics. Their arguments are held to be obtusely speculative. We refer to them for the sake of inclusiveness. But the first opinion, however, the one of the ratiorealists, has cultural and historical value. Culture and society have unequivocally pronounced their judgment here.

cultural conflict. When we adduce statistical evidence that 209 women have murdered their husbands—the women were psychologists and could not bear any longer the slander of ratiorealistic husbands—we can already judge, to some degree, the importance of the conflict.

With or without his house key, Paaltjes could not get to his bed that night. In front of his house he delivered the following monologue (not textually, but according to popular tradition): Since, first of all, I squandered my money, secondly, discovered my home with the aid of a cabdriver and much effort, but in the third place cannot find my house key, I will have to introduce a positive element in my evolution at this point in order to preserve equilibrium. Since I am furthermore obliged to stay the night in a hotel, I don't see any reason why I should do so in an ascetic and egotistical fashion. I can coordinate these two conclusions by searching for the last whore, the only one who probably has not found a client yet, and share my bed with her. I find it idiotic to spend the night alone in a hotel. I think that sleeping by yourself is simply stupid and, furthermore, champagne has a strong erotic effect on my system. I pay homage to fate, which made me lose my house key. If it hadn't happened I might have forgotten that champagne is erotically stimulating.

In a mood of world weariness, Paaltjes found whoredom's last example. Good, old world weariness. (The reader is kindly requested to read this last sentence aloud, with full and broad intonation.) When Hasdrubal spoke to her, however, she began to flicker again. Doused with new spirit. Tomorrow, she thought, she would know how to lure new ones by saying, yesterday Hasdrubal, you know Hasdrubal Paaltjes, slept with me.

Yet she did hesitate for a moment when he spoke to her. A light. And gone. Paaltjes did notice it, but made no attempt to fathom it. That's life, so what do you want. Later he thought often, that's why she hesitated.

They had a beautiful night. Hasdrubal was content with having followed the champagne up to its last consequences. She was happy to possess Hasdrubal. She kept on saying: Hasdrubal, my Hasdrubal. Her voice a vanquished Lorelei. And Paaltjes was also content for the next few days. The escapade did not have any repercussions. He pondered.

One loses nothing by waiting. And a solid dose of syphilis should not manifest itself immediately. The name guarantees quality.

That's why the whore had hesitated to accept the light for a moment. Compunction or a scruple of conscience? Sure. Hasdrubal too. The glory of the city. The living poem. Like a thunderbolt, it was clear to her that this escapade would have great influence on the further development of the city. And it came to pass. As in the thunderbolt. Hasdrubal observed. Then a doctor. And then a professor. Finally the dean of the faculty. The lecture was spelled out for Hasdrubal. Very difficult cure. And especially a sexual diet.

Hasdrubal repeated the words. A sexual diet? That means a diet which is not sexual? Or what? What did they mean by this paradox? Vague, deep in dreams, he felt like a captured eagle. Torturers and hot awls in the eyes. Inquisition. Was that a sexual diet?

Hasdrubal understood: either keep a diet or commit suicide, this or that, but it was all the same. His fame. He never thought of a diet. He had to hold on to that fame. *Taureau ardent. Ardent torrent.*² Sure. Women who had read books about cowboys and Indians called him that behind his back. It wasn't just giving up his fame. It also meant making himself shamefully ridiculous. He had obligations to himself.

That's the way things were. He was Hasdrubal.

The diet proved to be impossible.

Come what may. Such was Paaltjes' fatalistic concluding sentence. And he acted quite normal. What for him, Paaltjes, was quite normal.

Once on the path to perdition it is difficult to turn around. Paaltjes was on the road to perdition. And now he even began to help many other people down this path to perdition.

First a few women got on the path to perdition because of Paaltjes. Which is really nothing extraordinary.

One fact is indisputable: the women had an unlimited faith in Paaltjes. They didn't check. Precisely—this is weakness. Why not be objective? A state-like organization such as, for example, tariffs, cattle control, control of foreign import. Because of that, all the women in Paaltjes' city carried its consequences.

The specialists' bell rang all the time. By doubling their fee, these specialists thought they were doing a good deed. As well as giving practical warning. Think about it, because it costs this much when you don't think about it. The women would be more careful. However, it was just a drop in the bucket.

Gradually the caravan of men began to move too. Because the

women who had loved Hasdrubal were in the know. Conflagration of love. Not a little fire. And Hasdrubal was worth ten others. If Hasdrubal broke down, they had to balance quality by quantity. And so the parade of men became endless. Finally this multiplication by ten sufficed to lead those women who had not been with Hasdrubal onto the same path as his loves.

And so the waiting rooms of the specialists proved to be worthless. They accommodated the honorable clientele in the diningroom, the bedroom, in the kitchen. The clients formed long lines in the street. No street cars or other type of vehicle were able to move in the streets where these specialists lived. It was finally necessary to build hangars where the clients could stay overnight without losing their place in line. These places in line became a usurious business. The unemployed stood in line and reserved a place for the rich. The city and the state levied taxes as on markets and fish-auctions. A good idea. Restored the shaken finances of city and state. Folding chairs were sold like shrimp. Countesses employed Kaffirs for the purpose of carrying their lace upholstered litters. They brought refinement to the new situation. A new fashion. Gambling casinos were opened in the neighborhood. A new industry flourished—litters, mobile casinos, mobile libraries, mobile bureaus. Eccentric ladies even dared come out with mobile bedrooms. The streets smelled of perfume. Literature too. The secret of the mobile casino. Such a situation could not fail to worry the heads of state, the guardians of the citizens' well-being. In parliament the question was brought to the fore. Too late, was the opinion of the Right and Center. This interpolation is an assault on the freedom of man, was the judgment of the Left. Everything is pigeonholed in advance. Perhaps this is an excellent thing. In any case, it is pleasant. The jovial life.

The discussion degenerated into a purely political conflict. The Right called city X a danger to the state. Measures to isolate the city were called for. The Left made lots of noise. Yelled: morality and Papists' force. The leader of the Social Democrats gave a lecture about human rights. An ethicist argued that one should cure mankind by good deeds and good examples. But not evil against evil. No ethical homeopathy, gentlemen. One should show these erring people the a priori superiority of the good. The Right answered with a well-rehearsed *a cappella, libera nos, Domine.*[3]

The Right takes the trick of course. The Right always takes the trick. This is tradition. That this is necessary can be proven *ad absurdum*. Just imagine for a moment that the Left takes the trick. Yes, the Left. You laugh. You see, that would look like a censured film. And so the Right was triumphant. Finally the Socialists accepted the Right's proposal, with the understanding that the Right had to promise that the problem of a law for child and female labor would eventually be considered, to be studied in the central collegium of their party as soon as convenient.

City X became a free city. A clear term—what is important is the correct criteria for interpretating it. Everybody can discuss the fate of a free city. Except the inhabitants of a free city. That is precisely the reason why the name free city is chosen. When a characteristic absolutely does not exist, the word which expresses this characteristic is repeated a hundred times in order to convince others and to convince oneself. The creating word balances that which doesn't exist. A polarity.

Within moments this free city was granted unequaled infamy. She provided the fuel for the most important debates in every city on both continents. Yes, even in every village and hamlet. No wonder the newspapers thought that there was big business in getting as much news as possible out of the new free city. War, sports, politics and obituaries—everything was overshadowed by the new column, "Life in the Free City of X." Psychological works appeared. And three-penny serials. Everything X. There were ads: Journalist needed— only those who can write up life in the Free City of X using short telegrams will be considered. Or: Publisher is interested in all manuscripts concerning the Free City of X. A new movement appeared in all the arts, which was sometimes called neofantastic-naturalism, because it tried once again to present scenes from nature, but only those which were more a cerebral continuation of empirical experience than the plain notation of optical illusion. But in general this artistic movement was called X-ionism and was strongly attacked by the conservatives of all nations. It was simply the attempt to represent the City of X, unknown to most artists, realistically with the aid of fantasy. The conservatives could not understand that people who lay claim to good taste and to comprehending the esthetic idea, let themselves be fascinated by such a theme, even misled. It is the debacle of art, they said.

Every newspaper sent its correspondent, the large ones several correspondents, to the City of X. Most of the nations of Europe, Asia, and America thought it their duty to close their borders to the returning journalists. Soon only bankrupt people, discovered card sharps, and other persons from the free occupations were hired as journalists. They bound themselves never to return to their homeland. For which they received very nice bonuses.

More people fled to X than to any other city. Just think for a moment, so many unfortunates found a home there where they were no longer the outcasts of society but instead the healthy norm. The few (according to our notions) healthy people who still lived in the free city were naturally soon marked as scurvy sheep by the larger majority.

From America special ocean steamers left full of emigrants. The Japanese requisitioned the Trans-Siberian Railroad. Soon the City of X was called Megalopolis.

The City of Megalopolis flourished with an entirely new life. The superpowers did manage to isolate Megalopolis, but further interference in internal politics of the city soon appeared to be out of the question. For that matter, after the superpowers and neighbouring nations had carried on like mad against Megalopolis, inspired by an urge to destroy without mercy, an idea—launched by the United States—suddenly won general acceptance. That the city should be conceived of as a receptacle for those elements which in other cities and nations were considered to be dangerous to the state. The American proposition read: Instead of destroying Megalopolis, we should contribute much more to the growth of the city. The Supreme Court came to the conclusion that Megalopolis had to be isolated and that the foreign affairs of this city had to be put under the control of the great powers, but that, internally, a free political system should be left to the Megalopoleans. Economical assistance to the city was acceptable, because it could be used as an external prophylactic—the existence of the city disposed of veneral diseases by concentrating the carriers of the disease. And so it came to pass that after a short crisis Megalopolis flourished with an entirely new life. All opinions were the result of a totally changed way of life. One cannot say that these opinions were completely new. They simply came from the opposition and were, therefore, in terms of absolute reality, as old as the other opinions, since no pole exists without its opposite. But as

manifestations they were at least antipodal to our generally current
opinions. Especially ethics. One can consider this ethical turnabout as
the decisive factor. It is essential. All the other inverted views of the
Megalopoleans can be traced back to it.

A cult of fetishism to honor the great among one's compatriots or
fellow citizens is a characteristic which every people and every city
has made its goal and glory. And the Megalopoleans were no different.
They simply had a different set of values. Is it wrong to establish the
tree of good and evil as the beginning of the human differentiation of
values, at least the tree of a certain good and a certain evil? Shouldn't
good and evil be considered abstract poles with a constantly changing
concrete interpretation according to milieu, peoples, and individuals?
Hence good and evil simply as a symbolic representation of pole and
opposite pole. Our concrete Judeo-Christian interpretation of good
and evil has probably placed the abstract recognition of this supra-
polarity in the shadow.

Megalopolis knew no less a hero-worship than other cities. Only
the heroes were different—not in person but in principal, i.e.,
measured according to a different ethics. For example, it is un-
imaginable that the archbishops of Paris, Cologne, and Mechelen
would ever have the faintest idea of presenting Hasdrubal Paaltjes as
a local blessedness, not to mention desiring his canonization. The
Megalopoleans were totally different. Even during his lifetime
Hasdrubal Paaltjes knew the veneration which befalls great men.
Neither bishop nor king, but much more than that. Whenever
Paaltjes spoke, others were silent, and whenever he was silent, they
were silent too, so much did even his silence impress. When children
were born they were brought to Paaltjes to be christened. He
fondled them and said, hold in your heart pure and faithful the mores
of Megalopolis. A monumental statue, something like the statue for
the Battle of the Nations in Leipzig, was erected on the occasion of his
sixtieth birthday. It was a piece of work from the school of the only
real X-ionists. They had abandoned the ancient symbols, Phidias as
well as Archipenko,[4] in order to force the contemporary life of
Megalopolis to the height of a new mythology. On the pedestal were
four bas-reliefs. One of these four depicted Hasdrubal Paaltjes losing
his house key. Underneath was inscribed, "Birth of Megalopolis."
Another was entitled, "Development of Megalopolis." This bas-relief
was divided into several squares: the procession in the streets in front

of the houses of the specialists, the Trans-Siberian Railroad, the overseas service, and a panorama of the free city of Megalopolis. The
structure of this division was formed by a key. On the third and
fourth bas-reliefs were textual mementos and beneath were inscribed, "Know thyself," and "Unto thine own self be true." Which
speaks for the ethics of the Megalopoleans.

The streets in Megalopolis were named, Key Street, Lost Key
Street, Hasdrubal Paaltjes' Key Street. The square in front of city hall
was called Lost Key Square. Later one simply said, Key Avenue or
Street, number so and so. Finally the word "Key" completely dis-
placed the adjunct "Avenue." The Megalopoleans had made their way
of life into a quintessential myth. The great road—to lift everyday life
to the level of eternal symbols. And Megalopolis took this great road.
A myth was never as logical and natural as this one. Megalopolis was
an ethical unity. It can be said that we ourselves sadly lack such unity.
A concentrated myth, an ethic which each Megalopolean had in his pith
and marrow and of which the social, political, and artistic life were the
specific consequences.

Let us take marriage as an example for a moment. Here we can
already note the strongest antithesis between the Megalopoleans and
our civilization. Everyone among us acknowledges that marriage as it
is at the present time is immoral, at least in a large percentage of
concrete instances. And yet this institution remains. A presupposed
principle is quickly forgotten in marriage when other advantages
appear. Here and there one still sees an old evangelical king who
opposes his children marrying Catholic royalty. His conviction disappears when good opportunities announce themselves. Everyone
criticizes such an attitude. With reservations—everyone finds plausible reasons for doing the same thing when he is offered the opportunity. Which produces a complete rupture between ethics and social
habit. Megalopolis is totally different. If someone postulated his future
in-laws, he had to present immediately a medical certificate, proof
that he, as an inhabitant of Megalopolis, was no exception. Anyone
who could not present such a certificate was immediately shown the
door. He was considered a scurvy sheep, someone who betrayed the
entrenched habits and honored morals of Megalopolis. Not only the
parents, but also the children acted that way. That's how deep this
way of life had struck root in Megalopolis. In our culture we often see
a girl defend her lover against her parents, even get her way, if

necessary with a drastic argument. No such thing in Megalopolis. The first thing the girls asked for when they liked someone was his medical certificate. If he couldn't prove himself to be in the usual condition of Megalopolis, then there was a block against the possible development of her liking him, or what is called loving. Most girls hated such a man. Women are by nature conservative. And young girls are romantic into the bargain. And thus the girls had to hate such an uprooted man with the blaze of a romantic conservatism. Women of a riper age simply pitied him—although an inhabitant of Megalopolis, he was in reality without foothold, a poor creature who lived in Megalopolis without understanding the ethos of the city.

Of course no physician in Megalopolis ever thought of attacking the disease preventively. One individual who tried it was lynched by the women. The physicians had simply found a quick way to make the disease bearable. Necessity creates the means.

An American philosopher once said about Megalopolis: immoral because of consequences, this city has again become moral. On the one hand the Megalopoleans were glad that their morality had to be acknowledged. But then they could not understand that it was reduced to a consistent immorality. They laughed at the childish philosophy of the American.

It was an axiom in Megalopolis that the population had to be increased through immigration. So many homeless people were still wandering around the world. They constituted an inexhaustible source for Megalopolis. They also knew that entire tribes of Negroes belonged to them. To concentrate all these people in a happy fatherland was the dream of the true patriots of Megalopolis. This did not mean that procreation was ruled out. But anyone who was past child bearing was considered a real paroxysm in Megalopolis.

The Megalopoleans were a peaceful people. Only a few who were fanatics about their way of life dreamed of wiping out the old way with the aid of the Negro tribes. They formed the extreme Right in Megalopolis and even their opponents had to admit that they had an idealistic point of view. But the others felt that the new doctrine could be spread in the world by peaceful means. They called the Right, "Apostles who had lost their calling." Megalopolis was in danger with all this pacifism, as long as the free city was dependent upon its neighbours. Not with a piece of bread, but it had to do with higher goods. Two ways of life. And the time was not ripe to press the matter as the Christians had in the time of the catacombs.

Megalopolis was created in the distant past. Precisely around the myth or the reality of this creation developed now the most difficult problems. Sceptics felt that one could never get any further than a paraphase of the hypothesis. Proofs. God help us.

We already mentioned the friction between the psychologists and ratiorealists. The latter's opinion was shared by eighty out of a hundred people. There was also a third group: the nominalists. They adhered to the belief that Hasdrubal Paaltjes was a mythological figure. The lost house key symbolized a family (in the ramification which was now the thoroughly healthy norm in Megalopolis) which had fled to Megalopolis as the result of a banishment. The lost house key was nothing more than the mythological representation of the fact that it was impossible to return to the fatherland. The head of this family had rapidly gained prestige and influence in Megalopolis. The followers of the nominalistic belief could be counted. The true Megalopoleans not only mocked them, but also hated them. Decadent and uprooted, they said. Some fathers declared that they were Belials who wanted to undermine the ethical unity of the people.

Once someone who defended the nominalistic standpoint was accidentally appointed as a professor. The students—the kernel and the hope of the nation—stripped him and dragged him through the city with a team of horses. The nominalists were never entertained in the better circles, an honor which did befall a psychologist once in a while, even though it was only to mock him. The situation of the nominalists seemed very vaguely like that of the Jews in our society. But the greatest rivalry existed between the two major groups. The psychologists pretended to be the gourmets of the truth. The realists were undoubtedly in strong numerical superiority. The university professors, the nobility and the lords, the farmers and the day-laborers from the areas surrounding the free city were realists. The artists, a few Jewish bankers, the ladies from the various social levels who are called *mondes*, the wives of university professors and of the middle classes were psychologists. For both of the latter categories the erotic interest was a matter of concern. That is to say, many realists, for example, the professors, were impotent. And the middle classes allowed love only a small portion of life, something like from ten o'clock to five past ten. And so the wives of the university professors made an erotic compromise with the Jewish bankers. And a Platonic one, as a matter of course. They knew pleasant hours, while the professor sweated his energy away on a new book against the psychologists.

One can easily summarize the doctrine of the psychologists. Starting with Hasdrubal Paaltjes' individuality, it is easy to show that it is impossible to maintain that Hasdrubal had *accidentally* lost his house key or perhaps had. been unable to find it. The reason is clear. Hasdrubal was much too careful a person to handle house keys in such a fashion. Paaltjes had to be drunk, was their axiomatic assumption. And then it follows very clearly that he had not lost his keys, but had not been able to find them in his drunken condition. And, for that matter, said the psychologists, those discussions about the local history of Paaltjes' house key are ultimately useless. Not history, but the psychology or, even better, the immediate consciousness is of importance. You have to gauge the causal relationship between the outward manifestation, which becomes history, and the inner psychological necessity. And this necessity *is*. It only remains to investigate the kind of psychological mechanism. For example, it can be assumed and then deduced that Paaltjes had a creative or formative relationship to the idea of the nation. The losing of his house key is the ultimate incentive to creativity in Paaltjes' passion to form the state. Or something like that. The loss of the key is ultimately fated, without psychological value. Value has subjective necessity in contrast to this story, which is like effect versus cause in comparison.

The realists laughed about such a doctrine. Why would Paaltjes have been drunk? Of course chance did not play a role in the loss of his key. That was their opinion, too. But nothing in all this demonstrates such development. It is childish to start with the assumption of axiomatic drunkenness, based only on the empirical experience of a detail. It is absurd and adolescent. And then this psychological nitpicking with a new conclusion, inspired by empirical experience, that drunkards do not find their keys, so Hasdrubal Paaltjes did not find his key, either.

That is pure nonsense or dilettantish philosophy. Hold on to what is most elementary: Paaltjes could not reach his bed because he had lost his house key. That's the way it is written down in a naturalistic manner in the charter and that's the way it was. The charter, however, was too close to the event to trouble itself with the causes of the loss of the key. Something like that is to be regretted. But watch out: frequently one sinks into the speculative when researching such causes. The cause is probably very simple. The realists readily admit that. But various simple causes are possible. That so many Mega-lopoleans are redheads might possibly be associated with the fact that Paaltjes had forgotten his keys when closing a mahogany desk. The realists kept on searching very carefully in this direction in order to come up with an indestructible argument. And then the psychologists exploded it again—they also called this being speculative. But most of the realists were almost insanely convinced of the mahogany truth, though it was, in reality, nothing more than a cerebral game.

But the realists! A realistic philosopher of art had written a very strange book. He pointed out that all artists from Megalopolis had a preference for red, flaming red, as in mahogany, for fiery red. The realists see mahogany everywhere, said the opponents, so they could use this too for an argument. Such irony was naturally very welcome with the women and the revolutionary students.

The realists had to admit that the story as it was presented in the charter did not penetrate the ultimate reasons. There was a very dangerous gap. For speaking in ultimate terms, Megalopolis lacked the foundation on which the generally valid and distinct development of the Megalopolis-ethos could be built. The psychologists said, Why don't you admit that he was soused and leave it at that? The psycholo-gists proposed inebriation as a genetic postulate.

And thus there arose yet another nuance, realists who admitted that Paaltjes had been drunk, but stuck to the *losing* of the key.

In this connection, one final thing needs to be noted, a battle between a realist and a psychologist. It was ended when the psycholo-gist smashed a mahogany nightstand to splinters on the head of his opponent in the debate. The gesture of the incensed debater was so violent that, after a few moments, nothing was left of the opponent but a little heap of philosopher brains in the midst of woodsplinters and porcelain shards. But the realists obtained new proof to provide grist for their mill. Didn't this murder, committed by someone who had very consciously taken a position against the ratiorealists, clearly point once more to mahogany? Didn't his entire subconscious exist-ence pressure the psychologist at this point to a confession? And with his psychological weapons?

The philosopher committed suicide in his cell. He felt the blow all too well. And with this blow the views of the ratiorealists took giant steps forward in the public's opinion. And gradually the lost house key held out its hand to the mahogany desk. In a manner of speaking, as one is wont to write.

---

1. There are four historical Hasdrubals, all Carthaginians. It would seem, however, that Van Ostaijen had the first one in mind. He was the son-in-law of Hamilcar and the brother-in-law of Hannibal. He greatly extended Carthage's influence in Spain and founded the city of Carthago Nova, present day Cartagena.
2. An example of sound association. The French phrases mean "ardent bull" and "ardent stream."
3. Church music without instrumental accompaniment. The politicians in the story sing the hymn, "Deliver us, O Lord."
4. Van Ostaijen ironically conjoins the master of classical Greek sculpture and a radical innovator of twentieth-century sculpture.

# Portrait of a Young Maecenas

There are many Maecenases.[1] That's why one has to specialize. Portrait of a young Maecenas: by a young Maecenas I mean someone who possesses the untouched core of a Maecenas (and the latter is a well-known figure), but who has not yet added the stereotyped elaborations of the older Maecenas to this core. The common causes of the condition are material want or an as yet uncured romanticism. The most common cause, however, is a combination of these two. Material want necessitates the incurability of the romanticism. One is psychologically according to what is physically necessary. This romanticism is very serious. Serious as a matter of course. The temptation of the holy St. Anthony is also very serious. Shadow from light. Eroticism is really merely the shadow of light, asceticism. Well and good, I am understood. Why shouldn't I be, for that matter? I can't find a single reason why anybody should not understand me.

Teas in the afternoon or evening are a regular attraction for artists when they don't have the money to see acrobats. That's where the young Maecenas appears. Precisely because he has these two characteristics. An old Maecenas buys and does not appear. A young man from the same milieu as the young Maecenas does not appear either, because he is merely a young man. One has to have the two characteristics. That is clear. And then the appearance of the young Maecenas is also clear.

His entrance is conspicuous. That could be because it is absolutely not conspicuous. Who knows. It is wrong to affirm such a thing without elaboration. It is correct to say that his entrance is extraordinarily conspicuous because it brings the normal inconspicuousness of said person into relief. He is torn. He immediately faces a choice: Who is the most enviable man, he with an empty or he with a full stomach?

People with empty stomachs are either extraordinarily tame or extraordinarily wild and jaunty. It has been said that Roman emperors starved the wild animals before sending them into the arena. Art critics resemble Roman emperors quite a bit. They argue, for example, that for certain artists hunger is an essential creative factor. Perhaps they are right. Artists, however, couldn't possibly admit that they are right. What would become of the world (the artist) if they had to admit that critics were right? The bourgeoisie has, by way of the critics (or who knows, perhaps by animal instinct), inherited the teachings of the Roman emperors. That's why many artists starve. Because society wants to preserve their creative powers. It is therefore wrong to believe that society does not worry about artists. On the contrary. It even goes so far as to accept the sad necessity of a negative role in order to make room for the creative force to develop.

Hence the entrance of artists is either extraordinarily tame or extraordinarily jaunty. One should not be fooled by this jauntiness. The jaunty ones starve just as much as the tame. The jaunty ones make good use of their characteristic by throwing themselves with the same jauntiness (always consistent) discreetly (!!!) at the few cakes. The tame ones are caught by surprise. Discreetly means that the tame ones leave the business to the jaunty ones. Individuality must be preserved. The tame ones leave the company regretting that they could not have enjoyed themselves a little bit more. And their remorse tames them even more. The jaunty ones are happy because they have been of consequence. And this realization of the rigid line in their lives makes them even more jaunty. They no longer cease being jaunty. They are in a café with the same jauntiness and with a tame one who pays for their coffee. And so on. Those people who can be categorized, are so according to a very easily discovered mechanism. Jauntiness breeds jauntiness. Tameness, tameness. A chronometer is a chronometer and a Swiss watch is a Swiss watch. The entrance of the Maecenas is very jaunty. Not as aesthetically jaunty as the artists' (the jaunty ones) but still simply jaunty. One notices immediately the difference between the two kinds of jauntiness. The young Maecenas is jaunty from self-knowledge. The young Maecenas knows that he is on that level where he is invulnerable. The young Maecenas is propelled by an instinctive knowledge of his kinship to Achilles.

His jauntiness is not a mask. It is a very real existence. It has its goal in his life. That is a lot. In comparison the jauntiness of the aesthetes vanishes. Poor Pagliaccios!

But the Maecenas is good. He furthers tradition. Wealth must marry the good in order to be beautiful. The Maecenas wants to be beautiful. To be good is therefore a necessity in this case. Goodness expresses itself in expansive gestures. One must know the expansive gestures.

That's why the young Maecenas has expansive gestures. Even a blind man can see that. He vigorously shakes hands with the artists. His handshake says: "You don't need to thank me for the last canvas I bought. That piece of business was settled long ago." He then laughs very kindly.

He himself is aware that he cannot pay enough for the enjoyment of enjoying art. For one cannot really pay for art, says he. (That's why he says when he buys a painting, "Don't forget, at the price a friend pays." Which has the double advantage of friendship and economy. For friendship must be based on the healthy foundation of economics.) Immediately he offers cigarettes. In this manner, very reasonably, he immediately knows how to attract attention. If one refuses, he persists until one accepts. He has never doubted that artists can only refuse because they are timid.

Sometimes he discovers an artist who is too timid. In such a case he relinquishes his principles. "We who are not artists have the duty to take care of the lives of artists. What greatness can we provide in this life? The greatest thing we can do is to make the life of the greats agreeable. That is our duty. So take this cigarette."

If begun in this way, his evening is happiness. He becomes very romantic. When he has money he will build villas and studios for everybody. Underlining his heavenly voice with a sombre note. He clearly feels that he is nothing. There are thousands of people who make money. But an original artist is unique. What is he in comparison with an artist. Suddenly he also feels an enormous guilt. To own the paintings. He has only paid so much. He really owes the artist tens of thousands. And that is only a minimal sum. For art cannot be paid for. (The same basis serves him also when he pays 100. Whether one pays 100 or 10,000 it's exactly the same. It remains, practically speaking, just as far removed from the absolute value of any art.)

To think this way makes him even happier. The others buy or support and think their duty finished. He understands art because he feels eternally in debt. The others buy art the way they buy fat and candy. Not he. Oh, certainly not he. He knows art. Confidentially he informs me, "I know my guilt. The others think their debt is paid with a few coins. Idiots! As if one could pay for art! And it is for this reason that ultimately I am still satisfied. That I at least know that this debt can't be repaid. In this way I distinguish myself from those hundreds of Jews who support art. I have a feeling for art because I am not a Jew." A voluptuous expression adorns his face. To admit his guilt is like a tender coitus for him. That's why he wants to remain eternally in debt to the artists, in order to preserve this coitus.

---

1. Although the date of origin is not known, I would venture to suggest that "Portrait of a Young Maecenas" was written during Van Ostaijen's Berlin years. The theme of financial support must have been close to his heart during those destitute years in the German capital. Another clue is suggested by *Bankruptcy Jazz*, in which the name of Garbaty is mentioned. A very rich cigarette manufacturer, he bought up works of art for a song during those years of extreme poverty.

# The Prison in Heaven

Once upon a time there was a man who had spent twenty years in jail. This man had adapted himself so well to his prison existence that on the day he was set free he left the prison with what can be called a heavy heart. He had been subjected to the regimen of the great criminals. White and red striped clothing, linen visor, and chains on his legs with weights, exactly the way one sees it pictured clearly on the screen.

This man did his utmost to acclimate himself to his new existence. That wasn't at all as easy as pie. On the contrary. The man let himself be told several times that he was free, apparently without being particularly impressed by this affirmation. He did say that he found freedom to be very beautiful, but his intonation was then exceptionally sad. He liked best to go to the bureau for "comfort of released prisoners." There he felt himself at least a little bit at home. He had to stand in line and was properly yelled at. With a little imagination, he could see in the noble ladies who were in charge of the work his former prison warders. These ladies just couldn't understand why no. 200, now such-and-such, smiled in such a friendly way at them. Magnanimity is rewarded, they thought. They were very simple, religious ladies from the best families. Since they held mirrors to be a tool of evil, it did not occur to any of them that they bore a physiognomical resemblance to the prison bosses. And since they were magnanimous, it also did not occur to them that their work, as epilogue, strikingly conformed to that of the prison.

To lose all the habits of his former life, which he recalled not without great melancholy, became too much for no. 200. First and foremost he bought himself a green eyeshade for his eyes. He thus imitated as best he could his prison visor from the good old days. His greatest joy was the public swimming pool. Not for the pleasure of swimming. He abhorred water. But the white and red striped bathing suit was a great joy to him. He didn't even go into the water. He would sit on a bench until the guards told him that he had been sitting there long enough and that he had better get a move on. No matter how painful it was to leave his bathing suit, this warning was very agreeable to him. He simply loved the guards.

The problem of finding a place to live gave him sleepless nights.

Finally he found something ideal. A bare little room with an iron cot. There were even iron bars in front of the little window. But what made him most happy here was that this little room was situated in an enormous tenement building. The house was built around a rickety little courtyard. The little courtyard lay very deep between dirty red walls. For no money in the world would no. 200 have relinquished his early morning walk, from nine to quarter past nine, ever making the rounds of this little courtyard.

And so life already seemed more bearable to him, although he was still very much tormented. Finally he paid a visit to a doctor. He chose a particular clinic because it had much in common with the infirmary of the prison. He formulated his ailment as, "I don't know what's with my feet. They weigh so much." The doctor was not a psychiatrist. He reassured his patient. It was only natural that the ankles had become a little weak from the eternal dragging of weight and chain.

This opinion made no. 200 muse. He pondered the entire day, and, as still happens once in awhile, his pondering was crowned with a fruitful result. He needed his chains and weights as a fish needs water and a bird air. Could a fish swim in the air or a bird fly in the water? No. Could he live without chains and weights, feel himself unhampered? That was likewise impossible.

He immediately and with unflagging industry set to work. He didn't allow himself the slightest extravagance—no pipe, no chew. He scrimped. Among his buddies he was suspected of arrivistic goals. "The scrimper." One Saturday afternoon he asked for leave and went forthwith to the junk market and the district of the rag merchants. It was easy to see that his soul was troubled by heavy battles of conscience. He stopped at every display of the junk dealers. He tested the strength of the chains, the heaviness of the weights. He looked displeased. But if anyone had met him a little later in a junkshop a short distance from the market, he would hardly have recognized him. So much did happiness drip from his mug. As even the proverb tells us, happiness makes one stutter. Which no. 200 did. "Those sure are weights, those sure are chains!" No. 200 could utter no more, overcome with joy. He readily paid the price the secondhand dealer desired.

Now a new life began for him. The workdays held little enjoyment for him. Only the evenings. But Sunday! What a holiday that was.

From the wee hours of the morning he could feel his chains around his ankles. Sunday was exactly like it used to be. Everything was there —folding up the iron cot, cleaning the room, walking in the little courtyard and then lying in chains. Often no. 200 could not restrain himself from rubbing his hands. But since this gesture hardly suited the occasion, he usually controlled himself. He had a subscription to the *Abbey of Tongerloo*,[1] which for twenty years had been his favorite reading. The issues of this magazine were perused Sunday afternoons.

This was a very happy period in the life of no. 200. Someone who slowly builds his own cathedral. He smiled with self-satisfaction when he remembered the difficulties he had overcome.

"But all things pass," sings Polin.[2] The directress of the S.R.P. (Society for Released Prisoners) had heard of no. 200's life and drive. She presented the case at social evenings, since it was a very rewarding theme. Lively debates. Priests and professors found the case very interesting. The priests said that the Lord our God had surely sent them this man in order to suppress the monstrosities of modern unbelief. And professors from official and nonofficial Catholic and Protestant universities found an interesting proof here to support the proposition that intellectual freedom is the greatest good and that there is no such thing, of course, as a tangible or absolute norm. Intellectual freedom, the concept and the conviction of being free, harbored by every person in his very own carcass, had hereby been proven. Priests and professors delivered their thesis with this brilliant argumentation before emperors, kings and presidents. Without exception, they all were convinced that this wonderful evidence would no longer be kept from the people, so that one could start dealing with unbelief and confused notions of freedom which, unfortunately, had already seriously undermined the mores of the people.

And so it happened that no. 200 appeared as a galley slave at country fairs and universities. At country fairs he was presented to the common people by a literate Holy Joe and in the universities he was presented by the professors as triumphant proof that their theory was not alchemy, but that it was indeed founded on physical observation and actual experience, to wit, no. 200.

The Holy Joe was a fat, round guy of the order of the Redemptorists. He beat on the sign, made the clown roll the drum, and spoke at length about modern unbelief, the undermining of faith, and loyalty to king and country. He clasped his hands together and shouted, "Why I ask you. Tell me why. Can anyone explain to me what freedom is? Can anyone give me a tangible proof what to be free is in relation to God and King? For surely I say unto you, there is a higher freedom than this Godlessness and unpatriotic behavior. It is the inner freedom of he who strives to praise God and serve the King. I have in my tent here the erstwhile galley slave no. 200, who can be seen by everybody after paying ten cents. Servicemen and children pay half price. This galley slave does not bother himself with what constitutes your entire striving for freedom, the decline of our religion—freedom which you also express in not doing your duty to our illustrious King and our dittolustre royal house, freedom not to work any longer, freedom to whore in the fields and anything else which is sold as freedom, but which is simply licentiousness. This galley slave harbors his own freedom and is therefore much richer than all of you who seek freedom outside yourselves. He himself, of his own free will, wishes to be in shackles. Proof that your cry, when a political agitator is sentenced, is unjust. Prison is a function of the state and of religion. And if prisons didn't exist, don't you see, we would be forced to make one for the people who, of their own free will, want to go to prison to praise God and to serve the King by their example of loyalty. This simple galley slave has acknowledged that the prison has a necessary function in the state. He wants, so to speak, to feed the prison, that's why he goes to prison of his own free will. From the depth of my heart I ask you, does there exist a higher freedom than this one, of going to jail of one's own free will? And a greater? For ten cents enter my tent and let us praise the Lord. Servicemen and children praise for half price." And the clown rolled the drum with all his might.

The professors at Catholic, Liberal, and Protestant colleges said the same thing in more obscure terminology. The example could be brought in direct relation to Kant's categorical imperative. "Act as if the maxim of our action were to become by our will a universal law of nature." One couldn't find a better application than the will-to-prison. For, said the professor, if, for the moment, you begin with the hypothesis that prison equals the Alpha and the amen of a general law, you will, by means of this special instance following the general problem, quickly acknowledge that this hypothesis is in fact an ethical axiom, that even in such primitive people, to wit no. 200, it becomes *unconsciously* accepted as a guideline of their actions. A natural law, an ethical axiom. Thus we arrive at an entirely new formulation of the ethical phenomenon. Prison is the axiomatic focal point of all ethics. Since man's existence within the state has an ethical origin—or from a psychoanalytic viewpoint has an ethical-erotic origin—prison is the soundest support of our civil life. The Hegelians were every day roaring drunk, that's how pleasantly surprised they were by this case. Their reasonable-world equals order-system was with one stroke proven in a concise fashion. Prison was as reasonable an institution as any of the others. The world was created according to a reasonable order. Just think for a moment: if, for example, there were no prison and no. 200 wanted to go to prison, that would go against reason. This was a glorious period for the philosophers.

Within a short period of time no. 200 had become a famous man. Being a social and philosophical proof, he was offered a lot of money. But he refused it, since it wouldn't be of any use to him. For no amount of money in the world would he have exchanged his meager prison fare, with anti-erotic pigments, for a complete dinner. And he needed few clothes. At the exhibitions he showed himself in white-red. It was very unpleasant for him that he wasn't allowed to go home dressed in the same fashion. Finally he got it past the priest-impresario so that he acquired a van for no. 200, built like a prison. The profits easily compensated for this large business expense. It was then that no. 200 experienced his happiest moments. It is unnecessary to say that this simple man who preferred his prison to a beautiful hotel, his prison fare to a dinner from the hors d'œuvre to the crepe Mikado, made a great impression across the nation and abroad. This famous man could possess all the physical comforts, but refused this luxury and thus substantiated the theses of intellectual and moral freedom. The results were far-reaching—everywhere political agitators were lynched. Others were, so to speak, obliged to go to prison in order to prove to the people that their concept of freedom was also based on morality. The prison gates stood wide open—the agitators were obliged to draw, whether they liked it or not, the conclusions from no. 200's example. Communists, anarchists, and nihilists disappeared by the dozens into prison. Never did the royal house stand on foundations of such solid civil loyalty as it did now. Religion bloomed, many masses were said for peace of soul, birth, and abortion.

The several churches soon saw themselves obliged to assure themselves of a monopoly on the manufacture and retail of all religious objects, in order to prevent shameless dealers from using them usoriously. Now signs were seen:

*Roman Catholic Candle Factory. Beginning Course in Intellectual Freedom—Girls' Section—given by the Reverend . . .*

*The Teachings of Intellectual Freedom according to the Protestant Faith and the National German Philosophy from Kant to Hegel, Published for the Benefit of the People and the Military by the Prussian State.*

The king had managed to put his hands on a very satisfying monopoly, the publication of picture postcards of no. 200 in his various ecstatic situations: in bathing suit, in the van, etc. This sale constituted the most important part of his private income. The Redemptorists were in existence to instruct the common people. The Jesuits moved in better spheres—even among the most clever there is always one who is dumber than the others. Even among the common people, the concepts of priest, officer and state employee became the substitute for the former symbolic meaning of the word "millionaire." The priest-impresario in particular became a capitalist. But this happy period in the history of mankind also passed. It just so happens that on this globe good is in constant struggle with evil—or to put it religiously, the evil one—and apparently is often vanquished. These are the trials of Job, and when Job overcomes them he receives double the number of cows, she-asses, and camels. The Lord our God is a practical man and knows how to please mankind. This was quite correctly observed by the writer of the Book of Job.

The evil one began his fated work by clouding the mind of no. 200. No. 200 thought, obeying the voice of the evil one, that's all fine and dandy, but it is finally a miserable comedy. This van is really a lousy substitute for a real prison. And everything I do is only lousy aping. I am right in doing my best to think myself above and away from it, my desire for a real prison is stronger than ever. All this is merely artificial.

He explained this to the priest-impresario and also that he unconditionally wanted to go to jail. The priest didn't like this at all. "We still need you too much, young man, the people are not yet converted from their false doctrines. We still have to show you at many fairs and festivals. Do you want to leave us in the lurch now? Be content with your van prison. We cannot house you in a real prison. It would be equal to sterilizing a fruitful proof or refusing the miracle sent by God. We are the reclaimers of the miracles sent by God. We are the golddiggers for the souls of people."

And so no. 200 was put off. Of which the evil one made use to agitate the poor galley slave even more.

Then the horrible thing happened. The priest stood again on the stand in front of his tent and oracled:

"Let no. 200 come outside so that the people can behold this man, who cannot live without prison."

That was the fatal sentence. No. 200 jumped as quick as lightning at the priest and drove a razor-sharp knife up to the handle in his chest. "That's it," said no. 200, fully convinced, and he shoved the knife, proof of his crime, carefully through his striped vest, for you can never tell, perhaps the judges were of the opinion that no proofs of his guilt were available. "Since this priest does not send me to jail willingly, because he speaks big words about my will-to-prison, I have been obliged to seek refuge in effective measures, in order to realize my ideal."

The priest had flopped against the sign, "Servicemen Half Price," so that the sign had fallen over the priest. The dead priest and the sign formed a hideous still life. He had clasped the sign the way ship-wrecked persons would a crosswreck. It was like this: "See, I have always been good to servicemen. Now show me also military honor." Suddenly he rolled, with the sign, among the astonished crowd. An old man offered, "His reverence surely didn't expect this."

Strange, no. 200 was not immediately apprehended. He had become such a famous man and the pillar of the state, that common cops did not dare lay a hand on him. The entire evening he sauntered through the fair. In order to attract attention, he felt obliged to bring the dead priest to a Massacre of the Innocents Stand. He amused himself for two hours by throwing balls at the priest and having people do the same. By midnight he still had not been apprehended. He was obliged to report himself to the police. The police commissioner was extremely polite, offered no. 200 a cigar with a band which had a portrait of no. 200 on it, but said that he still couldn't take it upon himself to run him in. He understood, no. 200's will-to-prison was world famous. But even now, after the murder, he couldn't do this favor for no. 200. He had his instructions, no. 200 simply had to go back to the van.

Until the news reached the king, the bishops, and the judges. These highly lettered men immediately understood the situation. No. 200 had helped them build the real state. No. 200 came to commit treason, he had given this state the deathblow. His will-to-prison was excellent, one could use that. But in a real prison no. 200 lost all his use in convincing the community. The judges were obliged to sentence him. The advertising stopped. The possibility surely existed of finding him not guilty and of showing him again to the people, even of picking up his crime as a new argument. It should be clear to anybody, however, that the people wouldn't fall for this trick. The whole large-scale exploitation of the case crumbled. Already agitators voices were heard: okay, why hadn't they put no. 200 in jail, when he desired it, instead of monkeying around with that priest's tent? An archbishop, a famed Thomist, who had made himself especially felt by defending the Roman Catholic exploitation of the case by his government against the Prussian-Protestant (the Prussians had exploited this purely religious matter in a Machiavellian fashion in favor of their state-theodicy and hence undermined all moral bases—which was of course not the case in the Catholic countries under the influence of *Aquino redivivus*)[3]—this archbishop made it very clear, the clear argumentation of an almost eighty-year-old man—the trial, the pending case of no. 200. No. 200 was the cause of an imminent rebellion. Because of the fact that he, who at first had been the staunchest pillar of the state and morality, now played his own little Antichrist, he had placed them—kings, bishops, and judges who for the common folk were the symbols of state and morality—in a grotesque light. Here was no need of careful consideration of the matter. Pending case. Only the death sentence could possibly stem the rebellion. Since a stronger miracle than no. 200 wasn't handy, there could therefore be nothing like overshadowing him, not even if they could persuade a poor slob to murder a family of fourteen people plus the maid. Clearly, no. 200 was and remained the miracle. No. 200 always left the exploitation of his case in their—the wise statesmen and good guardians of the church—hands. Now this man, along with his miraculous case, went over to the other side. Imagine, honorable judges, that a rich rancher from the Argentine pampas puts his cattle at the disposal of Liebig.[4] Suddenly he breaks his contract and goes over to the competing firm. For the first firm it is a question of life or death. But the case of no. 200 is a thousand times worse, because our firm is called Religion, State, and Co. We cannot judge severely enough. May our verdict be a dike against the rising stream of immorality. In any case, one law must immediately be made public—the death penalty is reinstituted.

In the meantime no. 200 was in detention. No need to describe his happiness. It had only one shadow side. He thought, if the judges won't get it into their heads to sentence me to life imprisonment. If I am set free again in my lifetime, I am obliged to commit another murder in order to make my rights triumph. No. 200 had not yet the slightest notion of what was in store for him. Until the turnkey once said, "You can rest assured, hold on to your head, for you're gonna get the axe." "Excellent," answered no. 200, "in our country the axe means life." "Wrong, the axe is the axe again. The king no longer grants amnesty." "I find that a bit much," said no. 200, and he sank into thought. "And to think that the king used to receive me in special audience. And that I played jail for a quarter of an hour with the children. The crown prince played warder. He did it very well. I wish him luck. His royal highness can always earn his keep, I said. And I stuck to that against the socialists who will have it that kings and princes aren't good for anything. I said, as long as I live jail will have to exist and the crown prince is the best warder you can imagine. Now the king is leaving me in the lurch. That isn't nice. No that isn't nice of our chivalric king." But deep down no. 200 kept his spirits up.

But his situation was much worse than he thought. "Exemplary punishment to stem the revolution," was the word. Nothing could be done about it. And so the judicial authorities made short shrift with no. 200. A weak defense. Even no. 200 notices this. "That's weak stuff, lawyer, sir." And the counsel for the defense: "There's nothing to defend in your case, no. 200. Your crime can only be compared with that of Judas. In fact, Judas, speaking judicially, only betrayed a poor slob. But you have betrayed the entire country, church, king, and state."

The verdict was assured: the death penalty without amnesty. No. 200 lost his patience. That little game had lasted long enough. The business was really simple after all. Everyone was pussyfooting around. He wanted his rights, and that's why he killed the priest. Before they had thrown much praise at him, and he had wanted then exactly the same thing he wanted now. What they were doing wasn't serious. "No, gentlemen of the jury and judges, that isn't the administration of justice anymore. The law is here a virgin who is being raped."

For this pornographic expression, no. 200 was fined twenty-six francs. "Those twenty-six francs I'll gladly pay," said no. 200. "But let the death penalty stay away." But none of that helped.

Then the confessor appeared. He spoke in the following manner:

—No. 200 and my fine brother Eugene. I know, you have done much wrong in your life. But the good you have accomplished is not forgotten up there. There everything is, so to speak, written in big books.

—Where is that up there?

—There, pointed the confessor through the bars to heaven.

—Everybody lives there according to his desires, but the desires are purified there.

—That's what that other priest also said and that's why I had to live in a van instead of a real prison. No, I can't do anything with this heaven of vans.

Then the confessor went on:

—Up there everything is written down in big books. There is a credit book of the soul and a debit book of the soul. And when the soul comes to heaven, the books are balanced. Those who show a credit, remain in heaven. Those who are up to their ears in debt, go to hell. You can rely on your credit book. But surely there is also a lot on your debit side. That's why we will draw up together a short history of your life. There is first and foremost a great crime, smuggling with manslaughter, on your debit side. Even leaving the manslaughter out, that could have been bad luck. But the smuggling, i.e., stealing in regard to the state, is a large black mark against you. Stealing detrimental to the state is, after stealing detrimental to the church, the worst case of dishonesty. But later, when you were released from prison, a heavenly mercy surely hit you, so that, for years, you have wrought great works, through which, without being aware of it, you have greatly aided church, king, and state. I mean by that your will-to-prison, that great deed of your life, a great example which managed to turn the people from their error. This too has been entered up there. With golden letters in your credit book. This entry will be decisive in your favor at the final balancing of the books of your life. That you will be able to check for yourself within a few hours. Be therefore full of hope for the future.

—If we continue the history of your life, we see how suddenly the evil spirit takes possession of your soul again and brings you to rebel against authority. He uses you to mock authority, and we already see the effects—the monsters of unbelief indulge their passions. This is the fruit of your horrible act. Your punishment is deserved. If it were possible to chop someone's head off twice, it wouldn't be too much. But since you have taken the death penalty upon you with love, you are able to buy yourself free from this offense. You can give—be it merely silently—evidence of your pleasure, by going to your death for the rehabilitation of church, king, and state. If you can go so far as to say on the scaffold, "I deserved this"—and I expect that much from your Christian manliness—then you can count on a nice little place in heaven. If you solemnly promise me to call this out loud and clear, I will immediately write you a check for an easy chair in heaven. Here is my checkbook. You see: Administration of Heaven and Hell, Incorporated. Director: The Lord God. Nothing can happen to you hereafter, if you've got one of these checks of mine.

—I don't want an easy chair. I want a prison in heaven, no. 200 said simply and determinedly.

—A prison in heaven you can also have. We supply everything. You must imagine heaven to be like a great department store. Macy's Department Store in New York can already supply white elephants. But heaven is a much larger department store. Heaven is larger than the earth and its surface is, so to speak, one department store. Everything is for sale. You can also have a prison if it makes you happy. With this note.

—Let them come.

—Stop, solemnly promise first that you will say on the scaffold: "I deserved this."

—I can't promise that.

—Then you won't get a prison in heaven—and the priest pretended to leave, without giving absolution. The effect wasn't long in coming.

—Hey there, yelled no. 200, afraid that he had lost his chance to get a prison in heaven, hey there, not so quick, father. Why don't you give me some time to think it over. I'll say it. I'll promise.

—Good luck. The priest got his checkbook out and wrote a physical-metaphysical note.

---

### HEAVEN AND HELL
Incorporated
## Capital: X00,000,00

Social address: Heaven                    Administration:

Director: The Lord God

Note no . . . . .

Good for

One (1) PRISON IN HEAVEN

To be delivered: to bearer

Prison of . . . . ., the 25th of August . . . . .

The Solicitor,
Paulus-Franciscus Joostenius,
Prison Chaplain.

---

Full of confidence about the future, no. 200 climbed the scaffold. Care had been taken to assemble a large crowd. The crowd proved to be rebellious. That's where the bosses had gotten poor no. 200. They had exploited him. There was much sympathy for him. When the executioner had placed him on the guillotine, no. 200, understanding the seriousness of the situation, said, "Just a moment please." He turned to the crowd and shouted:

—I deserved it!

He saw the crowd standing dumb with amazement. "Oh, I'll have to add a word or two, otherwise I'll forfeit my prison in heaven." And he shouted very loud:

—I deserved it, the prison in heaven!

The executioner grabbed him. The chaplain had given him a sign. This no. 200 always had to ruin a good deed with some stupidity.

When no. 200 knew intuitively the proximity of the axe, he tried to give one more sign. He pointed to his feet—that's where the irons really had to lie.

When the axe fell, no. 200 thought: that is a miscarriage of justice.

---

1. An existing periodical. Most abbeys published a devotional magazine, designed for family reading.
2. Perhaps Paul Colin, who published the periodical *L'Art libre* in Brussels during the 1920's.
3. Literally, "St. Thomas Aquinas revived," that is, something forgotten (a philosophy, literary movement) which is brought back into public focus.
4. A German scientist who started the science of agricultural chemistry, and was particularly famous for discovering the principle of making meat extract.

# The City of Builders

*"Well, tearing down is really quite easy."*
(*A commonplace in committees, etc.*)

—Isn't it true, to tear down is easy? Anybody can tear down without the least bit of know-how. You get to work with a pick and shovel and the demolition is finished in no time at all. Not only are you through with the demoliton, but you can also say, the job is done. Such a profession is, as everyone will admit, quite easy. But not to tear anything down and build, to keep always building, with a vengeance, that is something entirely different, you gentlemen wreckers. Naturally, you are so hardened in wickedness that you can't even understand the joy which lies locked in constant, ever constant building.

The gentlemen senators who held the fate of the free seaport of Creixcroll in their hands were, from that point of view, fanatics about building and—it seemed to them a necessary corollary—enemies of any tearing down. Hence they decided to apply to the city of Creixcroll their philosophy of life, the antithetical conception in regard to building and tearing down. They didn't doubt at all that the city would thereby reach a period of great glory not known for centuries. The mayor of Creixcroll issued a police ordinance, which forbade all Creixcrollers to tear down anything—be it merely one stone of a chicken coop. Heavy penalties would hit those who dared tamper with the regulation. The senate, on the other hand, designed an enormous premium system to support all those who by building would contribute to leading the city of Creixcroll toward her period of glory. In order to scare everyone away from the disastrous vandalism of tearing down, the medieval punishment of pillory was reinstituted in Creixcroll's judicial system. He who dared to tear anything down was pilloried. This wise measure was taken in order to impress on the growing generation from childhood on the positive value of building, next to a contempt for the base and easy wrecker's work.

Basically, Creixcroll's citizens saw much truth in this. For that matter, if anyone spoke to them about the glory of their city, he always found them to be an obedient audience and perhaps useful material. That was also the case in this instance. The Creixcrollers rushed to work, i.e., to building. To be sure, soon there existed in the city a terrible shortage of architects, masons, carpenters, and all the other skilled men from branches connected with the building industry. After a short time things had already gone so far in Creixcroll that the literal professions were, so to speak, simply abolished. The young gentlemen from the better classes and from the middle class became architects, engineers, or building contractors, while all the working men switched to the building industry. No luxury trade seemed to be a match for the building industry, and no one could therefore guarantee its workers a decent income. Luxury items were no longer desired. If a Creixcroller had money to spare, he would invest it in a building. Gold and jewelry, a cozy house, and a linen closet filled to the topmost shelf—which used to be the ideal of all female Creixcrollers—were relinquished as being useless. Building had become the "measure of all things." The wealth of a person was measured according to the number of buildings he was constructing or, in the worst case, had constructed for him. Since the old harbor Creixcroll was financially a well-established city, her inhabitants had large reserves at their disposal. And all these reserves, up to that time primarily invested in bonds from solid overseas states, were used to finance this splendid, "uplifting" period of history. Everybody invested whatever he owned in liquid assets in buildings. As a matter of course Creixcroll's senate had to come up with something to provide the city with the necessary number of bakers and butchers. Galley slaves were called upon for this purpose.

If in the beginning usefulness, i.e., the necessity for and the need for buildings, still played the decisive role, this pragmatic consideration soon disappeared and the Creixcrollers built only pour l'amour de l'art, the glory of their city, the way it had been represented to them by the philosophers of the building theory. The Creixcrollers built therefore simply for the joy of building. They built so much that, after a short period of exertion of this industrious people, there were dozens of all possible kinds of buildings to spare, houses, palaces, concert halls, and churches. After three years of this sustained effort the city of Creixcroll had, among others, five court houses, eight city halls, ten slaughterhouses, as many asylums for stray dogs, and seventy churches, of which forty-five could not be used at present, and furthermore an enormous number of empty houses. The building of privies along public roads also got its turn now and then, in such a way that, in this respect also, the city of Creixcroll was well supplied in an exemplary fashion. Creixcroll's senate supported all these efforts as much as possible. It also had countless buildings erected at its own expense, including these privies. What was supposed to happen to all these building reserves would become clear in the future.

Against the objection of "uselessness" an architect had already found a technically brilliant answer, namely the building of an "abstract building," as he called it. The owner could, according to circumstances, convert this abstract building into a department store, a concert hall or a cafeteria.

As far as the wreckers were concerned, they were forced to notice, to their dismay, that the magistrates did not allow anyone to mock their ordinances. A pigeon fancier who had given up his hobby, thereby following for that matter the inclination of all Creixcrollers, and who now thought that he could tear down his dovecot, saw the offence punished with an entire day in the pillory. The following incident, however, gave cause for a lengthy legal explanation. An owner had a sock-worn house in the old center of the city. Like all Creixcrollers he liked the glory of his city and thought to contribute to its glory by answering the building order in kind. Since open land within Creixcroll's city limits had become scarce and, on top of that, because of the heavy demand was very highly priced, this owner decided to tear down his wretch of a house in order to erect a new one on the same spot. Sure. As soon as the workmen had made so much as a gesture indicating they might want to start the demolition, a police squad stood ready. They brought the whole bunch, owner, architect, and workmen, to the police station. From this action stemmed—for the Creixcroll of that time—a very famous trial. The owner deluded himself in thinking he had a strong position. He thought that the tearing down of a house was surely legal, when in place of this old house a new one would be erected. How can you possibly build a skyscraper on top of a medieval corbiestep. Even more so when the corbiestep, even without this experiment, would collapse under the weight of years. The owner argued that, in his judgment, he had done the city a service, for in the street where his house stood it was really not safe for either passers-by or occupants.

"This proposition is absolutely wrong," remarked the President of the Building Tribunal—an organism dealing exclusively with the execution of ordinances concerning building and wrecking. "For we should never forget that the Creixcrollers who have steered our city onto a new course started with the idea that tearing down is easy, hence unworthy of a people such as ours, and that building, always

building, is the one and only ideal which a superb city such as Creixcroll can aim for. No matter what reasons one could provide to
motivate tearing things down, they are a priori invalid. Tearing down
is, categorically, a reprehensible deed." And so the owner was
sentenced, after the tribunal had accepted the mitigating circumstances presented by the defense, to twenty years' imprisonment. It is
only natural that he, too, like all wreckers, was chained to the pillory
immediately after the sentence had been pronounced. His guard, however, his head full of plans for the "abstract building" which he would
build very soon, forgot the fellow in the pillory. The unfortunate
owner, after fourteen days of the most painful hardships, perished
there.

Want rapidly increased in the city of Creixcroll—we mean a want
of land to build on. It became urgent to do something about it. The
magistrates decided that now the builders of Creixcroll simply had to
attack the public squares—the health of the Creixcrollers wouldn't
go all that easily to the dogs. However great the emergency might
become, the citizens only needed to get it firmly in their head that
now, just as before, tearing down would be severely punished. If you
could not find any land anymore, you simply had to prop up the old
building which you owned in such a manner that it could support the
weight of a larger number of stories. If the house would give way
despite being propped up, you simply had to accept this natural
phenomenon. The rubble could not be cleared away, however, no
matter what. The ruins too had to prove the activities of Creixcroll.

A further cause of this intense building activity was that each
Creixcroller began to feel himself an expert on construction. And so
it happened that in the statistical returns of the city of Creixcroll the
cause, "accidents," soon took first place. For that matter, the word
"accident" had lost its original meaning. In Creixcroll one understood
"accident" only to mean the fact of perishing in the collapse of a
building.

In the end it became a bit much for some Creixcrollers. Especially
after the builders were busily building the public squares chock-full,
a movement was formed which, hesitantly at first, was called the
Anti-Building Movement. The propagandists of this movement tried
to demonstrate that it really was no fun to live in a city which was
being recreated into a forest of houses—an unhealthy forest—and that

it was necessary as soon as possible to put a stop to this building activity, which they called a mania.

As soon as the Building Tribunal had been informed of this rebellious talk they arrested the leader of the Anti-Building Movement. The Supreme Court, which had the jurisdiction in cases of treason, was assigned to the case. Since, according to the jury and judges, treason was proven as clearly as water from a well, it was quite unnecessary to make an elaborate trial out of his case. The sentence was the death penalty. The Court decided to administer it later by means of the rack. A didactic feast would be made from this putting on the rack, to teach all minds with rebellious tendencies a good lesson once and for all. A prophet is not without honor, save in his own country, thought the Anti-Building man.

Then the unexpected happened.

—Your honor, said the executioner, where can I set up the rack?

—In Central Square, answered the judge.

—Central Square! Central Square! You know, I'm sure, that Central Square exists only in name now.

—Put the rack where you want it, Hapmans.

—Sure, easier said than done, your honor, sir. There is no square larger than an apron in the city.

—What?

—I am saying that we cannot put this traitor, this rotten slob, on the rack, because we cannot set up the rack anywhere.

Indeed. The didactic feast had to be postponed. The zealots of the Anti-Building Movement used this occasion to incite the Creixcrollers:

—We don't speak for our cause. But think about it for a moment— the authorities arrange a beautiful feast. For the first time in ages you will be able to enjoy the rack as a public recreation. And what happens? The feast is off because we don't have a square. If you had followed his advice, you would have had a square at this moment, and you would have been able to put him very neatly to the rack.

A gang of Creixcrollers, with the executioner Hapmans among them, marched at night on the prison, rightfully angered by the idiotic organization of the present regime, and liberated the agitator. The next day he was placed at the head of the Senate of the city of Creixcroll.

—What do the people want? he asked from the balcony of the city hall.

—Squares! it rolled like a plainsong against him.

—You won't escape us for a second time, said a voice behind him. It was Hapmans. He stuck, defined in that sense by his job, strictly to the letter of the law.

# Prose Poem

## The Sirens

Not so long ago sailors succeeded in catching the sirens, a few miles south of the Azores. The sirens whistled heartrendingly, but the sailors, being literally deaf, remained unaffected. They wanted to purge the seas of these dangerous creatures and locked the sirens in a dark closed-off corner of the hold. In the harbors where their ship moored, after they had told of their catch, they were treated by sea-men with jubilation and hurrahs. And since sailors believe that a captured siren is a talisman, they had no problem selling the sirens in Lisbon, Liverpool, and Rotterdam. But only deaf sailors could lodge the sirens in the darkest corner of the ship's hold, the others know-ing themselves unequal to the task.

Everyone knows that sea captains are people who want to exploit everything to their own advantage. So it was to be with the captured sirens. A round opening was made in the wall of the sirens' brig, and from this opening a pipe carried the sirens' whistling far above the deck, above the sea, above the stream and the city. To make the sirens whistle when it was useful or pleasing to them, the seamen made a thin lance ending in three sharp needles. These needles were dipped in poppy juice and were thrust into the body of the captured sirens through a small opening in the brig. Poppy juice, when absorbed, produces an indescribable longing for space and an unlimited sadness. In sirens it awakens their memory of distant seas, their former power over men, and an ultimate sadness in which, as in another dimension, lie all of space and all delusions of power. Then the sirens scream very loudly. The endless vibrations of the whistling shoot sharply across the ship into space, suspended above the stream and the city. Seamen and people on shore say in the middle of their revels, it's twelve, the sirens whistled, the new year begins.

Yet, despite their captivity, the sirens have not relinquished their power. True, they are no longer able to entice blue jackets to the depths of the deep sea, where their song is an untimely death amidst the wonder of anemones and seaweed, shells and coral. But those who have once heard the whistling of the sirens high over the city, cannot for the rest of their lives suppress their longing for this lament. They have, like the mouse to the cat, fallen prey to the harbor, where they know the ships and the sirens.

Owners of factories in the country have brought sirens for their workers. They keep them captive in the cellars of their buildings. No matter what they try, they are not able to bring the sirens to make the plaintive wailing which these creatures let out aboard ship. One suspects that the sirens, lacking their ultimate pleasure, the smell of the sea, are slowly pining away. Besides, it is the water of the sea which gives their voices this sharpness.

# Four Short Tales

## Aquarelle

Aquarelle floats red. Blue and yellow. Around color bubbles swirls the water. In meeting the red and the blue become mild: mauve vibrates far up the limit of experience. Wattman paper flows mauve-saturated. The mauve paper becomes grains of Wattman paper. Or, the yellow runs childlike desire towards the solution of stability. Blue rests, borders the vibration and determines the ratio inwardly, kernel. Children glint very long glitterapples.

The joy of stroking the paper wilts from my fingers. Fingers want to go further to the knowledge of my eyes. Desire, to feel the peace of blue and to penetrate to the limit of girl-childlike depth mauve vibration. Their wish to be lips, quench, hands, thirst at the well of orange. This is the time of beauty for my fingers. Their total dissolution in their parasensual desire. They are no longer. They are only labile. They are becoming. Things which were fingers, now dissolved in the to-be-eye-striving.

Until the eyes awaken, the dictators yearn for uprising. Poor fingers, idealists of the transferral of the spiritual to the parasensual. The eyes kill the things which dissolved themselves in the lability of too real desire. The fingers are fingers again. They were not that all of the time.

Poor fingers, each failure resolves the question, wherefore this desire to awaken from exactitude. Fingers were always fingers. They will never drink orange and never stroke mauve. Dictators do not like uprisings. It seems to me that sparkle-eyes cruelly chastise once bold fingers. Full of animal shame, thus my fingers hide their desire.

Perhaps it is just as well that the ultimate limit of my fingers is temporary hypertrophy of their desire. Perhaps it is just as well that eyes are dictators. And rebels weak.

Yet despite weakness it is rebellion. That my fingers were able to vibrate for a moment, briefly, in the delusion of being labile and on the way to realizing their desire.

# Anaïs

That day the model Anaïs had received her monthly salary. She had postponed without effort every decision beyond this date. After brief deliberation it was now clear to her what little change her salary would make, and, quickly associating, she concluded that it was not worth the trouble. Even an affair couldn't be considered a defense against boredom. Until the tram for which she had been waiting stopped, she had been dozing in the partial peace of suicidal contemplations. Then, with a graceful leap, she was in the car.

Pleasure for her, to recreate her leap mentally, in taut and lithe tailored lines. To realize that she felt better on the platform of the car than inside gave her a sense of self-sufficiency.

During the short ride to her place, she enjoyed the thought of throwing the money out the window.

When she had taken her hat and jacket off, it had already become clear to her that throwing it away was no solution, because the gesture itself was disproportionate. A few fifties and twenties float above the street, then eventually fall in such a way that no one would notice them.

She found the idea silly, but just when she was going to relinquish it she was struck by the visualization of an act: thrifty banknotes over a street at twilight, the ordinary association scattered—this was, precisely, throwing money away.

Wrong: first to get the people, the shouting masses, interested by clowning and, after that, to throw the money by the bushel into the crowd—oh, the careful measures of the lavish scorner, to exchange the money for small change. The dissonance is clear between the psychic condition for this act—resignation—and the act itself—a positive rebellion with hope of salvation because of the rebellion.

This: twilight, you throw the few bills of your monthly salary out the window. There are a few people on the street. No one notices the bills falling. Finally, and as an afterthought, the last bill, which lies long on the broad back of the wind, falls. You close the window, casually flip the switch and make light.

Anaïs thought immediately that it was now fitting not only to think the possibility through, as she so often did, but simultaneously to put thought into action. She picked up her handbag. Through the open window the wind threw a few short waves of freshness over her face and moist hands. Anaïs thought emphatically, I am young. And once again, I am young. It happened with the banknotes as she had imagined. Anaïs rested for a moment on the rare equilibrium between pondering and reality. Slowly the bills floated away from the window, took a seemingly brief upward direction, until several hung midway over the street. In the space—between the four-storey houses on each side—the street was a vacuum around the few bills. Anaïs followed them with her eyes, with the interest of someone who is suddenly surprised by the structure of a common object. Because she was familar with the simple end of the last bill, which was still falling, she did not wait any longer at the window.

Alone in the room, she was uncertain. There remained in her a dissatisfaction like a slight nightmare. But her gesture had moved her such a distance from herself that, laughing, she realized that discontent was the only possible form of contentment for her.

## Convictions

It happened that an accordion player, so confident of his skill and, as they say, so much at one with his instrument, not only pulled his instrument open as far as it would go but also, so to speak, as the superlative of this motion, tore his arm from his body. This procedure was naturally a mistake and the result of a momentary defect of consciousness. That is indeed the way to explain it.

To repair the damaging results of this mistake the aid of a doctor was required. And so a doctor was sent for. But this doctor—it appeared afterwards—was no less a man of conviction than the accordion player. He was very keen on being a good physician and, moreover, was keener still to hear people testifying to his being a good physician. Extremely touched by the unhappy incident and wholly intent on averting as soon as possible the most dangerous consequences of this disaster—so that everyone would congratulate him after the success for his skill as a physician—the doctor worked with such speed and absorption that only on finishing the treatment did he ascertain his colossal mistake. The mistake was that he had joined the accordion instead of the arm to the body of the poor accordion player. Only when—in order to exhibit the affair as a clean and faultless job—he wanted to place the accordion in the hand of the accordion player, did he notice to his utter amazement, as they also say, that it was the arm that was left. He could not deny himself, however, the conviction that the arm and the accordion, from the point of view of causality, belonged to each other. From which it followed that, with the aid of a thin but strong piece of string, he tied the arm to the accordion.

Before departing he stroked the silk of his top hat with his sleeve and naturally in the right direction—that is, with the silk. He then took his leave of the poor accordion player's wife, saying there was no reason to be dismayed.

## Curious Attack

Stabile he is madder.[1] If he changes in such a way that instead of being he becomes becoming, he is carmine red. Such is he as soon as he moves.

He. The madder-carmine red. Not abstract, the madder. He is extremely concrete. Yet I would not be able to say in what manner he is concrete. Only, it seems to me, arching and oscillating on the perimeter-fragment. Movement is to displace weight from left to right and to oscillate. He could be a very baroque dachshund whose paws disappear in the belly. Natural desire for unnaturalness. A whim.

While writing I realize how incorrect it would be to express, carmine red. Precisely the concrete is the bizarre entity of this deformation of nature according to laws of the purely conceivable. But it is also incorrect, the carmine red form. As such he is again too defined, concretely appearing abstraction.

Separated from the madder red by blue, opaline, mauve, and manifold tremors of values lies the rose square. The rose square is peaceful. Subconscious cause of this is the delusion of the impermeability of the royal blue, the opaline, and the values. The rose thinks, *he* can't touch me. First of all there is the royal blue which is indivisible in hardness, after that the impermeable force of the undulation of the opaline and the values. The rose square is at ease, therefore. And lies island-secure in values, the closest waves.

Then it happens. The madder rises up and sways on his arch. Exertion to oscillate. Presses immensely towards the right and becomes croplike malevolent when he notices the ungainliness of his organism and the objective peace of the rose at the other side of the royal blue.

Inarticulate fury sticks in his—the madder red's—throat. The throat must be swollen. Only nothing indicates it. Where is the throat. The madder red is indeed only apparently archlike. The where of the organs remains unknowable in this baroque organism. What is knowable seems always the psychic cause for expression. Apparently unavailing and unrelated to the result he becomes carmine red.

Perhaps because it would go faster, I lose sight for a moment of the carmine red. When I find him again, he has, wonder how, advanced near the royal blue. He attacks the royal blue. With the beak. Where is the beak. Probably where line and perimeter-fragment meet. Did I not think before that there was also the muscle-end of the organ of motion. Beak and motion-organ. It is unbelievable, could one mean just as well that such a structure is purely cerebral. Nevertheless, I see the action of the madder red. Its positive result cannot be questioned. Much too clearly did I see the movement before, how he oscillated, and now the beak. Direct sharpbill in the compact clump of the royal blue.

The hardness of the royal blue greatly heightens the anger of the carmine red and, its inevitable result, his attack's sharpness. This happens suddenly. One half of the carmine red sticks right into the clump of the royal blue.

Now I seem to see the carmine red much clearer. He is completely mouth. I said already that the carmine red is probably archlike. Actively organic he is always completely that organ which is just then functional. The carmine red is in turn as much as left leg, right leg, mouth. Thus the carmine red has no organs. He is always organ. One single organ. Becoming-in-action. Not in such a manner that the form changes. From the vantage point of his alternately becoming organs he is the transcendentally given. To me he is archlike. But this arch experiments functionally in a very strange, I would almost say, crazy manner. He has now, suddenly completely mouth, swallowed a large clump of the royal blue.

The opaline notices this. It shudders. So terribly terrified is the opaline that its spine—its more pronounced tones—weakens. These tones finally disappear in an indeterminateness like the milky way.

The carmine red oscillates. He grins. Cruelly satisfied hunger rouses hunger. The archform is an open mouth. Licks his chops right in front of his prey, the mauve.

The rose sees the danger. Dream befalls the miscalculation in the certainty of the unconditionally being separated.

The rose rises straight up. To drive strength to center, a moment, to conquer desperation. Then—the die is cast—the rose makes the leap into neighboring values. The mauve guards the rear, the retreat. Balanced in the values the rose and the mauve dissolve.

The values vibrate. And a little later are again mirror-smooth rest. The carmine red winds up in the midst of the values. But the values are indeed impervious undulation. Where they become a hard resistance-proof mass, resilience compensates the lost ability of undulating. Hardened values evade the attack of the carmine red through a hard resilient leap—like a flea.

The carmine red is furious in the midst of this game—defense of the values. If they at least would defend themselves seriously. So nasty, while playing to escape the danger of being gobbled up. The carmine red oscillates mightily. The mouth becomes right leg again. Oscillation. Left right left. Left leg.

The carmine red is again madder.

---

1. A bright red dye, in Dutch, *Kraplak*. No pun was therefore intended in the original.

# Patriotism, Inc.

*In illo tempore.*

"To put it simply: the situation in Europe is swinishly bad. You can safely be platitudinous and say that any serious-minded person would agree about the situation. Agitators are now saying that ancient values, in which people have put their trust since time immemorial, are simply tricks of jawsmiths to fool the farmers. Patriotism, gentlemen, that noble virtue, these filthy bastards call the roll of drums on the tent of the faithhealer. And no matter what the authorities did initially to put a stop to this propaganda which is undermining the nation, we all know it was of no avail. The authorities, who were much too weak, were trampled on. The people worship the false prophets. Yes, in some countries it already has gone so far that these prophets hold the helm of the ship of state in their hands. *Inter*nationalists are at the head of the nation. Can you understand such a paradox, gentlemen? The king, the symbolic representation of the concept 'taboo,' is no longer taboo. Emperors and kings are in effect exiled. It seems that there are not enough islands on our globe to assure every ex-monarch an island for himself. We have already started on the peninsulas. This is the situation wherever the international riff-raff have triumphed. Unfortunately, it is also the case in our country. And now the absolute spiritual aberration—you will not believe it, but it is nonetheless true:

"A Court of Arbitration has been formed! Of course, in and by itself this still isn't too bad—even in former times the Palace of Peace was already considered a beautiful piece of architecture and at the same time the necessary proof to convince people of the good will of their governments. No, the *existence* of a Court of Arbitration isn't really so bad. But the fact that this Court really functions is horrible. Try to picture it for a moment—a Court of Arbitration which functions in the most realistic way! An absolute madhouse. Good God, unless you're a child you will surely understand that an Arbitration Court can serve all sorts of possible goals, except that of a Court of Arbitration. So the rulers can get together for a bull session—you can't quite go to Maxim's at eleven in the morning—or, for that matter, to see there a striptease, or raise rabbits, and particularly to deliberate together which report to put in the papers. In short, just between the two of us, the only goal of a Court of Arbitration is to give rulers the opportunity to pretend they are doing something. No, gentlemen, you've missed the boat completely. These characters who now hold the destiny of nations in their hands want to make it seem as if they are doing something more than the appearance of doing something. Isn't that a terrible mess?

"The internationalists have managed to carry things so far that, independent of the Court of Arbitration, an international league has been formed to fight venereal disease. As if the prevention of this danger *inside* the nation is not the task of the government, and as for *outside* the nation . . . well, outside the nation, shouldn't every upright and true patriot rejoice when statistics prove to him that the affliction of venereal disease in neighboring states is spreading at a rapid rate? Wasn't it therefore deliberately to undermine the energy of a nation that the interest of the people was aroused in something other than the suffering of the unhappy neighboring peoples? Hence the conclusion seems to be that to undermine the life energy of the nation is precisely the goal of these internationalists. And for whose benefit? Well . . . the enemy's naturally. And there you have it. The internationalists have sold out.

"But the worst is still to come, gentlemen. You are, like me, aware of the sad story. In eastern Europe two nations have decided to submit their dispute, which even concerns territorial problems, to the Court of Arbitration. The governments of both states have agreed to accept the decision of a jury which will be made up of two representatives from each state and a fifth member who does not belong to either of them. And there you've got the facts! And yet history is there to teach us that for ages nations looked for reasons to lay into each other, and that it wasn't always easy to find a plausible excuse— wherefore, however, the nations-which-were-not-in-a-state-of-decay did not give up and often went at each other without any excuse. But what is happening now? The complete opposite, gentlemen. Not just an excuse, but a real reason exists, under exceptionally favorable circumstances, to unleash a war like a dream—and yet these nations simply refuse, and submit their dispute to a Court of Arbitration, just as two poor wretches would do before a justice of the peace. What are the industrialists up to in these nations? Surely they can't ignore the fact that, from the point of view of industry, war is a state of perfection. Don't the agrarians see how, within the compass of one year, they could amass a fortune which under other, so-called normal, circumstances would only be the result of the effort of many generations? These nations are given the opportunity to eliminate with one stroke the entire silly social legislation as it now exists—the shorter workday, the reduction in female and child labor, the age-limit for workers and the countless restrictions concerning hygiene—to wipe out, I say, this entire legislation with one stroke.

In short, a unique opportunity to regenerate a nation, a people. Indeed, you wonder, are these industrialists and agrarians dreaming? Gentlemen! let us not deceive ourselves. The danger which is already a reality in the East stares us in the face in a most threatening way. Perhaps tomorrow our own government will submit itself to the Court of Arbitration. Where is this leading us? None of us would be able to answer positively, Romam. What awaits us is the exhaustion and decadence of the race—the stupid masses paralyzed by and living on utopian slogans and yet more slogans, and there you've got the picture. *Quo vadis*, Teutonia? I have spoken."

In this vein, only more verbosely, spoke Pameelke, member of the Senate, at a very secret meeting of the bosses of the Conservative Party, and he was so caught up in his own fierce delivery of these thoughts that after first having poured himself a glass of water, a few moments later he started the same action all over again, but executing it now in the opposite direction, i.e., from the glass into the carafe, which didn't prevent him, after his speech, from bringing the empty glass to his lips. Finally he even said, "Hum", apparently satisfied with the refreshment he had just savored. Thus the honorable member of the Senate at his best: realities were only subjectively existent, i.e., they existed as long as the subject clung to their existence. Indeed, every reality was a fiction, but all the more real because the ego constructed it. The strange thing about this contemplation was that it had entered the subconscious of the individual Pameelke in such a way that Pameelke, a fitting piece of evidence for Kant, could not be anything other than a very speculative politician.

His speech gained him a storm of applause, not to mention that those present agreed that the honorable member of the Senate had succeeded very well in diagnosing the disease which made Europe suffer, but that he had failed—may the noble goal excuse the sharpness of the term—when it came to the question of indicating a remedy. An Aesculapius for languishing Europe! a kingdom for an

Aesculapius! Despite strong coffee and curaçao none of the bosses came up with the saving idea—they couldn't ignore the lamentations. Only Prince Alp-Alp brought some light to the subject by arguing:

"The main question is a clear formulation of the question. Thus we say that Europe is in danger because it listens to internationalists and pacifists. Europe can only be out of danger when it listens to us, for, as is well known, we keep the concepts of state, nation and people pure, in terms of the strong emotion tradition has developed in them. Only in such an attitude lies the salvation of a people. What concerns us is to define the question within narrower limits, since our task is simply to make sure that our people will listen to us again. Although of international import, the task of a party like ours remains a national affair. In other words, and speaking figuratively, Teutonic patriots cannot be held responsible if the patriots attain power in Fochany. Since we must, for that matter, both in the first analysis and probably also in some direct way, be held responsible for our race—that race which, as is known to all of you, has been appointed the divinely sanctioned role of world healer—we have no reason whatso-ever for creating new means of expressing patriotism in neighboring countries. We hold the view that the action of the internationalists weakens the state, the nation, and the people. Such a weakening of neighboring countries, however, would please us tremendously. From which it follows that we can only be interested in the possibility that, if it comes from a neighboring country, internationalism has a better chance to get an easy hold on our people. Therefore our people ought to listen to us. But they do not listen to us. In spite of everything we have tried—erecting half a million statues of heroes, delivering patriotic speeches at a rate of $3\text{-}\frac{3}{4}$ speeches per day, spiritual con-juring with divination by monsters, films which show, black on white, that the neighboring peoples, as punishment for their licentious inter-nationalism (a pleonasm by the way, gentlemen, but the people adore pleonasms), were ravaged by all sorts of ailments—all of this was of no avail. The question is, does there exist any other means which we have left unexplored. If not, let us then quietly close our books, since the ways we have used up to now are indeed worthless. Today we are still permitted to beat the drum of patriotism, because our enemies the internationalists think that our drumming loses itself in the general inattention. It is clear however that this merely-being-

allowed won't bring the slightest relief. Tomorrow it might even get ·
worse."

Dr. Erich-Carl Wybau sat in a corner. He listened without any
apparent interest. After the prince's explanation there was a great
silence. Just as in the legend—an angel descended and it became
silent. None of the bosses could present a concrete proposal. The
silence lasted for a very long time. Only the occasional sound of
moving a glass or a cup. When the silence had become very oppres-
sive, so that the bosses had to feel extremely powerless—from which
it also follows that whoever could offer them the needed medicine
could also permit himself to utter a few harsh truths—when the situation was thus favorable, Dr. Erich-Carl Wybau asked permission to
speak.

Chance had willed that Dr. Wybau became the general secretary of
the Conservative Party. He didn't have the least interest in this or
that idea. According to him, whether an idea lost or won was just a
matter of the personal energy of the leaders. And furthermore,
whether you were a communist or a conservative was secondary.
That you had to have something to do in your life was primary. Life is
empty, fill it. If things don't go the way you want, fill it at least
ostensibly, and that is already more than sufficient. And of course life
can be filled just as well whether you propagate idea X or idea Z. It's
all a matter of thinking a matter through in a logical way and not
allowing yourself to be taken in by the harangue of a doctor at a
country fair. It all belongs to the realm of physiology. A sum of energy
postulates its being used up. For the sceptical spirit all proofs are too
weak and for a childish nature all proofs are cold cash. Ergo, that an
idea had value was baloney. Take any idea you want, keeping in mind
only while you think it through to its ultimate end, that it is merely
"stuff." There lies the matter, and now you, there, let's see what
you're made of. The only category admitted by the doctor was, you
can or you can't. The direction was unimportant.

How did this industrial knight get lost in the midst of these super
hygienists?—Wybau could not rely on his titles or protection.

Half-caste, son of a Teutonic father, mother a native of the Canary
Islands. Shortly after obtaining his degree, Wybau married. Six
months later he was arrested in San Sebastiano under suspicion of
having murdered his wife, Ursula Laff, famous for her beauty around

the world. Whatever actually happened, it was a case of passion, i.e., passion based on theory, and therefore incurable, unless such passion can be dissolved by a psychically impossible amalgamation. Wybau found his wife simply too beautiful, and the knowledge of this elusive comparative roused uneasiness in such a way that the murder had to follow as a physically determined reaction. That was the plea of his defense lawyer—while quoting Dante and Petrarch, Hafiz and Amaroe, Shakespeare and Goethe by heart—with the result that the jury, staggered by so much knowledge, forgot the case and by unaminous vote declared the defendant not guilty. From that moment on the *avocatuzzo* who had pleaded Wybau's case was deemed to be a specialist in derelicts of passion. More luck than wisdom, thought Wybau, who had been forced to fight very hard to convince the little shyster that he should pocket his own rhetoric and stick only to the memorized plea which Wybau had written. What to do next. "All avenues are open. The important thing is to be forced, down no matter what road. The rest is done by chance." And so he started as a cub reporter with a newspaper in the capital. It was the capital, as a matter of course. The provinces, God save him. After two years he was general secretary of the Conservative Party. His competitors had stumbled, one by one, over their own standpoints.

And now, he thought, a fantastic opportunity was offered to him to become one of the most representative men not only in Teutonia, but also in all of Europe. The time had come to go straight towards his goal, not sparing anyone. That's why he asked permission to speak. The chairman granted him the favor gratefully, though a little sus- piciously. Gratefully, for deep down the chairman was convinced, like the other bosses of the Conservative Party, that for about two years all the ideas had originated with Wybau. Which was no more than his duty. He was paid to have brilliant ideas. But still a little leery, since experience had taught them that Wybau never got them off the hook without using his aid to cut a few throats among them. Naturally you had to take Wybau as he was. The idea of nationalism was a sport to him, but God almighty, if now your one and only sportsmanlike industrial knight was a genius, then you couldn't do anything else but to go along. Only this—just so he doesn't cut *my* throat. That's why the chairman was both grateful and leery.

Dr. Erich-Carl Wybau began in the following manner:

"The honorable member of the Senate Pameelke, whose good will and devotion to the patriotic cause is beyond reproach (there we go, thought Pameelke, I am the one, and the chairman smiled with satisfaction) belongs to that peculiar class of people who pretend to be doing things—an action which should by no means be disapproved of, if it were not correlatively connected in such people with a second action, which consists of being absolutely sure that they are doing something. In this correlative, in this second action, lies the great danger. You could barely suppress your laughter when you noticed that Mr. Pameelke, after his speech, not only acted as if he had taken a drink, but also that, after this apparent action, he seemed just as contented as he would have been if he had actually enjoyed a refreshment in reality. Mr. Pameelke behaves the same way in his mental life, in the realistic transformation of it, politics. Yet a thoroughly understood code of ethics does teach us that we are permitted to betray others, but never ourselves. I am a bit sorry that such elementary wisdom still needs to be stressed, since we are after all among people in whose hands rests the preservation of the patriotic values of our nation. For values are only safe when he who is entrusted with their preservation stands above them, when the preserver is not a dupe at the same time. The true king knows—because of the relativity of his kingship—that he is only a symbol, the mythical paraphrase of an idea of the state. He himself doesn't have to believe in it as if it were an *absolute* value, because he is merely a petrified expression of it and has the function of ensuring its preservation—just as the stone externalizes a way of being, or, put in yet another way, the king has no other function but preservation. The creator believes in his thought, but he who has the function of preserving it does not. Outside the fact of being personally interested—a factor which however is decisive in most cases—the preserver is conservative, because he believes that, like an individual, a people either has to have genius to break with tradition or it cannot be allowed to break with it. Furthermore, since a human being cannot believe a priori in an individual, let alone collective genius, it follows from this axiom that he who is disposed towards preservation is inclined to this disposition because he cannot and may not make allowances for the very vague possibility that his people may have genius. This genius can only be proven a posteriori. But the breaking with tradition has to occur before the facts. In order to accept it there would have to be a reason to believe in the a priori existence of genius.

"The skeptic does not find this reason. Seen as an individual, he who is disposed towards preservation is always a skeptic and, strangely enough, when you turn the formula upside down it still fits: the skeptic is always disposed towards preservation. Sometimes unconsciously, and often so, abstractly disposed towards preservation that he is averse to our patriotic phrases, which already smell to him too strongly of demagogery. For that matter, true patriotism, the kind that has not lost itself in an ultimately meaningless abstraction, is common, plebian. Such love is unconsciously attached to basic things, climate, landscape, fauna and flora, and to the spiritual expression of these specific values, i.e., the swampdweller is attached to the song of the fisherman, because it is the spiritual expression of his climate, the swamp. But such childish attachments to basic things is not for you, gentlemen. You are not the leaders among, but of, your people. And you can only be that when, as defenders of the national tradition, you think truly anationally.

"In fact, there are some among you who think not only anationally, but who don't even think at all. (Pameelke felt he had to grin.) Did not the honorable member of the Senate Mr. Pameelke say that the internationalists had sold out? This would be excellent if this were said in a public meeting. But here among ourselves we should not have to prove to each other that we are incapable of thinking an idea through a little bit. This phrase would indeed fit perfectly in a public meeting, since the masses love slogans the way girls love chocolates. The masses never test against reality whether a slogan is true or false. They accept the slogan as is, because they like punch, bravura. So truth does not need to go look for a slogan, but punch does. That's why I like Mr. Pameelke's slogan, it has punch. This punch should nevertheless not forget that after the sentence about being sold out, the question follows, 'To whom.' And the answer, 'The enemy,' again appealing to the masses, has indeed no substance, because this would mean that the Teutonian internationalists would have sold themselves to the Fochanian government and that on the other side the internationalists from Fochany would be in the service of our government. Well, it is unnecessary to fool each other with such nonsense. That way we just lose precious time. It is of utmost importance always to keep the following in mind, that there are truths for the others and truths for us. This latter category, those truths pertaining to us, comprises in reality only one, namely, that even relativity is relative.

"Now to get to the heart of the matter. I hope to be the spokesman for all of you, gentlemen, when I give thanks to His Serene Highness, Prince von Alp-Alp, for his clear exposition of the problem. Hence I have finally arrived at an affirmative answer to the question of His Serene Highness whether there still exists a way to bring the Teutonic people back on the right track. Yes, there is a way. I hope to be able to show you with my modest means that I speak the truth —really gentlemen, you need not smile—the relative truth, if you like."

The forthright tone with which this confirmation was spoken pleased the auditorium greatly. Even Pameelke looked again with great interest at the orator. The concept of "Motherland" was so close to his heart that, when someone offered to save this abstraction, he immediately forgot his personal grudges. Pameelke is a very idealistic man, both in the popular and in the philosophical sense of the word. He is so possessed by his idea that he completely forgets the meaning of or even the concrete reason for this idea.

Dr. Erich-Carl Wybau continued:

"There is a way. But I must correct the hypothesis stated by His Serene Highness, Prince von Alp-Alp. His Serene Highness thinks that as Teutonic patriots, we should be very glad when the internationalists and pacifists become the masters in the rival country of Fochany. Allow me to answer this immediately. Such a notion is childishly false, gentlemen. It is totally unrealistic, not even tested against reality. It sprouts from an idealistic conception of patriotism, hanging painfully on to its meaning which has become folklore, instead of seeing in this idea merely the sensually clarified pose, a tactic of a party for the preservation of the state. Therefore, if we pose the question, 'What do we want,' the answer will be, 'We want to be the boss.' Why do we want to be the boss? Simply because we put more faith in ourselves than in the others. What do we want to accomplish if we are master? The supremacy of our oligarchy in Europe. This is a correlative of our belief that the Teutonian people has been chosen for a world mission. However, since we are at the point of losing everything, we will have to dismiss this ultimate goal for the moment. If I am presently successful in showing you how to become boss in Teutonia, then is there no further need for you to investigate whether this way is—strictly national or, as I would put it, in a folkloristically, national sense—patriotic. That is, when the end, 'a patriotic, conservative state,' has been saved, the means, hidden by the end, escapes criticism. Or, to put it even better, a means is always patriotic when the end which is to be realized by this means is patriotic. A property of a property of an object is a property of that object itself, isn't that so? And without deluding myself that I am pronouncing an axiom here, I mean to say that, seen politically, the end stands to the means in a predicate relationship.

"Contrary to the opinion of His Highness, I say that we have the greatest interest in the fact that, in neighboring countries, the conservatives should man the helm. And I prove that the masses do not have the slightest interest in abstract national values. Such values leave the masses to Mr. Pameelke. The masses have no sense of fair play. They do not conquer for the sake of conquering, but only when they are forced into this conquest, or when this conquest can be presented to them as the result of defense. The masses are realistically patriotic, not idealistically. To warm the people to a cause it is necessary to find a concrete symbol, a formula as neat as the infamous three eights of the Social Democrats.[1] The masses are such that they subconsciously wish the racial cause to coincide with the cause of absolute justice. In the democratized nations of Europe the sense of justice has become—since it was driven as a wedge into the heads of people by the proclamation of the Rights of Man—the most pronounced characteristic of the masses. But if you know kids, you know what illusion offers salvation. It is sufficient to create the illusion that our patriotic cause is also the cause of absolute justice. Now, gentlemen, we all agree that justice yields to the preservation of the well-organized race. The state and the conservatives of Fochany think the same thing. In that case these conservatives have to make themselves guilty of a trespass against that which the people feel to be absolute justice. Then we have the illusion of defense. The people need this illusion of defense and follow us meekly where this feeling of justice is satisfied. Gentlemen! *chauvinism is an international affair.* What are chauvinistic excesses here are reasons for chauvinistic incitement there. Patriotism, thus developed in two rival states, is like a pendulum that develops its movements in geometric progression. To speak in practical terms, what, according to you, is the most advantageous to us, that the draft be reduced in Fochany or that it be increased more and more? If you don't know the answer, gentlemen—though in fact, being the leaders of the Conservative Party, you should know it—I will tell you. The second alternative is the most advantageous for us. If you can prove that the rival country is armed to the teeth—and proving it does not imply that the situation has to be so in reality—then credit will be readily granted for a massive arms build-up of the nation, even by the Social Democrats. That proof will make short shrift of the pacifists.

"Now I will also attempt to prove my thesis—for my hypothesis has already become a proven thesis—*ad absurdum*. Imagine, totally defenseless rival states. We, the patriots, appear with a program which includes large credits for the army and the fleet. In the rival states, however, the words fleet and army still convey a folkloristic idea—children play hide and seek in what remains of former fortifications. Do you think that we would reap much success with our program? Do you really think, if we were to enter a defenseless country, that we could easily keep the soldiers separated from their house and home—that is, that when we are not supported by a concrete symbol of justice, the soldiers would make the sacrifice without a murmur, exchanging peace and hominess for a nomadic soldier's life? The masses obey after all the same laws of naïve morality as individuals. If someone strikes a cripple and is overcome by a feeling that he is a Neanderthal, but who nonetheless desires to strike, who would dare defy the public criticism of his action? Granted that we could talk our people out of their collective morality consciousness—no flattering hypothesis, gentlemen—and be able to lure them into a purely barbaric campaign, then the masses would still become irresolute from fear of shocked public opinion, from which follows the terrible feeling of isolation for a small mass of purists in the midst of a league of all the other collectives.

"I conclude: let us adopt the methods of internationalists. I have already said that chauvinism is an international affair. *Chauvinists of all nations, unite.* It is obvious that such an international action of the conservatives has to remain a secret organization. In the eye of the people we are patriots. Publicly we disapprove of everything foreign. However, we have acquired the knowledge that patriotism cannot thrive along only one side of the border. It thrives simultaneously along both sides or it doesn't thrive at all.

"Since we are primarily interested in the rivalry between Fochany and Teutonia, we have to form a *Fochano-Teutonic corporation for the exploitation of patriotism*. By forming a trust of patriotism both here and there, through reciprocal services of the Fochanian and Teutonic chauvinists the patriotic feeling in the people will be roused. Naturally, you do not seem totally convinced. I expected that. You find it a dangerous business to find common cause with the Teutonic patriots, right? One question—do you prefer to make common cause with the Teutonic internationalists? Fine, the general disapproval I expected came just as spontaneously as I had expected. Well, then there is no alternative, you will help each other to deceive the people in order to bring them back on the right track. But be sure to consider the following: you will help the Fochanian patriots, but they in their turn will help you banish decadence from your people. What possible advantage would we, as Teutonic conservatives, have in the decadence of the Fochanian people, when this would be equally the case for the Teutonic ones? Rather, a bellicose Fochany keeps ours on its toes. *Non delenda est Carthago*![2] In this way the Conservative Party becomes again master of the country. And you gentlemen agrarians and industrialists . . . precisely, you understand. In order to reach a model military state, both Fochany and Teutonia need forty to fifty years. To render accounts never falls on your shoulders, but the profit is always yours. And then again, both nations will have in this supreme case an equal chance to win the suit. To divide the chances equally is the function of the trust, And now, gentlemen, place your bets."

Obviously, at first the Fochanian patriots would not go along with putting Dr. Wybau's plan into action—an understandable fear of falling into a Teutonic trap. Wybau thought, "Double or nothing" and put his papers back into his briefcase. "I am very curious, gentlemen," he said, seemingly as a farewell, "to hear what results the upcoming elections will bring to your party. It seems out of the question to me that the battle can be won on the basis of slogans. My opinion is the following—I am sorry to see that it is not shared by you—that the national block, as you are pleased to call your party consortium—my congratulations by the way, a fine name—that the national block could surely use a couple of heroes. The only concession I can make to you as far as my party is concerned is this: we are willing to commit the first chauvinistic crime, if you can give us a slight reason for it. What do you think of sending two losers to Teutonia, with the label

'Fochanian patriots.' We'll take care that they are dispatched. To be sure, I know that you fear a trap. There is indeed a trap, but it is hardly meant for you. My task has ended, take me for what I am, a simple travelling salesman in patriotism. Nothing today. *Merci et au revoir.*

He bowed and left.

After Wybau had gone, one of the seasoned leaders said: "I see no other solution than the one presented by this young man. Whether the Panteutons will also profit from this solution is of secondary importance to us. As Panlatins, ultimately we are after all closer to the Panteutons—honest patriots from their point of view—than to the unpatriotic rabble of our pacifists. And furthermore, we know that until this young man turned up, the victory of the latter appeared impossible to halt."

When Wybau reached the station at the border, he was paged: "Le docteur Vibau, s.v.p."

A telegram. Fochany's Conservative Party kindly requests an interview with Dr. Erich-Carl Wybau.


When you develop an oilfield, you start by drilling a few oil wells. You don't drill the entire surface which is to be exploited. Why not? Practice makes perfect. The liabilities are too great if you exploit a large area without countermeasures. Slowly but surely, as experiences teach.

When the material you are developing is an idea—you see, ideas are "stuff"—then this law of the nonsuperfast tempo applies even more. When you exploit an idea you must think, all beginnings are difficult. But once you're past the beginning, nothing is so unbelievably easy as the exploitation of an idea. It is not very easy to get the masses to move, but once they're moving it is a pleasure to see how you can accelerate the tempo—mechanically quite a perfect merry-go-round. Start with a moderate dose of morphine. All by itself the result will be that the morphine addict demands his needle and syringe every half hour.

As far as the trust is concerned, for a few months you let the newspapers do the preliminary work.

Create atmosphere. You can also look at an idea as a vegetative growth.

Is it possible that someone at the busiest traffic center of a metropolis—the capital of Fochany is the largest metropolis of the continent
—could be murdered precisely at noon? Nevertheless. Hear the
screaming. The voice betrays an old man. The voice screams, "It is a
shame. A shame. It is an undefinable shame. A shameful shame." A
girl calls, "Mother, they're saying that something is shameful. Come
on, mother, let's go see what shame is." The mother says: "Yes,
child." When the girl who is curious about shame reaches the spot,
she finds an old man standing before a newspaper stand destroying
newspapers. Is this the shame? Her childish mind made her expect
more. She was betrayed at the boarding school. The girl yells,
"Mother, I have lived through shame, am I pregnant now?" But the
old man doesn't stop screaming, "It is a shame," while he keeps on
destroying newspapers. When you get closer you notice—such
strange newspapers. And you associate—Gothic print, damn it, they
are Teutonic newspapers. And sure enough, now you can even hear
the man cry, "The government should forbid a thing like this from
selling krautpapers here. Remember Sedang. I am a veteran of
Sedang.[3] I captured three Teutonic banners there. That's the way I
am. That was an honor. But this is a shame. Boiling tin should be
poured down the throats of traitors who read krautpapers. Where
are our traditional torture instruments. Thousand times shame."
Loafers. Discussions here and there. Interest in this strangely agitated
gentleman. Cop: Keep moving. Ten past twelve, everything is normal
again.

If you take the other side of the coin . . . at midnight in the capital of
Teutonia, a bustling unknown on other days. Something is stirring in
Fochany—So what sir—To be sure, sir, don't you read the newspapers?—But I do once in awhile when my sandwiches are wrapped in
newspaper—But, sir, how can a man in our day and age . . . no newspapers . . .—Yep, that's the Teutonians for you, they don't know their
ass from a hole in the ground until it is too late—You're right, sir,
when the barn door is stolen, one shuts the horse—Excuse me sir,
you look quite dark, are you perhaps a Fochanian subject—Sono
italiano—You see, I told you, it is a Fochanian. Down with Fochany—
Würstchen mit Sauerkohl gefällig?[4]—What's happening? Read. "Die
B.Z. um Mitternacht. B.Z." Read about the horrible anti-Teutonic
manifestation at Montparno! Five dead and twenty wounded. A
Teutonic nursemaid abducted by the Fochanian rabble! A little hat

and a little flower were found in the Saine—Can I take a look for a minute, sir—Hey, you there, stupid cluck, can't you see where you're walking—By all means sir, do what you want, I pray you—There you have it alright.

The *B.Z. um Mitternacht* has a headline.

HORRIBLE ANTI-TEUTONIC DEMONSTRATION IN MONTPARNO

and gives the story as follows:

"(By telephone, from our [—] correspondent): Today at the stroke of noon a gang consisting of fifty-odd members of the patriotic league of Fochany stormed the newspaper stand, situated at the corner of rue de Paris and avenue des Pays Bas, in the center of the city. The attackers were armed with truncheons and blackjacks. The reason for the attack was that the newspaper vendor had paid no attention to an order *not to sell any more Teutonic newspapers*. While some of the demonstrators were occupied with destroying Teutonic newspapers, being apparently especially after the *B.Z. um Mitternacht*, others dragged the poor newspaper vendor from his stand and attacked him physically with truncheons and blackjacks. Still others addressed the crowd, which at this hour and place is very large, and voiced threats aimed at Teutonians residing in Montparno. They spoke of pouring boiling tin down their throats. The public did not remain indifferent, but loudly showed its approval. There were screams of 'Down with Teutonia,' and here and there even 'Revenge.' A procession was formed. It made its way down major streets of the city. Curiously enough, the police seemed to have been forewarned of what the patriots had in mind, for they immediately took measures to maintain law and order during the march and to nip potential counterdemonstrations in the bud. The march lasted precisely an hour and forty-five minutes. The number of demonstrators was estimated to be between twenty to sixty thousand, which proves that really the entire population of Montparno—as far as is possible with an improvised march—participated in the demonstration. It would therefore be terribly inaccurate to represent the demonstration as being purely chauvinistic and thus to lightly deny the importance of the event. Several complaints of Teutonian citizens were filed with the police. The latter seem to pay little attention to them. A Teutonian nursemaid has been missing since yesterday."

And twelve hours later the Fochanian afternoon press: CAMPAIGN

OF SLANDER AND ACCUSATIONS IN THE TEUTONIAN PRESS. At the same moment in the Teutonian capital. A telegram delivery boy at a run. Lübeckerstrasse 51a. 49, 50. Look, bell, cord, pressing and leaning against, first floor. Sign: National League To Raise the Fallen Girl. Rings bell again. Office girl. Dr. Wybau, please?—All right— Urgent telegram—Thank you—A knock at the door of the private office—Come in—Doctor, very urgent—Thank you, Miss Schiele— Wybau deciphers the secret telegram. It reads, "The four girls found two in San Remo two Cairo returned prepaid border request to accept at that point tec."

Which, when translated, means, "Are sending you clods, made out to be two leaders, and two secretaries of the national block, but the scapegoats as promised. Please murder at least two, preferably all. Situation favorable. T(rust) for the E(xploitation) of C(hauvinism)."

Yes, such a thing could now be dared. The situation was favorable indeed, so favorable in fact that you could easily keep people a little out of breath. With the four future victims of nationalism the case was as follows: a soapmaker and a rural notary were accepted as candidates for the upcoming elections by the party committee of the national block. To enhance their candidacy they received a confidential assignment, a trip through Teutonia for the purpose of reporting on the political situation there. "I hope you will succeed," as the chairman of the party committee had said, "in gathering material with which our party can prove conclusively that the inclination of the Teutonian people has evolved sharply to the right." "We do our utmost," assured the soapmaker. That they would indeed do their *utmost* neither he nor his travel-companion, the rural notary, suspected. But they did do their utmost. Without knowing it themselves, just as Mr. Jourdain[5] writes prose. Truly great figures, for that matter, never know the great deeds they perform. From their point of view their greatness is an accident.

The soapmaker and the rural notary were very neatly killed, and one of the two secretaries badly wounded, but ultimately saved. This happened right in front of the Adler hotel. *

A chock-full restaurant at eleven o'clock at night, which would otherwise be filled by a third. Chock-full means, two-thirds filled by

*The Fochanian has just sent the Teutonian government a note demanding that a memorial be erected in front of the Adler hotel. It is expected that the Teutonian government will refuse. The averages on the stockmarket are hard pressed.

the cronies of the T.E.C. Someone yells to the band, the national anthem. The two-thirds applaud. The soapmaker can't make head or tails of it. The bandleader says, bitte schön, Herr geheimer Ober-sanitätsrat. Press the button, all the cronies stand up. The soapmaker and the notary simply ignore the tune. Consequently do not stand up. The cronies scream, stand up. Threaten. Hell, when krauts say stand up, then we gotta sit straight first of all, don't you agree, notary? You're absolutely right, soapmaker—A bottle of champagne—tut, tut, real champagne in Teutonia!—smashes between soapmaker and notary. Splinters clink bewilderment. Then bottles, dishes, chinese vases, chairs. And screams, stand up. Throw this bunch of foreign bums outside. On to the good war. To arms. War is war. And there you are, pistol shot. Soapmaker, whadya think, going outside—Thank God, the manager and the waiters form a row. The foreign guests escape. To be sure, they escape. A car. The door slams shut. The danger is . . . someone jumps on the running board of the car. Glass splinters. The notary sees the barrel of a pistol. Four shots, one right after the other. Something falls off the running-board. Walking. What's going on. What has happened? People. The cop. Who is the murderer, gentlemen. Where is he!—In the park—a young man adjusts his clothes a little. Has he fallen to his knees? Quite excited. Rests a bit. Okay. Puts the collar of his overcoat up. Cigarette. Finished that one nicely, too.

The police didn't find a trace. The chauffeur said that when he heard the first shot, he simply lost his head and therefore had not thought to brake. While the Teutonic press thought this explanation quite acceptable and made the belief gain currency that the Teutonic police had acted properly, as far as was possible—and that one should on the other hand not lose sight of what strange characters one was dealing with here (indeed, weren't the murdered men spies? who can say?)—in short, while the Teutonic press exerted itself to relieve governmental responsibility, the Fochanian press saw instead in the fact that the murderer or murderers had not been apprehended, proof—two times two is four—that there existed a holy alliance between the government and the hideous gang of murderers . . . . For it appeared all too obvious that the murderers had been assured immunity by the government. Thus the Fochanian press queried, what can be learned from this event? First, that the Teutonic government hardly bothers to disguise its ultranationalistic tendencies.

Secondly, two deadly honest Fochanian citizens had been dispatched by the Teutonic people, which means for the Fochanians that they fell on the field of honor. Léon Baudet,[6] the famous leader of the *Action Fochane* raised the suspicion that the murder of the two Fochanian patriots was planned by Fochanian defeatists, who were presumably headed by the infamous financier-traitor Blaireau. These defeatists would have secured for themselves the cooperation of the ex-monarch of Teutonia, who, with the idea of organizing the plot, would have been smuggled again into his country. The press of the national block, however, called this suspicion fantastic, and Baudet received from the T.E.C. a serious reprimand, that he be very careful in the future not to anticipate the facts, i.e., not to make the dumb masses digest more than the training of their stomachs—figuratively speaking—would allow for the time being.

But the victims, the heroes without knowing it themselves!—You never saw so many people in Montparno. And flowers on and behind the bier. Lord almighty, what flowers! The entire Riviera was shorn. Thank God it was spring and the tulips between Leyden and Haarlem could, if I may put it that way, be mobilized en masse. The crown of deep violet tulips which had been sent by Maurice Marrès,[7] the famous patriotic poet, crowned everything. You've got to be a poet to come up with a thing like that, don't you see. That Maurice Marrès has always been a very original man.

Man! did you see that procession along the Champs Elysées—Champs Elysées,[8] that's great, why didn't they stay there, they had reached their destination—What, the gentleman dares to poke fun at our national heroes?—Defeatist—Traitor—I recognize this fine gentleman. He is the lover of Mata Hari—To the gallows—Death to traitors—It really was not proper to mock the eternal values of the nation on such a day.

An avalanche over the nation, the election campaign of the national block. Millions of copies of portraits of the two national heroes slain on the field of honor were distributed. The soapmaker's widow commemorated her spouse royally—she had his likeness reproduced on all the cakes of soap. In a jiffy the statue of the two Castor and Pollux types adorned every Fochanian city of at least 5000 inhabitants. You got them on stamps, on decks of cards—the soapmaker was the king of hearts and the notary the king of clubs—on street-organs and ice cream carts. The cinemas showed a guaranteed true-to-life depiction of their heroic deeds and deaths. Their dignified behavior in the restaurant where they refused to greet the Gessler hat,[9] then the Teutonian murderers surrounding the car, the heroic defense of the victims and the police, at a great distance, allowing the murderers to complete their business while looking the other way, and even the moment when the car was going to escape and a policeman lifted his stick in the air and thereby stopped traffic, delivering the heroes in the hands of their executioners. Throughout the entire country it became a triumphal march for the candidates and propagandists of nationalism. The *vox-populi-vox-Dei* verdict destroyed the defeatist-pacifistic monster. When by ten at night the outcome of the election in the capital was certain, young men of the patriotic organizations trooped, followed by the people who now meekly listened to their orders, to the People's House and to the buildings of the newspapers which had sold out to Teutonia (their having sold out appeared to everybody a clear-cut case). The place was smashed to pieces. A couple of traitors —happy channelling of the people's fury—could be finished off.

There! There you are. As I told you. The internationalists didn't say, kill me please, I deserved it. On the contrary. They defended themselves like wild men against civilization. The worst thing was you couldn't make short shrift of them, for whatever the case was in Fochany, patriotism had not yet penetrated the Teutonic people. So damned difficult to make the Teutonian people feel nationalistic. That's why the killing of this unpatriotic rabble ran into certain difficulties. But not insurmountable by a long shot. Thank God, one can count on the help of professional soldiers, the clerks, and the judges.

Down with the traitors! Kill the swine! Beat the swine to death! Arise, arise, youth of Teutonia! High school and college students, midwives and whores, all of you who are interested in a solid nation, arise! On to the good war. Organization C has taken it upon itself to kill the swine!

Indeed, Teutonia could not fail. The honor of the nation. And mark my words, when Teutonia does something she does it right—guaranteed production work—and as wholesaler. Within three months 6785 Teutonian defeatists had been murdered. Of these 6785, 6784 were, as the police report indicates, struck-down while attempting to escape, while they—suspected of propaganda dangerous to the State —were under special police protection. Well, you see that's fate, trying to escape is for a defeatist the surest way of getting killed. The

6785th—he suffered from paranoia—had been finished off by the soldiers for humanitarian reasons.

We can already permit ourselves a few fantasies, thought Wybau. Who sows shall reap. The most notable Fochanian politicians of the national block, with interests in heavy industry, saw—to their not so trifling joy—the truth of the proverb once more confirmed. After the smashing victory of the national block, the change in the draft laws was mere child's play. These laws were not changed just once, but ten times. This was a result of Wybau's method: every increase in the active service of Fochanian draftees was answered by the Teutonian government with a new proposal concerning the country's prepared-ness for war, and, in order not to be outdone by Fochany, it raised the service of its young men yet a bit more than the government of the national block had for the Fochanian draftees. This behavior of the Teutonian government then gave the Fochanian Cabinet a reason to revise yet again its recently revised draft laws, on the basis of the "situation created by the Teutonian desire for war." In order not to suffer a shortage of arguments concerning these revisions in the draft laws, another exceptional wellspring existed, the spies. If you know how to handle it, you can get the folk-psyche to imagine "the spy" as a very vicious, sneaky, animalistic man. And such a depiction in the manner of Bosch is always a viable argument. To the people, vice is never a reality, but always the dragon with seven heads.

The police of the Teutonic capital nabbed a dangerous gang of spies. They had specialized in photographing the documents of the Teutonic secret service. A spiritualistic spy and his medium were arrested in the Pantheon of Montparno. At the moment the spy was busy interviewing deceased statesmen about the secrets of Fochanian diplomacy. If they refused to answer—which might normally be expected of deceased patriots—he would, threatened the spiritualist, desecrate their grave. A spirit whose ashes rest in the Pantheon is very sensitive to this sort of thing, hence the erstwhile statesmen gave in to this spiritualistic blackmail. Once arrested, it was difficult to restrain the spiritualist. Luckily an occultist-cop was found, who succeeded in neutralizing the fluidum of the black magician—five Fochanian engineers were arrested in the Teutonian mountains. They had been entrusted to fill the Two Towers Peak with dynamite. In wartime a pilot would be able to turn more than half of Teutonia into a pile of rubble—No less important was the arrest of two bacteriologists at the moment when they each brought a suitcase full of typhustuberculosis and cholera bacilli across the border—But the strongest spy-stunt was undoubtedly this: Teutonian engineers and pioneers disguised as workmen had penetrated Fochanian territory up to the redoubt Ronveau. They had already carried the cupola of the redoubt across the border when General Gourdot showed up, true to his habit of inspecting the forts of his sector twice a day. Consulting only with his courage, the general went up to the Teutonians and ordered them to surrender. The general's virile language made such an impression on these barbarians that they immediately fell into line, letting themselves be led as prisoners to Fort V of the third sector. "The heroic conduct of Your Military Excellency* saved our country," said the President of the Fochanian Republic in his telegram of thanks and praise.

After things had alternated in this fashion and over a three-year period spies were arrested and military service extended by turns in both Fochany and Teutonia, the result in Fochany was military service of 66 months for the cavalry, 64 for artillery, and 62 for infantry. In Teutonia those eligible for the draft were faced with 74, 72, and 68 months, respectively. As a matter of fact, the experts had declared that this time was needed to produce a good soldier.

However, it was only when the orders for equipping the army started to come in that an industrialist could begin to notice some of the benefits. Especially after the Fochanian parliament, in order to alleviate the manpower shortage, had passed a bill which provided a nice solution: soldiers could henceforth be used in factories. Their wages, which were just about *ad libitum*,[10] were to be deposited in the treasury . . . how logical, since the state was responsible for the maintenance of the soldiers. Similarly, heavy industry was also able now to lower the wages of the workers who had not been drafted. If people grumbled sometimes you could always—not to mention the fact that you had means now to take drastic steps—point to the danger of the neighboring nation which was busily arming itself to the teeth. Really now, do you think that is the fault of the government. But a free people should know that freedom is the most supreme good which a free people can possess and worth your sacrificing your

*In Fochany a general is officially called His Military Excellency, General So-and-So. This expression has, however, not yet found its way into the spoken language.

entire freedom to defend it with your last breath. It is a matter of course that concrete freedom will always be sacrificed to abstract, to moral freedom.

At the first lustral feasts[11] of the T.E.C. the heads of true patriotism from both of the now very powerful militaristic nations were united, the leaders of the conservatives as well as the directors and limited partners of the company. The balance sheet was quickly drawn up. Exports, which now no longer had to be allocated by the leaders concerned but which, under the heading of "secret funds," were taken care of by the ministers of interior and foreign affairs, were always carefully balanced by the imports. The goal of the T.E.C. was not to be directly a profit-making business, but those who through T.E.C. actions had indirectly received substantial dividends had therefore not forgotten their obligation not to be extra mindful of Dr. Wybau and his helpers.

A spirit of plucky comradery reigned during the lustral feasts—all fine socially-minded people who had transcended rivalry. After the gala dinner, when it was time to toast, the Fochanian chairman drank the health of the Teutonian patriots, lauded their capacity for work, thereby concisely summarizing what the Teutonian patriots had achieved from the attempt made on the notary and the soapmaker. At the mention of this event there was some hearty laughter. Marrès was not the one to enjoy it least, the poet of the deep violet tulips. To the abduction, as the chairman put it, of the redoubt Ronveau. He finished his toast by expressing the wish that the Teutonian patriots would soon be able to welcome back their beloved imperator-rex. To this end, if it proved necessary, they could count on the help of the Fochanian patriots. The chairman of the Teutonian party thanked the speaker. He too expressed himself without constraint and in a spirit of comradery, or better, *gemütlich*. Several orators praised Dr. Erich-Carl Wybau. The honored participants of the lustrum also paid a visit to the magnificent mausoleum of the first two national heroes since the existence of the T.E.C. Flowers were placed on their grave by the Teutonian delegates and the board of directors of the T.E.C. But in order not to wound the Fochanian population, the bow with the names of the eulogists on it was not attached to the flowers.

Only one unpleasant incident interrupted the otherwise continuous joy of the lustrum's festive spirit. A Fochanian industrialist argued during the general meeting that, since the desired results had now been achieved, the T.E.C. should simply be dissolved. He said, "In both countries the reins are in the hands of the patriots. We now have a strong nation and a strong army. Therefore the T.E.C. no longer answers a need. On the contrary, this company can only be detrimental to the ultimate goals of patriotism. Since we have achieved this jointly, winning our peoples back to the national goal, the moment has come to say farewell. From now on every state is responsible only for itself." This speech gained terribly little support. Psychologically, too, it showed little insight, since it paid no attention to the fact that the influence which had emanated from the T.E.C. for five years had changed things, to wit, now the people had taken on Pameelke's role, while this Pameelke felt himself very much at home in the role of international trustee of patriotism. Hence it was quite sufficient that Dr. Wybau made the situation of five years ago come diagrammatically alive to give all those present goose pimples. But going straight to the point, Wybau argued, "The honored interpellant is right insofar as that the T.E.C. can easily be dissolved without our immediately bearing the harmful consequences as patriots. The masses are for the moment quite into the swing of things. Five years ago they were, on the contrary, already quite a way on the path to internationalism. But the masses are now into the swing of things and *remain* on the right path only because, with the necessary tenacity, we point out to them the harmful consequences of an unpatriotic attitude. We go with a whip after them. But drop the whip. The masses will not *immediately* realize that there is no longer a whip after them, no, but they will do so ultimately. Then what? True, we have the power, and there's no question that when we hear rebellious voices, we will have nothing to fear at first. Our power, however, our material power, is the people themselves. Ultimately speaking, we no longer control this material without this moral force, the consciousness in the masses of the undeniable fact that the sacrifice has to be made. Dissolve the T.E.C.—outwardly our armies remain just as strong as before, but by dissolving it the process of demolition has already begun. It means going to Capua.[12] After all, you can try it just as well as Hannibal. In my opinion, the T.E.C. should be a permanent organism. Indeed its existence is especially justified in times of war. What do you think of a jolly war with international law alternately violated by the Fochanian army, and then by the Teutonian? You have no idea of the potentials the Trust has. The Trust can shorten or perpetuate a war at will. And, perhaps most important, the Trust can regulate the end of a war in such a way that even the vanquished patriotic government will no longer fear a revolution. Instead it will remain gloriously in power, which is also important for the victorious nation. The conqueror has no interest in a revolution in the country of the conquered party. After all, that's just like a fire in your neighbour's house. And from a positive point of view, it also is really of interest to the conqueror that the partner be back on his feet as soon as possible. Above nations, elevated above the vicissitudes of peace and war, the T.E.C. should be the regulator which allows us to hold the fate of Europe in our hands forever. It should be the metaphysics of nations. Approximately what, according to the great Leonardo, necessity is in nature: 'maëstra e tutrice, tema e inventrice, freno e regola eterna.'"

Wybau paused for a moment, then he concluded with a smile, "The meeting can be adjourned until tomorrow, don't you agree Mr. Chairman? We have already lifted the required quantum of heavy theories for today. Shall we take a stroll through Montparno? You should know that I have reserved a small surprise for you, a cabinet document which, I hope, will always remain a souvenir to remind you of this first lustrum. Nothing, a game—but intellect is nothing but a game."

In fact it wasn't until they were walking down the street that the gentlemen of the lustrum asked themselves, What does this mean? In the streets of Montparno rules a quite unusual uproar. People who don't know each other stand in groups talking away. You see sluts being familiar, but at the same time all excited and in the same company as high society ladies. Gestures: the Eighth Wonder of the World has happened. Desperate gestures. The Eighth Wonder of the World *was* a terrible wonder. In cafés waiters are talking with customers. Buses have stopped in the middle of their routes. The drivers and collectors are also caught up in the general commotion. Underground stations are deserted. And you keep hearing, persistently, Neiffeltower. Neiffeltower? The famous Neiffeltower. All right, so what's all this about the Neiffeltower? Until the gentlemen have reached a point right across from the *Gazette du Soir* building. And there it is: in monstrous neon lights. And you can hear the fury and despair of the people. An old gentleman has a brainstorm. The entire square yells with one voice, The Krauts have stolen the Neiffeltower!

No matter where you turn you find despair and dismay. You get the impression that a national disaster was never so deeply shared by a people. If you enter a house, you find a pool of despair soundless with dismay. All presence of mind has left the people. Right over there is a man who buys a newspaper and keeps on running, leaving the bank-note with the woman who sells papers. Here you've got kids hawking newspapers who don't accept money. In this café right here the customers sit on the tables and have their refreshments on the chairs. There are ladies who—still at their dressing tables when they heard the news—painted their eyes red and their lips black with leadblue shadows around them. And one lady: hat, bathrobe, one shoe, and one slipper. She does not notice the cold and no one points out to her that she was probably in a great hurry. She participates in the general commotion quite naturally. Not one person thinks of making use of the occasion. Not a single wallet is stolen. Nothing but despair, fury, and dismay.

—But the Neiffeltower stands right there, yells Pameelke suddenly waking up, and proud to have discovered this naked truth all by himself.

—Come on, don't bawl so loud, Wybau says calmly. If people hear it they'll yell like a chorus. Man your posts and we'll have ourselves another big mess.

—The truth . . . Pameelke ventured shyly.

—Baloney. Look.

The people are standing right in front of the Neiffeltower. Women who sell newspapers call, the Neiffeltower stolen! The same for everybody—the Neiffeltower is stolen. The Neiffeltower stands gray in impotent reality. And the telegraph operators, far away from the noise of the streets, transmit from the station on top of the Neiffel-tower: the Krauts have stolen the Neiffeltower.

The multitude had completely stepped into the world of Pameelke, the idealistic patriot.

—Well, what do you think of that, Wybau asked Pameelke.

—Very nice. Incredible. I didn't expect anything like this.

—Expecting is always wrong, Pameelke, just like waiting. From a human point of view, the one implies the other. When you don't expect anything, you don't wait either—you do something. *What* is irrelevant. "The misfortune of these people lies in the fact that they are incapable of remaining quiet and alone in a room." No, to be sure, this wisdom of Pascal is not for me. Act, even though you know that all your actions are merely trivialities.

—Who is this Pascal, doctor?

—The same who said, Know thyself. But when he said this he was much younger. That's the reason for that boldness.

—You know everything, Wybau . . . Tell me . . .

—Well . . .

—Are you going to the girlies tonight?

—Haven't you understood yet, oh man Pameelke, that I don't like artificiality?

---

1. In 1914 members of the Belgian Socialistic Party sang a party song which contained the slogan: "eight hours work, eight hours rest, eight hours off."
2. Literally, "Carthage needs not be destroyed," which is a variation of the phrase "delenda Carthago." This means "Carthage has to be destroyed," and stands in general for something which has to be brought to an end or destroyed, and to which one returns again and again in order to accomplish that mission. This may be compared with the words of Cato the Elder who closed every one of his speeches with "Ceterum censeo Carthaginem esse delendam," meaning "I am furthermore of the opinion that Carthage has to be destroyed."
3. Allusion to the famous battle of the First World War, fought at Sedan, wherein incredible losses were sustained by both the Germans and the French. The entire story is a thinly veiled attack on France (Foch was the military leader of the French in the War) and on Germany.
4. "How'd you like sauerkraut and sausage?"
5. Hero of Molière's comedy, Le Bourgeois Gentilhomme, a vain and stupid man who takes lessons in becoming a man of quality. He learns from his philosophy tutor that he has been speaking prose for the past forty years without knowing it.
6. Léon Daudet (1868–1942) became famous as a political journalist for the reactionary paper L'Action française.
7. Maurice Barrès (1862–1923), novelist and, like Daudet, another French super-patriot.
8. This sentence contains a pun on the literal translation of the famous Parisian boulevard—Elysian Fields.
9. The governor of Switzerland, Gessler, put a hat on a stick as a symbol of authority, specifically that of the Austrian Emperor. He insisted that every Swiss had to salute it or suffer the consequences. Wilhelm Tell refused and was ordered by Gessler to shoot an apple from the head of his son. This and subsequent events emanating from the incident are the legendary beginnings of the fight for a free Switzerland and the basis for Schiller's famous play.
10. Musical term meaning, "to your taste, at your discretion."
11. Celebrations which are held every five years and also, in Roman times, rites of purification.

12. Capua became proverbial for its riches and its corresponding pride, rivalling both Carthage and Rome in power. When Hannibal, one of Rome's most famous enemies, was defeating Roman legions, Capua revolted and joined his cause. After Hannibal had been defeated, Rome recaptured the city in 211 B.C. and punished it severely. Prominent citizens were executed, its territorial holdings were confiscated, and it was stripped of all political rights. It never recovered its former glory.

# Hierarchy

The k. und k. Command of the umpteenth army corps understood the situation. It was obviously critical. Pessimism was warranted. For no one could argue that boys will be boys. *Et nunc et semper.*[1] You have to assume that they are virile. You must especially assume this of martial soldiers. Soldiers are men squared. Though not necessarily squares.

It isn't much fun in Cattaro. Cattaro in a state of war. The soldiers know nothing but bugs in their beds. And they would gladly have something other than bugs in their beds. The imperial and royal Oberkommando could do no less than find this wish reasonable. A brotheller found the solution. That is how he got the title of Engineer of Erotic Affairs.

Here's what the difficulty was in establishing a public brothel—officers and enlisted men. Plus an incidental difficulty, the total absence of women and space.

The engineer was a smart fellow. He found a house and even four women: a blind one, a lame one, a paralyzed, and a hunchbacked one. They were assigned to his establishment for one year. By contract of course. On sealed imperial and royal stationery.

The greatest difficulty remained—officers and enlisted men. Officers cannot, as is well known, have intercourse in a bed where soldiers have done so previously. Question of hierarchy and prestige. Render unto Caesar the things which are Caesar's. And officers have just as much right as enlisted men. On the other hand, it would be unwise to keep the brothel open only for officers. Result: destruction of the spirit of tolerance among the enlisted men and, who knows, maybe even mutiny.

There were only four rooms in the house. One for every woman. How to attune this to the spirit of hierarchy, the nerve of every important army?

As noted, the engineer was a clever man. With a sense of hierarchy. He reconciled the decoration of the rooms with the hierarchical principle: a bed and a sofa were allotted to each.

So what, you might think. That is no solution—the sofa is for the first act of wooing, the bed for the second act or knot. Come now!

The eroticism of the perfectly healthy umpteenth army corps is not that complicated.

The sofa is for enlisted men. The bed for officers.

The statistical reports of the women read as follows: Today I had two beds and five sofas.

That's what I call hierarchy. Indeed, even objectively, that is hierarchy. Synthesis of hierarchy: a bed for the officers, a sofa for the enlisted men.

That an army with such discipline perished!

Cattaro[2] brothel, myth of our civilization!

---

1. Part of a longer formula used in Catholic church services, "Gloria patri et filio et spiritui sancto, sicut erat in principio, *et nunc et semper* et in saecula saeculorum, amen." "Glory to the Father, the Son and the Holy Spirit, as it was in the beginning, *is now, and ever shall be*, world without end, amen." The irony in the context is self-evident.

2. This is the Italian name for the Yugoslavian city Kotor, a seaport on the Dalmatian coast. Besides being an important harbor for maritime and inland traffic, it has a fort which was important during World War I. Called Hercegnovi (in Italian = Castelnuovo) it changed hands many times during the centuries, finally belonging to Austria as a military citadel of the Austro-Hungarian Empire. In 1918 Slav sailors in the Austro-Hungarian Navy mutinied there. The uprising was supressed and many sailors were shot.

# The General

**B**y what chance the general was brought to our city, I don't know.[1] It is absolutely certain, however, that it was not by chance. People simply use the phrase, "by chance," when they really mean there was a cause or effect. It is a question of knowledge. And to show you that I know, I'll explain it briefly. It is all very clear. I suspect that the general's political and military life is finished. I told him so once. He began to scream like a maniac, grabbing alternately at a beer glass and at his (beloved) yataghan.[2] He was going to dash my brains in, or so he promised me in his anger. His role began only at that moment. Everything else had been a game. Now it was going to be serious. Every serious person starts with fun in the beginning. Up to now he had only fought local wars. And was responsible for the death of only 100,000 people. Now he had a plan which, without a doubt, would set off the real world war—even the Bushmen and the Tibetans would join in. And only then would he force his military and political strategy on the world, and obtain its homage.

The general is kindly disposed towards me. I have concluded this, without further investigation, because he did not dash my brains in.

Many who thought they knew claimed his name to be simply Ricardo Gomès. But he gave me his card himself. He is called Ricardo Gomes de Santa Cruz (naturally). And below his name appears, General of the Peruvian Army of the National Committee. He asked me to crush the legend that his name was simply Ricardo Gomes. "You can see for yourself," he argued, "It is entirely different on my card." He did not find it necessary to show proof of nobility. His logic was enough for both of us. If people like each other, they come so easily to an agreement!

I usually met the general between four and five in the morning. He was a regular customer at those places where the night people and the nightworkers—the nightshift, right!—girls, waiters, pimps, cardsharks, have a last supper or their first breakfast. The concept of time has slipped so much in such places that you cannot distinguish an evening meal from breakfast. You *could* say, of course, a *last* supper or a *first* breakfast. Both these definitions are really qualitative terms. As such, they do not have an independent temporal value, only a relative one.

The general is often tipsy. You cannot say inebriated, however. There again is a large difference. People who one day per month live it up, as they put it, are inebriated. The gentleman who celebrates at five every day is tipsy. The two extremes of the dignified and the commonplace clash here pitilessly against each other. The general, I must say, is *the* example of the tipsy gentleman, that is to say, his tie can be a tiny bit crooked, but then his monocle is even straighter. When he is tipsy he stands out because of a correct, but not caricatured, posture and because of an exceptional clarity of mind. The best impressions which I have of him are those which had such tipsiness as a foundation. He constantly controls himself when he is tipsy. If he says anything about anybody you can be assured that his judgment is the result of a real expert's deliciously thought-out psychology.

When not drunk he is something of a hermit. You can't help thinking then that those who maintain his role is finished could be right. When not tipsy he attempts to be stoically fatalistic, which he can't bring off—he has too much Latin temperament to forget his grudge against life completely. Then he degenerates (very slightly) into hypochondria. But when tipsy he is a Plato type, pessimistically idealistic. He is very human, with a Latin bent for the bon mot.

Enough! With all this I have succeeded more in proving my subjective propensity for such people than producing an objective picture. But one cannot be done without the other. You cannot give an objective picture without being in love with the object. You can also hate it or find it a caricature. All that belongs to the same category.

It is five o'clock. I don't know where to go. But at Richard's, *chez Richard, à la réunion des artistes*, I'll probably find the general. Naturally, he's sitting there. Just as naturally he is tipsy and greets me in a very friendly fashion, without forced cordiality.

"From your hesitant step I notice that you feel somewhat strange, as a poet amidst these artists. Thank God, because they are not real artists, you can feel the cozy intimacy of this place even better. For no one knows himself more a stranger than an individualistic artist among popular artists. Praise God that these artists are merely waiters and cardsharps, barmaids, and rakes. True, as an author you can't demand half price for artists, but on the other hand your appearance inspires more respect."

And a woman whines to a dancer-pimp, "I have my friend who

keeps me in high style. But I am prepared to follow you and leave everything behind."

The dancer kisses her and swipes her diamond brooch.

The general tells me, "This man thinks differently about it. He means: You must follow me in order to leave everything. Everything depends on the conjunction. That this couple knows enough to put the accent on the correct conjunction is the best proof that, as man and woman, they belong to each other."

The woman, however, makes a last effort. She obviously doesn't want to fall under the spell of the young man without a struggle. To be conquered only acquires meaning in terms of the value of the battle. Everything is transitory and also its own opposite, says Heraclitus. Thank God, Parmenides says the contrary.

The woman cries louder, "I didn't mean it that way."

The man has a yen for philology. He stretches his left hand out as if he has something hidden in it. With his right hand he swipes this imaginary object—that was precisely what I meant at that moment. The general acts the wise man. Not to reconcile the parties. He extracts the quintessence from their short dialogue.

"The worst," he says, "that can happen in the world is that the word 'meaning' is pronounced with two different meanings during one conversation."

But Richard, the bartender has the last word. He synthesizes for an audience of three bellhops, "That man is a general, a philosopher, and a drunkard."

The general pulls me to the side. We sit by ourselves. This is a sign that the general is in a talkative mood. He begins immediately. "My young friend, I notice with pleasure that you're a bit tipsy and, furthermore, alone—I mean, not in the company of a lady. The latter is proof that from time to time you succeed in being sober. And the first is further proof that you are usually sober when you are a little tipsy. All hail! Not only that. My pride is also tickled because I notice that when you are at your best you look for my company. *Te juvenem laudamus!*[3] That there are moments in your life when you prefer the company of a greybeard over that of an indifferently good-looking girl is proof to me of your search for knowledge. For our conversations could hardly be less wise than whatever fun takes its traditional if nonfatalistic course in the bedroom of a pickup. A little tipsy, however, and you see how pointless that tradition is. Sober, you argue

too much, purely empirically about the given of your little philander-
er's world. Then you think, without copulation this is just some more
wasted fun. If you are a little tipsy, your thoughts are on surer ground
even if your legs give way at some point. If they do give way, the
reason is that they can't carry the greater content of your
thought. But your spirit sees the senselessness of this penis-politics
being the goal of fun. The true goal of fun is asceticism. It's fine to dress
the spirit from time to time, like a clown. You discover its worth and
regret having made fun of it. Then you realize the pettiness and
comedy of your life. For natures like ours, which basically do not
long for asceticism, repentance is a blessed event. The way this night
is going, you have at least come to realize your incredible stupidity
and the destiny of this stupidity. You use copulation consciously or
unconsciously, as a means to prevent the recognition of this stupidity.
To be stupid isn't so bad, but not to recognize your own stupidity is a
tragic happiness. But let's stick to the present: you escort a barmaid
to her bedroom and by imagining the tale you will have to tell, you
get at least some dubious pleasure out of it. That you declare your
love, or she declares hers for you, is at least material for a good
anecdote. And if this does not happen, you still find copulation,
without such a declaration of love or lust, quite pleasurable. From the
empirical will, the speculative rising of pleasure. Should I congratulate you and all your pleasure-seeking companions?

"In our century, wisdom is the recognition of one's own stupidity.
The would-be ascetics only discover their own wisdom. Between two
people—the first of whom finds his ideal in copulation and the second
answers each temptation with a 'hence daughter of Babel' and then
transforms all day his unfulfilled, repressed eroticism into hypochondria—the first is still preferable. If copulation is the parent of
laziness, insofar as it detracts from the knowledge of your own
stupidity, then current asceticism is colorless, an optimism achieved
without a struggle—or even with one. It is therefore without value,
or worthless, because the eroticism remains just as obstreperous
and comes to light as hypochondria. Hypochondria is eroticism in
atrophied form. The stronger you thunder against sin, the more
ardently does the battle consume you and the repressed eroticism
revenge itself. Someone who has truly conquered, faces someone who
still struggles with an immense pity.

"You must begin with the complete void to know the senselessness of your life. Cell and bed detract from this knowledge. But now you choose the only possible road, the road between. I do not praise you. You don't deserve the slightest credit. Thank the hand which led you. So you lived it up for a night and drove away the senselessness of your actions with continuous drinking and gratification, without realizing that thereby you also magnified it. Yet suddenly you refuse the final thing which would help you get over your own foolishness: copulation. And so you stand at five o'clock in the morning in a Harlequin costume, realizing that there is no carnival. There is a direct casual connection between maximum stupidity and minimal wisdom, which is the recognition of this stupidity.

"Now you look up an old man, even a broken man, according to you. A Peruvian general who wastes his life in a harbor town. You won't get far with such connections. Just as Socrates preferred the conversation of boys to what was commonly deemed the twaddle of the Sophists, so you come unto me. Even erotically you choose me above the most gorgeous girl you met tonight. The intellect is sick of being just a complement to the penis. Now we can talk."

The bartender taps me on the shoulder: "The general is plastered. A minute ago he paid a bellhop to listen to him talk."

"Yes, these three kids were arguing about contemporary wars as if they were talking about truly ideal wars. They talked constantly about the strongest and the weakest. Absolutely. They came away from war as if it were child's play—that, by the way, is the only true way of waging war—child's play is the archetype of true war."

"Then you surely have put this concept into military practice?"

"Unfortunately that was not possible. I was even forced to become a Marxist. In our time, war is just a weak replica of the archetype. Man is a product of economic circumstances, says Marx. And the entire philosophy of modern war is 'l'argent c'est le nerf de la guerre.'[4] Poor mankind, sinking to such a low opinion of war! But worse yet— it really is so. War, the pure test of power between two masses which have become as one, no longer exists. War has no ethical meaning any longer! You find that, my young friend, a terrible paradox, don't you? Don't you see that here lies the secret of why I am a wreck? I belong to the type known as warrior. Such a person is just as tragic in our century as any other pure person. Napoleon was the last warrior. He was the last of our kind who could exercise power. He was the last general who really played chess. You are a poet and seek man's essence somewhere else. You want to know if people are just pawns of chess-playing generals. Your question sounds to me like something beyond my world. Therefore I do not hate you. I learned empirically that there are people who long for another kind of happiness than this game of chess. I cannot understand it. It is terrible.

"I am a wreck. I could not carry out my ideals. I dreamed of applying the *idea* of war to nature, to the world around us. I gave in to one thing after the other. And once I even reaped my laurels because of this militaristic Marxism.

"I was at war with a neighboring republic. Directly behind the enemy lines were valuable oil wells. Deep in the republic's interior were other even more valuable ones. Our situation was terrible. British financiers advised me to buy up the shares in the interior oil refineries under cover of neutral parties. I then massively attacked the entire front, my last effort. I occupied the first refineries. Their reserves having arrived, the enemy forces were able to throw me back, but paid the price of my destroying the captured refineries. I gladly allowed myself to be thrown back for this purpose and sacrificed 20,000 men. Then I stubbornly held my old positions. The shares of the destroyed refineries, all owned by interior capital of the enemy republic, went down in an amazing fashion. Mine rose proportionately! The enemy republic was without a cent. I united as many volunteers as possible and granted, after a month, peace. Now, is that war? I am ashamed.

"Between what truly constitutes war and its present debasement lies an immense difference. Marx said once—I repeat his most significant wisdom—'I am not a Marxist.' Neither am I. Only our senile century can trace war back to mere social and economical conditions. That these now play a large role is a fair judgment. Such a thing you can always prove. Our century is a regression to infantile romanticism. Listen, for example, to the laments of the vanquished about the cruelty of the conquerors. That shows a total lack of knowledge of the concept of war. Total war is a mutual striving towards this supreme moment: I am the conqueror. Cruelty or compassion are two extreme possibilities in the psyche of the conqueror. Lamentation or praise from the vanquished is totally insignificant.

"If you proceed from a pure idea, for example Condorcet's, that man is susceptible to an unspecified evolution, you can hope to conquer war. At least you could prove it theoretically in this way, and therefore be true. Theoretical knowledge is truth. With biology and ethics—with ethics as a human addition to biological fact—you can approach the problem. Pay no attention to the pacifists who haven't the slightest knowledge of mankind. It concerns the removal of something essential in man—his love of war. How silly anyone is who thinks he can combat this with statistics about casualties! It is scientifically proven that cruelty is a purely human attribute. Man's love of war is either passive or active. If it is passive, it remains the worthless lamentation of pacifists; if active, their babbling stimulates the others. The love of war and cruelty are different things, but they are as one against such laments.

"What is war? War is the clashing of two parties with the goal of separating the conqueror from the conquered. There is no significant child's game that does not spring from the love of war. Nonsense to believe that we suggest the idea of war to children. A warlike element resides in the sperm. Children divide their game into two opposite sides, even when they do not play 'war.' That already is war. Every child's game is like that. The child's game is an archetype, let me repeat. What happens is an artificial division into two sides, instead of what is biologically correct. Anyone who is against war has to strive towards this, to replace the artificial division according to caste, nationality, religion, with the biological-ethical given differentiation according to man's value. The evil of war sprouts first and foremost from making everybody equal and from the artificial differences which follow necessarily therefrom. This is the only stand you can take against war: it represents biological degeneration. An absolute—and surely unbiological—equality leads to artificial distinctions, and these lead to war as the arbiter of values. Both sides are basically equal, and only the difference of defeat or victory determines their value. Pacifists who believe the biologically unsound theory of absolute equality ought to admit that man must give in to his warlike nature, since by war you can at least establish their worth artificially.

"Love of war is present. It does not need to be active, but it is now necessarily activated by the universal equalization of people.

"Some theoretical idiocies and aspects of modern ideas about war which cannot be proven are the following:

that there are defensive and offensive wars;
that war can be defined according to principles of honor, like a duel;

*that the abolition of the draft would necessarily aid universal peace.*"

The bellhops express a hope that the general will buy them a round of drinks.

"Gladly," agrees the general. "A general speaking about war is more unselfish than an old man with a long-awaited potency. Selfishness lies on another plane. I gladly yield to the peripheral what I can regain inwardly."

He proceeds:

"Certain plundering expeditions have been called offensive wars. That is a confusion of terms. The British psyche, for example, has conquered its warlike instinct with a rationally individualistic philosophy of life. They don't know what war is. They only know plunder. That's why you don't see the British wage a significant war independently—they are merely allies. If they were not theoretical conclusions, one could believe in the theses of the gentle dreamer Condorcet. But this individualism, which protects them from such human endeavours as war, also protects them from other ardors such as art and religion. As a result of their individualism they now have the substitutes of hypocrisy and a flat decorative style. Hence the essential quality of their psyche is both good and evil. With the British you can see very clearly how the circle was formed, you see where it is joined. But it remains, nevertheless, a vicious circle. You can never go further than knowing that you know nothing. Don't forget Socrates' suicide. The French are conceited loudmouths and also great artists. They are absolutists who are incapable of doubting their outrageously silly pretensions. And here the circle is closed again—precisely here—their absolutism is the key to their amazing art. Can't you see yet, my young friend, that the world is a hopeless sphere with no way out?

"There are plundering expeditions and then there are wars. The British only know the first. The continental peoples, only the second. A war between France and Germany will always be a completely primitive clash between two sides. Only the concrete situation at the particular moment of war determines whether it is offensive or defensive action. It is like the situation in chess when the game already has been started and is under way. The very act of commitment takes the game beyond the question of offensive-defensive. An offensive becomes at most plunder when the defensive nation does not respond with an equally strong will to war. The defensive nation relies just as much on the value -judgment war will make. War begins with the agreement that this clash makes a judgment possible—with each party thinking it is to its own benefit. You'll accuse me of still dealing with two parties as being offensive-defensive. The second party accepts the evaluation, acknowledging thereby that its urge for war is ripe and that it has weighed its strength, with the intention of waging war. Trying to be the stronger while preparing a defense is a beautiful mass propaganda device. But theoretically it won't hold."

He notices that I am not quite satisfied with his exposition and says, "perhaps my argument is not quite convincing. But one thing is clear: war is a condition of being, whereas defensive-offensive is an illusion, a quantitative relationship outside the realm of abstract justice. Every war is an empirical proof that these alternatives do not exist in reality. Again a compromise. The urges for war and for democracy confirm each other in a hostile fashion. Defensive war is the compromise between the warlike urge and democracy. In times of oligarchy, hierarchy, or monarchy, at least the economic or religious goal was stated very clearly. Our age cannot muster that much courage anymore. The urge for war remains. But it has to manifest itself against democracy in an atrophied form. Defense is an invention of British individualism. That's how one fools Frederick, democracy.

Secondly, a duel and a war are essentially alike. But different in their manifestations. Honor is a matter of expression. That's why you can make a duel a matter of honor, but not a war. The norm of responsibility is different in each case. In war honor has to succumb to the egotistic responsibility of wanting to be conqueror. In the duel they can be united, in war they are separate values. One springs from the other. The duel is fought according to abstract fixed laws, hence in a duel, honor can be a steadfast principle, without interpretation. War is heavy with contradictory components. Honor becomes relative. Once relative, honor can't be maintained. It is either an unshakable concept or it is relative. If it is thrown from one relative position into another it becomes completely worthless. Honor can only be maintained if it is absolute. And it is precisely there that it is in direct opposition to the possibility of war. Absolute honor in war would mean a frank declaration of one's tactics and objective, conveying to the enemy, for example, that I am placing my troops there because I am going to do *this*. You play chess, right? Well, then this feeling should be familiar to you: when the other party has wrought

considerable damage with a move which you did not foresee, you
cannot suppress a certain feeling of resentment. You probably have
not explored this feeling. *It is the feeling, not the knowledge, of the
disloyalty* of the other party. Outward honor has nothing to do with
the inner notion we have of it. Even in such a fair game as chess, we
are unable to suppress feelings of disloyalty. And our urge to win the
game becomes a little friend to make the opponent pay for his disloyalty by an equally harmful move. Our disloyalty is reciprocal in this
case. If, however, we are the ones to make the first harmful move, then
we are controlled by the following emotion—one which you have not
made an effort to understand. Namely, that by this move we are doing
something dishonest, something like a sneak attack. Isn't that so? Our
feelings about honor would be satisfied if we said, 'This move I make
with the following intention.' Generally, this is impossible. It is impossible to satisfy both chess and our feeling of honor. To be honorable is to expose the actions and the objective. Absolutely. If this unshakable principle is not to be reconciled with the principle of war,
then there is even less chance of transforming it into the empirical fact
of war. Isn't that so? From then on it is necessary to define honor by
means of arbitration. It becomes relative, i.e., small so-called honorable agreements are reached in the midst of the general condition of
the dishonorable. But it is of course possible, even a fact, to displace
honor from this general situation according to your own desire or
necessity. Psychologically, the inherent feeling of disloyalty strives to
break through the loyalty boundaries imposed from the outside.
Relatively, loyalty is shoved from one extreme to the other; absolutely, an antimony between the crime of disloyalty and the peripheral loyalty. I have spoken."

"With another cup of coffee and a Dutch gin you'll say more,
general. For example, the abolition of the draft."

The bellhops demand a new round. The general delivers. The bartender quickly raises his conclusion:

"The general is a pederast but he won't show it, the dirty old man!"
And the general:

"Silence, Richard, you are a lucky fellow. You have your wife. For
you the problem of life has been solved: a woman and a bedroom, at
a discount. Leave others at least the happiness of their unhappiness."

"You can say that again."

"*Alors*, my young friend, the draft. Abolition of the draft would only transfer the battlefield from the outside to the inside. Conscription itself has transformed the warlike urge into a permanent prepared-ness for war. In this way, war is degraded, it is now caused more by this preparedness for war than by the primitive and spontaneous will to war. The draft can be the temporary domination of a superficial militarism—in this case the martial spirit is not primary. The army of Miltiades was martial. People are martial when suddenly called to war —like the Romans when they fought as one against the peoples of Latium and Italy. During the flowering of the Roman Empire, the organization of legions in the Provinces was military, the flowering, and at the same time, the fine overture of decadence. Militarism is an academic trivialization of man's martial genius."

"Sparta?"

"You mean to catch me, young man, because you mention a state which was both martial and academically military. In Sparta, what was academically military was not exclusively and not even primarily causally linked with martialism. There martialism was a direct philosophy of life and did not sprout from the stupidly conceited, 'Si vis pacem, para bellum.'[5] Militarism was the esthetic expression of a manly, virile, erotic philosophy of life. It concerned, in fact, the passion for martialism and not the burden of militarism."

"He definitely is a pederast," mutters Richard.

"That state is martial which can count on the inherent warlike traits of its citizens. That state is martial where the people, the totality of the individuals, is martial. Where military exercises are laid as a burden on the shoulders of the people, there exists the greatest danger to the martialism of this people. The inherent, spontaneous martialism is repressed by the outward military duty. In the martial state military exercises are free; they are equal to the arts or religion, as these are regarded in Europe. Military exercises are the expres-sion of the martial will in man, just as works of art are of the esthetic. Only in this independence can the martial genius develop itself. There was no draft in Sparta. There was a general desire for military exercises, so men themselves devised the laws of the military state. Not free, but completely independent. In this state martial will in-cluded also the ethical and the religious strivings. Martialism was primary. One can't say that of the European states. The draft can only be seen in the light of 'Si vis pacem, etc.' Militarism by no means grew out of martialism as an ideal way of life. At best it is a striving for martialism, instead of a result of it. Thus you get strivers, opportunists. You, a poet, will understand when I say that the same relationship which exists between bourgeois art and art exists between militarism and martialism.

"Universal conscription shifts the inherently martial to the periphery. Given a good standard of living, a state which has less martial significance can conquer a strong martial state which is economically less well off. So Marx is right again. Economic conditions govern military conflict. But in pure martial war, *the* war, the most martial wins.

"Abolition of the draft disposes only of militarism, not martialism. The latter is inherent in mankind. Stronger in some, stronger in certain peoples, and they will win martially. Martialism is a matter of ultimate ends, like esthetics. Its realization is difficult. It depends on war, on battle between two sides. Its realization demands human lives. I am martial and do not find this fact important. If you are an artist you surely want to sacrifice your life for art. I am martial and do so gladly for war. Not to mention that martialism expresses itself largely by playing with the uncomplicated complex of life and death. Martialism means furthermore that you also gladly sacrifice the lives of your friends and subordinates. This situation concerns ultimates, which allow for no discussion, but which can be fought over.

"Universal conscription, under which I naturally include the entire military apparatus, is a solution for martially weak states. This means that the martialism of the citizens has been weakened there and needs an outward stimulus. He who carries God within has no need for a monk's hood. The truly martial peoples have no need for parades, only, at most, military exercises prompted by the citizens' own free will. Their only desire. The animal species man is part of the state. Species of this kind strive more or less strongly toward martialism. The stronger the martial striving the less necessary is enforced militarism. Martialism is a qualitative nuance in the animal species man. Militarism is essentially not human at all. It will always remain a shell—the result of the European philosophy that clothes make the man. 'L'habit fait le moine.' Modern states try to give witness to their martialism with a helmet or a pair of red pants. Clowns!

"Decadence occurs when the inner worth of man is degraded, one might say, by outward ornaments. Real wars are a battle between two sides and therefore truly war. But when two sides are not divided according to a martial, but a military, principle, it is the encounter of two ornaments. The warlike urge often plays a parenthetical role in the state, although the state has to count on the warlike instinct of at least part of its citizenry for, if it could not, war could not realistically be sustained. But such wars are superficial. And they repeat themselves quantitatively very often because qualitatively they have little meaning. They are peripheral wars. The pacifists combat only these military wars and, therefore, a secondary 'evil.' I don't fear them because they do not penetrate to the core. While they attack militarism, they leave martialism untouched. And it is exclusively on the latter that I, as a man with a martial philosophy of life, build my hopes. You might say that the militarists control Europe. Their opponents argue from identical militaristic points of view. As if militarism is the heart of the problem. The pacifists are the victims of the militaristic philosophy of life. The principle of honor, furthermore, is nothing more than a compromise between moderate militarists and philanthropic pacifists. And here, again, the latter are the victims.

"Actual wars are a cheapening of the ideal war. No longer does war sprout from the spontaneous warlike drive of two parties, but from a militaristic situation. A militaristic situation is a perpetually latent war with a small outburst which transforms latent into active value. It has no depth. Real war is the transformation into activity of a latent warlike drive. The latter lies deep in man and a colossal harmonious upsurge is necessary to bring it to the surface. Consequently, it comes from the depths of the soul and becomes suddenly and spontaneously active. The ideal war is closer to martialism than to the militaristic surface. It is the supreme expression of martialism. And yet a great upheaval is necessary to transform this drive into activity. A war which follows from an arms buildup is merely a thickening of this situation itself. Such wars are intellectual, while the others are the life of the soul. A comparison for you. Art and artist are alike. The work of art is projected into the world from the profound spiritual urge of the artist. In a period like the Rococo, everything is art—no spiritual urge is necessary to create the so-called work of art. Hence the work of art is created without much labor. The real work of art is very close to the real artist, and yet it only gains intensity when it grows out of this relationship. Constant production takes the intensity away. The greatest realization of the artist is to create the work of art; for the martial man, to wage war. But in both, their being human prevents them from *beginning* to create before they have reached the pinnacle of their drive to create. From drive to surface, that's where their intensity lies. By arguing this way I want to squash the opinion that true war, since it is simply the realization of the warlike drive, would be a curtailment in intensity. Active war which springs from the latent war of the militarized situation is only peripheral. War which springs from the spontaneity of the drive for war is inward and has intensity. One other example as an illustration. Take two spheres and leave them untouched. Take two other spheres and press them in such a way that their contents spread in width, so that they become almost like two circles, as flat as possible. The first spheres have less surface area but more content than the second. Which clash, everything else being equal, will be more intense? You should also note that the spheres are at a primitive distance and that this distance increases their ardor, while the others, through their expansion in width, stand closer together, which decreases the ardor.

"Actual wars are a test of economic conditions, not of martialism, and therefore of only a small number of the conditions which can eventually be involved in martialism. I do not deny the value of the economic conditions, you see, although my goal is to achieve the ideal war which can be experienced outside these conditions. I combat them in the absolute, not in the empirical. You see, I am a Peruvian. I still like ideas!

"Therefore I conclude that abolition of the draft has as its only result the removal of the militarized situation and its consquence, the peripheral war. In this way room is again created for true war, that of the profoundly martial nations. With abolition of the draft the way is opened for the removal of a general hoax, that wars sprouting from this condition would be a measure of the martial characteristics of a people. By abolishing the draft, the possibility is raised of allowing war to be a clash of the purely martial characteristics of two peoples. The martial genius will then provide the means of wars which are currently provided by academic militarism. In my view, the law of arbitration can only end economic, and therefore unideal wars. Wars resulting from martialism can't be judged by arbitration, just as the artist can't be judged by public laws of morality. Once militaristic wars have been abolished, true war will rise again in all its old glory. War from spiritual need. After admitting arbitration over economic quarrels, you will have to admit that martialism is a matter of ultimate ends. War will be waged for war's sake. I am all for that principle. 'L'art pour l'art.' There you are young man, what I mean is 'l'art pour l'art!'

"The American prophets of mankind (duds, otherwise) fight very clearly against militarism and pretend they've never heard of martialism. Perhaps they mean well. But they can't help being rich and in business. If it isn't bad business, war is good business. You know what the truth is: 'La guerre c'est le nerf de l'argent.'

"With the abolition of the draft, the possibility of life for martial people and martial nations begins. The stronger peace is, the deeper the drive for war is repressed and therefore the more intense the ardor will be when the drive for war transforms itself into war. That's why it is wiser to say: 'Si vis bellum, para pacem!'

In martial war the best one wins. Martial war is waged with pure means, creations of the military genius of the leader and the masses. The European nations are becoming even more decadent. They have to resort to militarism. We Peruvians are a strongly martial people. In the war which will be true to the *concept* of war, we will have to win. I have complete faith in the future of my supremely martial people. I drink to the health of the army of the National Committee. An army to be sure, but only because of its desire for military exercises. As a man who loves war I have been completely won over to the idea of abolishing the draft. Away with the draft or even conscription! Long live war! I drink!"

"Hail, general!"

"I also want to drink to the health of your nation, my young friend. To . . .?"

I hesitate for a moment. My god, I don't expect much from such a toast.

I look for a way out. I say:

"Belgium, general, to Belgium!"

Whores and pimps have tears in their eyes at this moment.

"To the health of Belgium," they weep.

"Wave on, my dear little flag," Richard falls into my arms as if he were my brother. The parrot glorifies the general enthusiasm by really whistling a battle hymn. A drunken barmaid disturbs the enthusiastic theme. A left from an order-loving pimp brings her unseemly intermezzo to silence.

That's how much the general drew everyone together with his

toast. "It is an important explanation," comments a cardsharp. This opinion finds general agreement. Everyone else is in a delirium of ecstasy.

The pimp who loves order gives the following speech:

"Les salauds de Prussiens veulent accaparer les couleurs de not' 'tit drapeau national. To put it plainly, those bastard Huns want to swipe our flag. Eh bien, messieurs, cela ne sera pas! They choose the same colours as ours. Even if we have to go to war again. We all want to volunteer. And the general too!"

Richard theorizes: "Yes, basically the general is for war."

The barmaid dreams. She wants to say something impressive. It comes out: "The general is an intellectual—an asshole!" Richard removes this scandal from his establishment.

What is a storm? You might answer that a storm is a unity, and the calm of the seas is merely the passive state of the storm. You could also say that the storm is a multiple phenomenon which contrapuntally breaks the calm of the seas, which is a unity. Whether unity or multiple phenomenon, the storm abates. What is the storm which breaks the calm of the human soul, is it ecstasy? Is it one thing, or is it a complicated phenomenon, as we said first, breaking the calm?

The general smiles at me.

"Behold Europe!" His voice a scraping violin.

"Enough. Closing time." Richard throws his last customers out. The general and I lost sheep in the midst of a lean herd of whores and pimps. The general laughs continuously. Gray morning fades the motley garments of dancers. One dancer, still in a Pierrot costume, dances drunkenly away in the gray morning. Wilted rococo of our century. Under the black of overcoats deathlight appears, a white tip of a tie. The general looks as if he's looking at me. He laughs. Good-naturedly. My good old Ricardo Gomes. Poor Ricardo! (I was the only one at his funeral after he committed suicide.)

The night people look after the Pierrot dancing away. Our symbol. While dancing, he babbles a song which sounds gray and misty, one and yet broken.

"Pallas Athena." The general stands there, a little lost baby.

"Shall we get some fresh air in the park, general."

"I still have to tell a lot," he says.

We leave the group. The group dies, hardly visible. A silent rain which gradually levels a ripple of sand. A tuneless song is whistled by a pimp. Gray stubbornness in the morning. Elusive resistance. A few grains of sand, we are driven away from our lifeless little group. The dying of this lifelessness is full of futile sadness.

Clocks toll first Mass. Miserable shabbiness.

We sit in the park. It is naked. It makes no sense without the familiar swarm of children. A shivering nakedness. What keeps us here? The shabbiness is the character we ourselves give the morning. We want our role in it to the end.

This is the garden of the olive trees.

The words of the general hardly make any sense in the midst of the grayness. Grayness which drugs speech.

"My young friend, I do not want to disillusion you. The problem of pacifism, connected exclusively with antimilitarism—and along with, of course, a few phrases that what really matters is the spirit and one's view of life—has been falsely stated. I believe that pacifism concerns not only overcoming a social phase which is based on the relative inequality of people, but also on overcoming a biological condition which is that of the abstract equality of all people, and that differentiations become social factors. Humanity is biologically different. Abstract equality precludes social differentiation. The cause needs to be combated, not the result. If you want to accomplish something you will have to break those clowns. You must uphold Plato's principle, without his localized Greek conclusions. Today people uphold the localized conclusions without the principle. Empirical existence teaches clearly enough, for example, that nothing is gained with the abolition of slaves and serfs. In Russia, for instance, they campaign for the abolition of the serfs. That's good and praise-worthy. Once the goal is reached, you say, *Gaudeamus*.[6] If that indeed is so laudable. A group with the sign, 'Abolish the Draft' is, from a higher plane, just as useless or as useful as an organization for keeping the ghetto clean.

"The most meaningful and universal trait of humanity, more so than love, is the urge for battle. Only in mystical writings is the duality of *I* and *thou* resolved: the Godhead and man melt into one. Everything which lies outside that is relative. You have to think things through to the end. Namely, that the universal desire for battle is an inevitable biological stage, which can only be exchanged for another biological stage.

"I believe, however, that mankind as such is an end which in itself is not susceptible to change. Someday they will have to give up the illusion of peace, provided that, speaking abstractly they remain as they are. (Social change changes nothing.) For peace is a contradiction of their present nature. Then everybody will be content with their martial being. And the knowledge that it must be that way will at least liberate them from struggles with their conscience. Then the era of great warriors will return."

"Yet it is clear, general, that mankind struggles at least to dam up this instinctive desire. The law of Moses is at least a synthesis of Asiatic and European thought, isn't that right? It states, 'Thou shalt not kill.' "

"Precisely. Mankind has confessed to this commandment and kills all the same. To begin with, the essence of every law is to aspire to curb instinct. Instinct wants to kill. Clearly. The intellect imposes its veto and this veto becomes a general commandment, a natural law. Man has an unshakable faith in the ethics of this commandment. And his mind aspires toward this ethic, which he himself projects individually, making it universal, to follow it as a natural law. Instinct is stronger. Ethics gives way to biology. With all this you have only proven: (1) that instinct wants to kill, (2) that ethics does not know how to dam up this instinct. The desire for ethics is just as primitive as instinct. But the latter is stronger. From this fact we can develop two theses: that this relationship is constant, that the role of aspiring is assigned to ethics and the function of realization to instinct, because it has always been that way; or that this relationship is relative. That is, since both are elementary, conquering the instinct for battle indicates only a temporary relationship of the two elements. That this relationship can be turned around, because both have intrinsically the same value. This is the last stand that an ethically striving human being can take—that ethics and will, in relation to power, are equal. He can go no further. Man is neither good nor bad. The will to power dominates at the present time. Its domination is momentary. Further it can't go.

"I'm not trying to present all of this in a logical sequence. I am only voicing my hatred for these idiots. Nor am I a professional philosopher. You have to take all of this in its kaleidoscopic perspectives. Altruism and humanitarianism are stupid words. Pure fictions, not existents. Secondary theories which prove nothing. By setting altruism over against egotism you have *ipso facto* already succumbed to a warlike mentality. Man thinks dualistically. Dualism is latent war. Humanitarianism has no meaning. It can only have meaning if it is a reality. Those people who currently champion humanity and promise to marry a girl, take her and disappear without a trace. Anything one does today is twaddle, all within the same frame of reference. The only person who has worth, in terms of the present argument, is he who deserts for the simple reason that he does not want to give up his life. The others become soldiers and write books. Look, today you usually ask someone who tries to realize something idealistic whether he does this selflessly. This is complete nonsense. You should ask whether he can gain anything from it. That is the only reality. The other way is to delude with false facts. It is a lie and a delusion. Gain is naturally identical with making no sacrifices. It depends on the structure of man's soul whether he will make the largest or merely the smallest sacrifices for his own benefit. What is important is the peace of mind of man on this planet. He can never reach it. He can only strive toward it. He strives toward his own good. To ask for this provides the measuring stick of his existence. To ask for selflessness provides no measuring stick. When I order breakfast, no one asks me whether a coat would do instead.

"Today you ask a man whether he is for or against war, for or against free love. All bullshit. What is important is how the man is. Ideally speaking, 'for' or 'against' are secondary. These alternatives are not based in the thought of man, but in his biology. They are the talents Christ spoke of. 'How' is the important thing, namely the development of the talents. The first thing you have to learn is the indifference of man to himself. Without this no objectivity is possible. This is what brings pain, the rest is crooning."

He pauses. An imperative Peruvian gesture signals the end for me. I want to rise. He holds me back.

"Enough of that. But something else."

I am waiting now.

"Do you know my great secret strategy already?"

"No."

"But how could you know. I tell it to nobody. I want to tell it to you. Who knows if my end isn't approaching. Then you must execute this plan in the great war which shall come between East and West."

"Who knows."

"Listen and feel the blissfulness of partaking of this manna."

"Martialism is a matter of the ultimate ends of man. War is the realization of this martiality. For war is the conscious or unconscious striving of martialism. It is false therefore to view war as a consequence of other causes, especially of such things as social conditions. etc., which are not ultimate ends. The war which results from such things is an abortion of true war. I am not talking about any such wars. Hence my striving is to achieve the one true war by avoiding these wars. You see at this point we shake hands. The militarist vs. pacifist split represents temporal politics without the least ethical value. That's why, as a martial man, I can even shake hands with pacifists. 'Mea res agitur.'[7] The aforementioned split is not visible from a higher plane. The antithesis which bases itself on martialism—the martial and the nonmartial man—is real, without being pulled into pity by space. This is existence. These people are like little ant men and ant workers. The common cause of those who have recognized their true being is to be able to think about the illusory splits. Pacifism vs. militarism is not being. Among my fellow men I stand in defense of my inwardness, martialism. I am not trying to surmount it but to live according to it.

"I want a return to war which corresponds to the *concept* of war. I want to bring the concept of war out into reality. I want to do what Plato wanted when he went to Syracuse, discard the ascetic idea in order to realize the idea.

"Martialism is a question of ultimate ends. If you try to realize it in war then you should never forget this fact. Since war sprouts from martialism and is removed from social causes, it cannot be waged with social means. The present economic wars, which are essentially decadent, are also degenerate in their means.

"Martialism demands the realization of its life in terms of ultimate ends. Eros is the means of true war. You understand, eros. Such a pure thing as martialism cannot be tied to illusions such as social institutions. The realization of martialism demands a pure element, eros.

"Eros is the basis of true war.

"Hence it is false to divide the battle forces which are at the disposal of the army's Supreme Command on any other basis than the sexual-erotic one. The initial division is the erotic one. A regional division of the army such as they have in Germany—Prussian, Bavarian, Silesian regiments, etc.—is ridiculous. For God's sake, what do these people have in common, if one considers 'common' in terms of an ultimate standpoint like martialism. Usually they hate each other because of eros, the different sexuality of both, which can't be bridged either in a social or intellectual way. Why can't they feel the helplessness of a homosexual who stands between two heterosexuals! What has that man in common with the other two? So, what is regional unity compared to erotic separateness? And which force is the stronger, the erotic, which scatters this force, or the regional community, which keeps them together? Do you notice the frequent inconstancy in troops which are formed on this social basis? That is inner weakness under a strong façade of an iron harness! The present armies are corpses. They don't have *one* structure, *one* striving, necessarily one, you understand, since the cause is *one*, *one* life and *one* blood. These troops have no human structure, they are not individuals. Each individual has eros. In these troops no attention is paid to the individual, with his elementary drives. These troops are a mishmash of dehumanized individuals. Where no attention is paid to the human within the multiplicity of the one, this multiplicity can't be crystallized into a unity. If you deny what is unique in each individual, you also deny what is unique in society. Only from basic similarities can you build a higher, communal individualism. Despite all differences, there are communal elements which permit the design of a primitive, architectonic, higher individualism. The element which separates or binds is eros. In order to express the life and ardor of the individual, the community must be built on human existence, not on social illusion. The latter is not binding, The nature of present armies is such that they will flee when they face troops which are unified by human bonds. Our armies only make a stand because the other armies are just as malformed. Our armies are rotten in origin. But try to imagine an army set up according to eros! Troops with the same love urge, that is, with the same spirituality! See the ardor of these troops.

"My army of the future will be arranged on a sexual-erotic basis. In subdivisions it might be possible to let conscious opinions be expressed. But the subconscious is what is binding. That is the trump.

"I will divide my army into heterosexual, homosexual, bisexual, fetishist, sadist, and masochistic regiments. There you are. A regiment of ascetics is also conceivable. Hermaphrodites are, as is well known, usually at home in any one of these categories. Narcissists are an exceptional case. Obviously you can't do a thing with exhibitionists at the front. At best, they could be used as the vice squad in the occupied territory.

"Just look at the advantages of such a division. According to Plato, eros is the desire of the soul for a better fatherland, for a better *Heimat*. Eroticism is the sexual realization of eros. But eroticism is not just sexuality. It has overtones of human culture, of political culture in the human-biological sense. Realize from all this the greater unity of people who are separated and bound together according to their eroticism. It represents a unity on all sides. We could speak of it as a metaphysical unity through transcendental longing and an empirical one through being similarly directed by the sexual expression. No split among these people. They can speak the mystical words, 'Your desire is mine.' Transcendental contemplation is achieved as the basis for ecstasy. My war is not waged without ecstasy. And only from this realistic erotic soil do I see the possibility, with hope for general consensus, of nurturing this mystical unity which is ecstasy, or at least the way to it.

"These troops are readily mobile. Their eroticism is one single motor which moves them. War gives these people the opportunity to fulfill their desire for a better fatherland. The large space of the battle-field plays along in this harmony, the stretching, the expansion of their desire. They have to feel the way a convalescent feels who for the first time draws a breath of air fresh. First of all, it is not important what the direction, the dynamic, of their life is. But how it is. The principal thing is that it does not necessarily carry its decline with it through the antithesis of the elementary forces. First and foremost it depends on the basic unity, after that on the striving of this unity. Each unity is useful. Only dualities are destructive.

"All these regiments can be used according to their characteristics. The practical side of war is waging war, and that is complicated clock-work. For each type of sexual existence you can find the matching area in warfare. Now for the relevant details, systematically arranged:

"I will place the regiments of masochists in the most dangerous spots, the front trenches, on bare slopes. According to their essence, they are quietists and wait for sexual incitement from the outside. That's why they can never be used as storm troopers. Storm troopers have to provide the ardor themselves. The character of masochists, however, corresponds beautifully to what is expected of defense

forces: to endure, even in the greatest danger. A preliminary initia-
tion is necessary. That's why I put the greatest emphasis on erotic
schooling, not by psychiatrists, but by those who can be called pro-
fessionals in this field—I'll be straightforward—for example, by
pimps. The point is, naturally, to adapt the individual sexual drive to
the general character of war. That is to say, you usually see sexual
gratification only between two people. You must learn to view a larger
scene. You won't have to look far, as long as you bring a masochist to
actions which are essentially sadistic, for example, the action of storm
troopers. But you can get him to view this essentially masochistic side
of war as a realization of his sexual drive. You could, for example,
argue that the masochist who is stationed in a dangerous position
would probably try to see his enemy at close range, to have the object
of his love near him. Instruction will remedy this danger. If the enemy
is close by, then everthing is over with one blow. So it is clear that it
is essential for the masochist to keep the enemy at a distance for as
long as possible. Only that will be a guarantee of his pleasure. According to his erotic character he is obliged to stimulate the enemy's
attempts, and he can only do so if he performs his duty well as an
occupation soldier. But if his drive is transformed into the realization
of his ultimate goal, then his joy is also gone. I have examined the
problem from all sides—I assure you that masochists are the most
perfect troops in the trenches. They joyfully station themselves in
places where no one else wants to be. In order to satisfy their
eroticism they are at the same time obliged to fire at the enemy so
that he can answer most accurately. And if the enemy attacks their
trench, it is a regular feast! They will defend themselves to their utmost, not because to do so expresses their sexuality, but because the
enemy is such that if they don't resist, they simply get slaughtered.
But to beat the enemy back, I have other reserves standing by, since
you can expect the masochists to defend themselves only insofar as it
is stimulating. As you can see, these regiments of masochists are of
colossal value. Without them you cannot even think of defense—no
one gladly lets himself slowly get killed. Furthermore, war is usually
not a rising tide of victories, but the ebb and flow of victories and defeats.
So you must be prepared for both. You should not sacrifice troops
needed for a victory at a position where strategically a defeat is
needed, or where defeat is definitely a primary necessity. In contemporary wars there is too little speculation about the psychic value of

defeats. Psychically, a defeat strengthens the sadistic eroticism of those regiments which I want to use, in particular as storm troopers. And my storm troopers will splash into the enemy troops which have just won, driven by the intensity of their desire to conquer and the wildness of their sexuality, which has risen to its zenith. Dynamism—a stronger force than dynamite. Quick and easy—*veni, vidi, vici.*

"I have already demonstrated that sadists make ideal storm troopers. To look at enemy troops as erotic objects is in their case even easier than with masochists. It is sublimation pure and simple. Don't forget the multiple appearance of their object arouses their eroticism correspondingly. The more enemies, the stronger their eroticism, and therefore their power to attack, for their eroticism is sadistic. If resistance is strong, then it merely stimulates their eroticism. Trying to obtain their sadistic orgasm concurs with their psychic striving to see the ultimate defenselessness of their object. All this needs no further discussion—the sadist's power to attack lies completely and directly anchored in his eroticism.

"The two extremes of war, defense and offense, can be expressed by the erotic concepts of masochism and sadism. All of war is a motion from and to the extremes. The natural stages in between are also valid. Pure defense and pure offense are extreme and rare cases, just as in eroticism, pure sadism and pure masochism. Both of these are perversions insofar as they are the hypertrophies of normal erotic qualities. After all, everybody leans either towards masochism or towards sadism. This leaning is of great value to me, of course. It makes an identical line-up possible with the defensive-offensive motion of war. My other regiments can therefore be subdivided into heterosexuals with sadistic leanings, heterosexuals with masochistic leanings, etc.

"Homosexuals are of the greatest importance in warfare. They form the elite troops. Because what is not the case for heterosexuals does apply to them, namely, that the erotic object and erotic subject are together in the same army. These troops are animated by a spirit of exceptional solidarity. That speaks for itself. A spirit of love hovers over them, fortified by the hours of shared suffering. To transfer more homosexuals to such a division in wartime is, believe me, to give their love its greatest potentiality. Do not forget that masculine eroticism has an undertone of melancholy, even when this masculine eroticism is heterosexual. If it is homosexual, however, then the melancholy is both in the object and in the subject. In masculine eroticism, suffering is inherent in love. And now, in war, their love stands suffering in the midst of tangible, incessant destruction. And so their love achieves the highest harmony and they live in this harmony. Miseries become a paradise, for every subject knows that each object bears this suffering with love. And the knowledge that perhaps soon the hour of separation will strike drives them into a paroxysm of love. Everyone wants to make a wall of his body to protect the body of his sweetheart.

"Now don't think that every soldier will aspire only to protect his erotic object. First of all, it is never certain whether he really has only one sweetheart, and even if he does have only one, whether he nonetheless desires many others. But this is nothing. A man's love is not absolute and object-centred, like a woman's. A man's love is cosmic, a woman's love is objective. And the love of the homosexual is even more cosmic because he knows the object shares the same essence he does. The suffering which man always experiences with love is a psychic formation of this cosmology. He therefore embraces the entire army with his love, not only the object. But won't jealousy split the homosexual army? Least of all, precisely because of the cosmic nature of manly love, subjectively present in everyone, objectively seen in everyone. But won't the homosexual when he discerns a beautiful love object in the enemy ranks or simply because of his cosmic nature, be crippled in his capacity to attack? Manly love is composed of eros and intellect, logos. True, you can't say of a man, this is eros, this logos. The fusion is complete. Eros does not want anything illogical. The well-organized homosexual life is after all the homosexual's ultimate realization of his cosmology. His cosmology has a goal. Anything that tries to force its way into his paradise, by means of sexual drive, is unconditionally viewed with hatred by the fused eros-logos. It is an intruder. *L'intrus*. By logical necessity, the categories of good and evil are at this dangerous moment decisively defined.

"The homosexual regiments form an organically closed world. Hence they are to be trusted no matter where they are. Reflect for a moment on the pyramidic foolishness which occurs in today's armies, the persecution and punishment of homosexuals. Anyone who treats them that way has no inkling of their traits and inherent qualities. In my army, not punishment, but the greatest development of their sexuality will be law. And then I'll take on the combined armies of

Foch and Ludendorff.[8] Their penal colonies will succumb in the very first moment to my one erotic living army. Hosannah!"

A churchbell strikes six. It must have a mechanical defect. For it is definitely seven. The general breaks the mystique of the clocks. "I have to admit that you can't do very much with onanists. At least I have not discovered yet in what way they can be pampered. They love to philosophize too much, like Schopenhauer. That is both their virtue and their fault. In the final analysis, they really do have too little sense of reality. Germany must definitely have the greatest percentage of onanists. The theoretical wisdom of these onanists usually leads them to be attached to headquarters. That is naturally a disaster. That's how they can theoretically prove that they will win any war. But in fact they lose one battle after another. They cannot be used even in that capacity.

"That fetishists can be pampered is on the other hand much clearer. I don't want to argue whether fetishism is or is not atavistically determined. The object, the fetish, certainly isn't. Maybe it is possible that someone comes into the world as a fetishist. But that he choses a woman's shoe instead of a woman's glove depends on his upbringing. Yet fetishism is probably still a pure perversion. At first the fetishist also loved a woman's foot. Later on he preserves only the shoe as a hypertrophy. Since the fetish is not essential, it can be removed by upbringing, suggestion, and other aids, and be replaced by another, gradually or suddenly, depending on the individual. The fetish can be sublimated. Instead of a shoe, a fetishist can be brought to love a cannon. He is then the perfect artilleryman. *C'est très simple.*"

"Indeed."

"Young man, I ask you not to joke—all of this has been deeply, seriously contemplated. You have to take away from the hetero-sexuals all hope of eroticism at home or in brothels 200 kilometers behind the front. But allow great bacchanals with new conquests of cities and territories. They have to become convinced that advancing is identical with satisying their eroticism. Then they will promptly sublimate their need and experience the attack erotically.

"Contemporary warfare is a total fiction and accident. Real war is a true event, and to put certain means under moral censorship is therefore fantastic and stupid. Every means which serves warfare is, from the point of view of war, realistic and not to be neglected. To neglect certain means in wartime is to playact, to be conventional. All baloney.

"When storm troopers have to make an attack, they are fed half a pound of meat. What does that mean? Half a gram of cocaine makes them worth a thousand times more than with five pounds of pork. The latter diet sprang of course from the narrowminded spirit of the German High Command, which has an eye only for quantity, not quality. Again my thesis: narcotics and stimulating pharmaceutical products are indispensable means in war. To deny the value of such means is stupid, not to use them is neglect of duty.

"Kola is already a sufficient means during normal attacks. It also suits heterosexuals better, whereas homosexuals need the additional spiritual working of cocaine. If a large-scale attack is planned, over-feed the heterosexuals with kola. Behind the front there is no satisfaction for them, but you give them a speech telling them that with the occupation of the first city they can carouse. Only one way remains for them—forward! Give cocaine to those who are more spiritually inclined, or whose love is more blasé, or stronger psychic-ally. Their eroticism transforms itself into a do-or-die attitude.

"Cocaine moves into the sphere of the ideal, and transcends empirical suffering. One goes into a rain of shells without so much as a peep, seeing only the activity of the storm, feeling only the satisfaction of the cocaine high, and not thinking about the split between normal suffering and normal joy.

Cocaine provides, as you know, a powerful *joie de vivre*. While experiencing joy soldiers bypass temporal sufferings. And cocaine also induces activity, so the soldiers march on fulfilling their duty while enjoying life to the full. Death doesn't frighten them, and killing is no longer murdering—conscience too has been put at ease. Everything depends on a certain cosmology. To be killed or to kill no longer counts as suffering and evil.

"This is a beautiful lyric subject, an attack of storm troopers high on cocaine. You yourself can elaborate on it. I merely touch on it here. But not a syllable can be uttered against my contention that cocaine is useful. There is no doubt that of two equally strong armies, the one that uses cocaine will win.

"Ether also is a useful drug. As is well known, an ether high con-sists mostly of formidable auditory hallucinations—in the midst of an advancing army you hear a hundred bells tolling. Their sound keeps on surging. So it can be utilized against drumfire. The noise of drumfire is absorbed by that of the resounding ether high. It becomes narcotically sublimated. Though it has an unnerving effect on the ordinary person, it works only as ecstasy on the etheromaniac. But there is a danger. Someone may point out: 'It is not enough that drumfire does not paralyze you. Ether should also have the power to spur you on to action. It's true that you aren't paralyzed any longer by artillery noises but on the other hand the ether narcosis itself leads to the same effect.' Ether is still a narcotic, but whether a high immobilizes you absolutely is not proven at all. For we have seen barmaids who are high on ether dance so sublimely that we forget such a dance was unthinkable in a 'sober' condition. What follows I have deduced from my own experiences. That it is always the case. I naturally do not want to maintain. Hence: an ether high affects an individual in the way he himself assumed it would *before* he inhaled. You can clearly see that a dancer etheromaniac, when she is high, has a different conception of space—it is much more expansive than usual. How much always depends on the particular personality—it's limitless. Now I know there are etheromaniacs who only fantasize without acting it out. I doubt, however, the general validity of this. What I find usually the case in an ether high is the realization of empty space. Nothing less than that. But how we react to this realization depends on the individual. That many are oppressed by this realization says everything against them. Nothing, however, against ether's principal use in pampering. And I always speak in principle. You have noticed this already. Furthermore, you could probably make use of a combination of ether and cocaine. The second would neutralize the paralyzing effects of the first. And so only the useful properties would be effective. When negotiating for peace, narcotics are unquestionably important. The so-called primitive peoples have already taught us this, who thereby give proof of their higher development. The chieftains gather together and immediately a pipe with opium or Indian hemp is passed from man to man. A peaceful mood cannot be far behind. So an agreement is always reached promptly.

"I am a very peace-loving person. The wars I wage are never the result of imperialism, but of martialism. Once the martial strength of my army has been proven, I naturally have not the slightest interest in the peace terms. Next to war, gentle peace is therefore dearest to me. And so I am willing to smoke the opium pipe. And so will all those others who have only waged war to actualize the personality they contemplated.

"But can peace be achieved only through negotiation? If so, then it is clear that the only mediator is an opium pipe. If Wilson had been serious about a just peace, he would first and foremost have demanded that Lloyd George and Clemenceau[9] smoke from the same pipe into which the German delegates had already drooled. That's the way it is. Without narcotics, no negotiated peace!

"As you can see, every problem is simple when you finally see it, and its solution is, too, if you take the right road. Anyone who is martial definitely has to be against contemporary militarism. Anyone who is must be equally opposed to pacifism. The battle of militarism vs. pacifism is a battle against windmills.

"I therefore present my proposal: let us form an organization. I for war, you for peace. We unquestionably belong together. We have common enemies, people who distract attention from the real to the immaterial. A vicious circle we can never get out of. The first meaningful war will be the one which is waged to liberate the dilemma known as war-peace from its irrelevancies."

The general shakes my hand. As he moves off, he says, "Make an outline of the organization's statutes. I do believe my concierge would like to become a member. We only have to assure him that we are also against the tax on dance halls."

---

1. This story, which mentions Plato frequently, may have had its source in the writings of the Greek philosopher. Consider the following passage from the *Symposium* (179): "And if there were only some way of contriving that a state or an army should be made up of lovers and their loves, they would be the very best governors of their own city, abstaining from all dishonour, and emulating one another in honour; and when fighting at each other's side, although a mere handful, they would overcome the world. For what lover would not choose rather to be seen by all mankind than by his beloved, either when abandoning his post or throwing away his arms? He would be ready to die a thousand deaths rather than endure this. Or who would desert his beloved or fail him in the hour of danger? The veriest coward would become an inspired hero, equal to the bravest, at such a time; Love would inspire him. That courage which, as Homer says, the god breathes into the souls of some heroes, Love of his own nature infuses into the lover." (Translation Jowett's.) The entire *Symposium*, as well as Book V of *The Republic*, would be an illuminating concordance to this tale.

2. A dagger or short sword with a doubly curved blade, worn especially in Oriental countries.

3. Pun on *Te Deum laudamus*, meaning, "We praise Thee, O God." Hence the phrase in the text means, "We praise thee, O youth."

4. "Money is the backbone of war," which the General later inverts, to mean, "War is the backbone of economics."

5. "If you desire peace then be prepared for war." Again, the General later inverts this to mean, "If you desire war, be prepared for peace."

6. "Let us be merry."

7. The correct phrase is from Horace's *Epistles*: "Tua res agitur, paries um proximus ardet," meaning, "Your own interests are at stake when your neighbour's house is on fire." It came to mean, during the Roman Empire, that the interests of the State are everybody's concern. As rewritten by Van Ostaijen, then, the phrase means, "My own interests (are at stake here)."

8. Ferdinand Foch (1851–1929), French General and Chief of Staff during World War I. His inspiring personality and military genius helped France win against Germany. Some of his aphorisms became famous and are particularly relevant in this context: "The will to conquer is the first condition of victory," and "A battle won is a battle in which one will not confess oneself beaten." It was Foch as General-in-Chief of the Allied Forces who commanded the final offensive in 1917–1918 which forced Germany to submit to an armistice. Erich Ludendorff (1865–1937), German General during World War I and the primary influence of the German Army in 1916 when his partner, Hindenburg, took over the supreme command. It was Ludendorff who masterminded the last German offensive of the war in 1918 which brought France close to disaster, but which ultimately failed. His adversary was Foch.

9. David Lloyd George (1863–1944), Welsh statesman who, in 1916, became the Liberal Prime Minister of Britain. His unorthodox personality and methods made him one of the most controversial political figures of this century and helped him push his country through the last years of World War I. At the conference of Paris, he, Clemenceau, and Woodrow Wilson decided the fate of Germany. Between the American's desire for a settlement based on international law and justice, and Clemenceau's demand to keep Germany as weak as possible, Lloyd George kept a middle course which incorporated both views of conciliation and revenge. Georges Clemenceau (1841–1929), French politician and Prime Minister. Famed for his blustering temperament and ferocious pen, he was nicknamed "The Tiger." When in 1917 the fortune of his country was at its lowest, he was called back from retirement to guide France away from the brink of disaster. Vigorously supporting Foch, Clemenceau refused to condone the prevalent mood of defeatism and took sole political responsibility for the conduct of the war. Being an intractable enemy of Germany, Clemenceau demanded harsh treatment of that nation during the preliminary talks leading to the Treaty of Versailles, and was the principal architect of the presence of Allied Forces in Germany to insure the faithful carrying out of the Treaty.

# Four Prose Pieces

## Small Forest

After an acquaintanceship begun fourteen days ago, this morning the little forest of not very tall pines became suddenly estranged and then, simply, strange. The sunbeams, abruptly warmer from one day to the next and—we are in the month of June—for the first time warm and bright, have almost completely prevented the possibility on the retina and in the brain of a relationship between the little forest of not very tall pines—there yesterday and saved in memory— and this forest now, with the light, which is so totally different. The difference is so great that, where yesterday you ascribed the most beautiful circumstances of this forest to chance, today you discern everywhere a connection, yes, a structure of which the sunlight would be the mortar. Indeed, from pine to pine and everywhere a gap could be, there is now the light, not as something accidental which could vanish—for instance when a cloud pushes past the sun— no, but as a durable construction. This is the relationship of the pines to each other and of the pines to the light. But there is something extravagant about it. So extravagant that you might think a prince— no, not a king, but a prince such as Hamlet was a prince—would have wanted a palace from such singular materials, or his parents might have wanted it, to meet halfway the excesses of their deedless son and his insatiable satiety. For they guessed that peace of heart and tranquillity of spirit could be his only after his retina became threadbare from the maddest realities of light.

You must lie on the ground. Thus, across the ground, past much ochre and brown, past much green, your eye gains the bark and again the green, the old and the young and finally this gray, this crazy gray green, which is so exhausting that your eye flees to earth and slowly, only slowly, awakens to the motion of a brown hay wagon in the midst of the yellow-brown bed of needles.

# Nicolas

Once upon a time there was a man. His name was Nicolas and everyone called him by his Christian name, Mr. Nicolas. Let me explain first that there is no resemblance between this Mr. Nicolas and the one who is the hero of a novel by Restif de la Bretonne. No, I do not mean a hero of any story, but a man who, though no hero, is in all honesty called Nicolas and to whom one says Mr. Nicolas. Now, one could think that being called Nicolas is neither terrible nor exceptional. I understand this point of view, but I do not share it. On the contrary, I do find it terrible and exceptional. I find it even terribly exceptional and exceptionally terrible. For when Nicolas enters the barbershop, the barber says: "Good day, Mr. Nicolas," and immediately thereafter, without a pause between, races the voice of the apprentice, shrill after it: "Good day, Mr. Nicolas." And, as if one were at the bottom of a narrow valley where the echo is bounced back and forth, the parrot calls after the apprentice and the barber, "Good day, Mr. Nicolas." Sometimes it happens that an old customer enters after Mr. Nicolas, and he greets, "Hello everybody. Hello Mr. Nicolas."

If he is at home in the evening and feels nice and cozy, alone with his wife and, for example, in the midst of memories of his youth ("Yes, that Harry Lammerse, he was a damned nice fellow"), he suddenly hears the maid lie to someone, probably just a friend who dropped by, "Mr. Nicolas is not at home. Mrs. Nicolas is not at home, either. Yes, they are probably at the opera. Yes, tomorrow you have a good chance to catch Mr. Nicolas." How heavily on one's conscience weighs such a lie, with the bright vowels and the stress on the last syllable. For every time the stress is like a hammerblow which drives the nail deeper into the receding mass of conscience, built on the loose sand of a lie, Nicolas! Once again there will come a prophet. He will be awakened in the middle of the night, and the voice of Elohim will call and the vowels will surely ricochet, "Nicolas! Nicolas! Have you heard my voice, Nicolas!"

For this name is worse than a name and worse than a shadow. It is like a name which has the power of the shadow and like a shadow that can cry. If you deal with such a shadow, you will never know whether you can trust its silence. That's why you're so terribly afraid. And you keep silent since you hope that it too will be silent, the shadow. But suddenly it is no longer silent. You hear: "Good evening, Mr. Nicolas," and before you have looked past the steam of your fear, the man who greeted you is already far away. That is nothing. But that those bright vowels, spoken only once, sound from wall to wall and roll from terrace to terrace in your conscience, ever deeper, and that they furthermore have the clarity which depth hangs around the things which already carry their own limpidity, that is terrible. For now you see, by the lantern of these vowels, your darkness and corners so black that the most tried tactile sense shivers and hides.

## Lines

You see a man in the street; he is not yet old, around fifty. He seems ordinary. And he is. For what you now see, and with amazement, you should have seen earlier, you should have seen just now. It is always present.

That is, how in this man's still ordinary gait lives the old man's walk. You see the ordinary gait now like a heavy inkline, but beneath it the other walk lies like a line of pale ink, and you know that time will darken this line when the other lightens. Like a caterpillar in its cocoon, so the resilient young walk harbors the old one. And nothing prevents the caterpillar from breaking through the cocoon, when the time comes.

And in the smooth rectangle of his shoulders you see a curving forward that is not visible to the naked eye, and yet you see it. Like a circle you might have drawn inside a square and then removed with an eraser. The line disappears, but the impression which the lead pencil made remains.

When you have seen this and the other, you see that the ordinary man walking there is losing his sturdy outline and that the contour of this man is changing perceptibly, just as a sheet of paper which, thrown into the fire, shrinks in baroque curls toward the kernel of its ashes.

With this man you see how the hull is being discarded and how his solidity is no different from the cocoon which hides the caterpillar from his presently old form.

You know now that you are still in the time of the unpierced hull. But you do not know or you forget that the caterpillar has already been living for a long time within the tissue.

Now and then it moves.

## O Thou, My Splendid Solitude

This is the first vernal evening of March, no longer fresh but humid, already humid. Perhaps you have known such an evening, experienced it in the same way I did, when aimlessness becomes the aim and settles with such forthrightness in the will, in a way that one very rarely— oh this rarity of the enduring consciousness—observes in oneself. Therefore, I am lured by this bench at the end of the lane, near the entrance to the park. You know, the lane which ends in a square behind which a woman stands high on a pedestal. She has a torch. She also leans heavily on one hip. It must have been a trying pose for the model. And there is the café at the left, where you leave the park and, there is light.

Nevertheless, this is an evening when you love the gathered darkness and place yourself in its midst with nothing but this full aimlessness. You are glad, for you know that this plenitude of aimlessness has its meaning in the rhythm of nature and that no matter what, you can do nothing today which would not be part of it.

There is a late bicylist. In winter it can also happen that you see a late bicylist. But this bicylist is totally different. He has a light with a red glow and you don't quite know what he wants with this light in our darkness, which is vernal and can hardly bear the lamplight.

There are also some people passing by, among them merely casual strollers. All those passing by wonder why I just sit there by the entrance, on any bench. It is strange that no one simply passes by. Finally there is a Jewish family, which scrutinizes me. The young man, the Jewish bridegroom, walks in front, and his bride next to him. Behind them come the old woman and the younger sister, obviously the sister of the bride. That makes four glances which slide across me, each with its own specific light. Then they become large at my level, and finally the glance is past. But I do feel that something in it remains unsatisfied. The bridegroom was, of the whole lot, the shyest.

I almost forgot one man who did just pass by without paying any attention to me. His face stood on a long neck, sharply forward and far from the trunk. He did not pay me my due.

With sure steps he carried the same aimlessness with him.

# Obsequies

When, in mid-August, it is not hot, but mild without being cool, we can no longer (as we did in June) regard this temperature as probably a short, intermediate stage of which, according to the few experiences we have had of this sort, the causes can be many and varied. But in this mildness we sense, in memory, the September day when summer really decomposes, when it happens in front of our eyes and in our organs that the elements of summer separate. Hence we do not say of this mild day in August that autumn is already visibly present in it, no, but we are like animals which, long before death, already smell decomposition. By eleven in the morning the sun has taken away much from the street, and we walk more easily and certainly more freely, on the sunny side, rather than on the spots where here and there the shadow still is.

And without being able to define the feeling precisely, we feel now that there is nothing contradictory between this mild August day and the obsequies which one is called upon to attend in the distant church.

The rural church lies stretched out in the distant unsieved clarity. Such clarity we would be inclined to hold unusual in a church, but we do not. We find it quite normal that it is very light everywhere, except for a few slanted shadows in the aisles. The knowledge we brought along this morning becomes in this church a clear experience. The notion of death as a bitter finality against this experience of equitable light commands no longer this synthetic power, which, in us, could formerly order the phenomena according to this accompanying notion. It is totally different. This notion of death bobs almost visibly against the clarity of the church, like a cork bobbing on the water's surface. Two values stand suddenly side by side, death and light, and we no longer succeed, as before, in thinking of the phenomena of this notion according to the order of the other one. But instead the flood of light washes the cork constantly to the beach.

Suddenly we stand with the accompanying value judgment of death as with a telescope in a room.

# Bankruptcy Jazz (A Film Script)

## Part One

**1**

The room of a little seamstress in Berlin. Sewing machine. On the wall gallant pictures cut from magazines. Wilted bunch of forget-me-nots. Atmosphere as in novels. Little seamstress industrious in front of the sewing machine. Singing. Orchestra plays softly. When you think the moon goes down      though she won't go down for awhile      it only seems that way.

**2**

Brussels. Same scene. Through the window a view of St. Gudule°1 or the municipal hall, representing the city. A canary in a cage. Industry. Singing. Orchestra perks up. Little bird, thou art in prison.

**3**

While the orchestra plays this tune, the scene changes to room of a third little seamstress. Window looks out on the Montparnasse cemetery, or something of the sort. Genre *Marie-Claire*.° On the screen the same melody serpentines° with the original French text, *Nicolette à sa fenestre.*

**4**

Dream scene. The little French seamstress is seen in an easy chair.° A shepherd. Curtsies. Wooing, etc.

**5**

The orchestra breaks the sentimental song and cuts in immediately with a Brazilian Matchiche.° The screen: a large rotating neon sign, from bright to dark.

SMOKE NICOLETTE CIGARS

A shot of boulevard at an oblique angle: domination of the monstrous neon sign and tiny people.

**6**

A back-alley in Berlin's Alt-Moabit.° The display-window is seen from

the inside, with the letters: Ye Olde Family Restaurant. Real Patzen-
hofer beer.°
First a few heads. Rakes. Pimps. Then these people around a table.
Debates. Disappointments.
A Gallic Jew° bangs his fist on the table. Triumphant, eureka expres-
sion on his face. Surprise.
Do you know Dada?
                        Pimps sober down. Speech by the Gallic Jew.
No, Dada is not an artistic bluff, but our solution to the financial
problem after all. Ambience. That is Dada. Expansive° gesture by the
Gallic Jew:

CABARET DADA IS THE FUTURE

Approval. Dadaism as real a value as an oil well. Consortium for the
exploitation of Dadaism is founded.

## 7
The Polish banker goes to the bank by car, followed by three trucks
loaded with Polish marks. Solemn entry. Transactions at the window.
Just as solemn, the banker leaves the bank. In his hand he holds one
single note.
*U.S.A. ONE DOLLAR*
Some twenty clerks unload the trucks of their Polish marks.

## 8
The Dada consortium in the midst of putting their plan into practice.
Buying of houses. Redevelopment. Beautification. Berliner scepticism.
Until Silverbroke shows his dollar. Change in the rate of exchange.
Respectful bows. Silverbroke's car surrounded by marriageable
daughters and tarts.

## 9
Billboards.
           Handbills from cars.
                     Weird sandwichmen. Ensormasks.

**10**

The little seamstress of the first scene is seen. She quickly closes the sewing machine. Mirror. Puff. Powder. Happily down the stairs.

Already a large crowd of similar little seamstresses in front of Cabaret Dada. Clerks. Travelling salesmen.

## Part Two. Cabaret Dada

**11**

Jazz starts languidly.

Slow

shuffling. Feet                                    Legs.

More assurance in the movement when the saxophone becomes stronger.

Stronger car horns, bars, megaphone, answered by the dancers with rhythmic assurance.

Pistol shot.

10 pistol shots.

The little seamstresses and the clerks feel at home. The

uncertainty of violin Puccini Butterfly is gone.

Assurance on the platform. A new period of positivism: Jazz.

The saxophonist yells. Hellooo! !

And everybody: Hellooo. (Close-up of the mouths.)

## 12

Neighboring houses. Typists and clerks working industriously. For a moment the music falls silent, so that the typing is soundless. Extremely intense typing, but soundless. Then

Shot

10 cracks.

The wall thins.

The rhythm breaks through. The typists stiffen their hands above the keyboard. Rigid, with their pens in their hands, the clerks are not writing.

Close-up of Dada in quicker tempo. The wall very thin: paper.

The typists slam the typewriters shut. Clerks leave the desks without balancing the books.

The clerks and typists going down, in couples, and in jazztempo.

The deserted office.

An almanac falls from the wall.

Into the wastepaper basket.

## 13

A boarding-school. An auditorium. A professor giving a lecture about *Götterdämmerung*. And to sum up    Richard Wagner is a good Teuton. Teenage girls: sleeping, eating candy.

Pistol shot.

10 Pistol shots.

And all the teenage girls: immediate understanding.

Shot of teenage girls' mouths: Halloo!

As a password rushing out.

The professor alone. He closes the books: *Götterdämmerung*.

## 14

The street in front of the Cabaret Dada. From the right come the typists and the clerks, from the left the teenage girls. Fraternization. As one, the group shoves into Dada.

## 15

Dada bar is chock-full. Nondancers strengthen the orchestra. With glasses, sirens, chairs, dogs, forks, and knives. And the invention of Mr. Browning, which only now comes into its own as a life-affirming sound. On the floor dancers as sardines in a can. Too small. Jazz on tables. Jazz on the stairs.
Shot of this movement in concave and convex mirrors.

## 16

The house *DADA* seen from the outside. Shot: the façade very close. The windows vibrate.

> Kettledrum.
>> The façade moves.
>>> Cracks. The cracks

develop like an animated drawing over the façade.
Cymbals.   Rattling.   On the screen: windows break. Doors burst. Or are thrown forcibly off their hinges.

> *THE JAZZ OVERFLOWS INTO THE STREET.*

Pell-mell the now strong jazz band and the dancers. The magnified tube of a saxophone and body of a banjo are visible.

## 17

The abandoned hall.
> The abandoned piano.
> The chandelier falls. Point right through the piano.

Clavier slammed together in a sharp angle around pivot-point-chandelier.
The walls. The deserted feeling enhances the billboards.

GARBATY.° CHOCOLATE ICE CREAM  FREAK  SHOW

SPECIALTY

What is dada? DADA is universal  reason°     DADA
which                                                    IS
the superidiocy of everybody                 NIETSCHE
can attain                            WITHOUT
Dada is not                                              NIETSCHE
bankrupt, but
BANKRUPTCY°        *Bourgeois*

DADA is not an artistic
Business, but the
FORMULA of BANKRUPTCY     **D**

*hail*
*Dada*                                      **A**

Dada is                                                                  **D**

the PainLess                          JOIN          **D**

# bankruptcy 75     DADA     **A**

**18**

A silent street. Suddenly, the tube of a saxophone. The body of a
banjo. And the jazz. Clerks, typists, models, schoolboys, teenage
girls, dadaists, dummies, a piece of Debussy's statue, somebody all
dolled up,° extras from *La Juive*.° An elderly man who looks like
Tirpitz.° The harmony of Zehlendorff.° The famous king of the onanists.

All the jazz-steps of dancing schools are gone. Supreme lyricism.

Everybody jazzes instinctively. Central European exertion to
become Negroes.°

In the middle     Sadi Ride     the beautiful Negro.

Dominant.     Superiority.

Concierges join the dancers.

Piano teachers leave Schumann with one jump.

A Negro scans. Movement with a bamboo stick. Rhythmic movement
of shoulders. Of hips.

The jazz accompaniment yells.
   Ticatoc
      ticatoc
(which means in Swahili: to move your hips rhythmically.)
The bourgeois raise the black-white-red flag.° The Bavarian, the Prussian, the Papal one. The symmetrical eagle with the crown.
The entire scene. Then the eagle alone. Then the crown alone. While the crown remains on the screen the jazz image comes out of the well-known soft focus. Rapid clearing. The crown falls amidst the jazz.

## 19

Revolution?
    Dada-jazz revolution?
Noske° is seen marching forward,
         Noskites, grune Polizei,° Sipo,° Sipol
etc.°

Machine guns. Flamethrowers. Handgrenades. Military law.
  *The revolution is to be fought with every possible means.*

Panoramic view of the street.
Jazz comes from the left.————Noske (Justav) comes from the right.
At left, banjobody enlarged.  At right, machine gun.

Slowing down of jazz rhythm. (And the bruited° accompaniment in the orchestra is silent.)
     Slow swinging
       of the  hostile  groups.
This is a panoramic shot.
  Two animals
   the
   groups
 facing each other  *UNTIL*

A little ahead of what
  happens on the screen
      *Orchestra*
          *KETTLEDRUMS*
bUrst of homeric laughter.

Perspective moves from left to right, shifting upwards and into shot of gaping mouths. Laughter in accelerated motion. A man from the mass, hand at his mouth. Calling.

*The Noske racketeer.*

Panoramic or angle shot of the jazz mass performing the Noskestep. A sudden stand-still. The shot.

Shrinking back in one-two-three step.

With the scanned chant.

Noske

Noske

shoot    some    more.

The Noskites. Dumbfounded. Faces as if the world were topsy-turvy. Atlas dangles from below, instead of bravely shouldering. The agents of provocation now on the side of the public. The Sipo is provoked. To provoke the Sipo . . . .

The jazz group makes use of this confusion. Streams into the Noske group. Peace on earth. At first an unclear tangle. Gradually (what can be called "gradually" on film, not a Marconi-psychology) the jazz rhythm breaks through the chaotic clump. Typists catch sweet Noskites. Then the Noskites, now themselves master of the situation, embrace typists.

One after the other the bruited instruments strengthen the jazz rhythm. When they arrive at the moment, Noske, Noske, shoot some more, the soldiers point the machine guns upwards. Fire. Displace the jazz into a more encompassing unity. Machine guns as bruited accompaniment of jazz. The Armed Forces swallowed in the dance. Triumphant jazz.

## 20

The now large mob in the relatively narrow street perforce regulates the jazz. The jazz steps *determined* by the number of people in the street space.

In front the initial banjo and the initial saxophone, flanked by machine guns.

Movement closed by the rolling field kitchen of the company. The vehicle rolls by, the back-wheels large, shot along the slope of the street.

## 21

Square, Church.

For music, only a bell.

Afternoon ceremony. Women. Polish immigrants. A gentleman with a silk hat. Organ music. Churchlike melancholy.

The two corners of a street which opens into the square are shot without depth of field. On the same level as the street corners, the banjo, the saxophone, the muzzle of a machine gun.

Depth from below: a thousand jazz legs.

While on the screen the jazz engulfs the square, the orchestra consists of two forces, the bruited jazz and the bells.

On the steps of the church, the gentlemen of the church committee protest violently. The sexton appears with the banner of St. Michel. The first motion of the faithful—primarily women—is to recoil. Then something like the gesture of "rape me please." The jazz rings round the drivellers. Noskites break through the ring. Embrace the drivellers. It's so wonderful in the arms of a Noske guardsman.

Bells toll desperately, and the jazz bruitists try nervously to outshout the bells.

The sweet gestures of the teenage girls get the gentlemen of the church committee in terrible roundelay.

A moment's hesitation: freeze framed. Wind still.

But in the orchestra expression of struggle. Bells—and jazz: machine guns, kettledrums carry banjos and saxophone.

The teenage girls mimic gallantry and guide the gentlemen of the church committee. Little hands around fat wrists. Dotards, childishly uncertain, dare the first steps in the new life=jazz. The sexton leaves Michael in the lurch. A teenage girl, with a sulky

mien, says, Why isn't Mister Michael dancing with us? She takes the banner. The banner of St. Michael—the holy warrior and the trampled snake—flaps with saintly protection over the jazz.

During the paroxysm of the struggle the music—bells and jazz—falls silent for a moment while

the screen shows the great action.

When the church is consumed by the jazz, the jazz music begins softly with banjos only. Growing assimilation. Saxophone. Bruitists.

And the bells. *Frère Jacques* melody consumed by the jazz rhythm and the noise. The bells replace the jazz in a more encompassing unity.

## 22

Bells carry the jazz over the city.

On the lower half of the screen, panoramic view of the city; above it tolls, won-lost, a bell.
Down from the square the jazz engulfs the city along many streets.
The main church and four small ones—a hen and chickens. Five towers. Five bells. The large one tolls first, then the four small bells answer.
Evangelical church, Calvin, Luther, Catholic, gnostic, neo-gnostic church—all bells toll jazz.

## 23
A bell sows tolling jazz over a workers' quarter. Cinematographic metaphor—grains of corn cleave rapidly through space, fall amidst groups.
The people push out of the housing projects.

## 24
Suburbia. Above it, bell tolls jazz. Simultaneously Venetian blinds are bashfully rolled up in many houses. Windows are opened. Heads.
Two adjacent interiors with mathematically identical scenes. Round table. Card players. The swinging movement of the bell makes the scenery tremble. The gentlemen put their cards aside. Brief, definitive tragic gesture. It's going to happen. A gentleman holds two fingers up. He speaks. *Now the time for playing gin rummy is past.* (Overture to *The Flying Dutchman*.)
Tentatively they dare step into the street. Try out a step in jazz tempo. Always out of step.

## 25
Scene a panoramic view of Berlin.
Isolated jazz groups in many streets.
Concentric movement towards the main arteries of the city.
Alexanderplatz.° With the contingent of the proletarian jazz jews.
Rosenthalerplatz. The proletarian jazz.
Kurfürstendamm.° Jazz of bankers and call girls.

Pederasts jazz.
       The waiters.
           The doorman.
                The cocaine pushers.
                    Etc.

**26**

Tilted and closer panoramic view of the Potsdamerplatz.° Higher, from the Alexanderplatz, the Wittenbergplatz, Alt-Moabit, from Neukölln° the jazz bands stream towards the Potsdamerplatz.

From the Potsdamerplatz through Budapester Strasse through Unter den Linden,° up to the Schloss, a long jazz band chain is formed.

The historical cannon of the Zeughaus—°Ulm, Austerlitz, Jena—fire accompanying jazz.

The Cathedral totters, the Cathedral falls.

The Kaiser-Friedrich Museum totters, falls. Schloss.° Tottering. Falling.

Cars, buses accompany the dance with nervous stationary idling.

Commuter trains roll in jazz tempo.

The ground trembles: shuddering and murmuring of jazz in the subway.

**27**

One moment—the empty room from 10. Almanac. Wastepaper basket. A still shot remains a relatively long time on the screen. Polarized tension.

**28**

Symbolic scene.

A street corner. A cop. The Wandering Jew° comes. (Exactly like the one by Eugène Sue.) He approaches the cop. Questions:

     Is it far from here to Spandau.

Nightstick direction. The Wandering Jew disappears in the direction of Spandau.°

# Part Three

**29**

The belfry of Ghent.° The bell. Roland's bell.° Tolling. Soun . . .ding! Tolls fire and sounds storm in Flanders.

                           Jazz storm.

**30**

The screen a map of Belgium. Above it sounds the bell of Roland. The map trembles.

**31**

St. Gudule. Bell. Tolling.
Brussels: the "cozy" life. Bars. Sidewalk cafés.
Newspaper vendors. Newspapers. Headlines. *WAVE OF INFLATION*
                    *Read the Wave*
Conversations. Brussels' mime. Everything has to become cheaper.
The franc is dropping back to the peace rate. Keep that in mind.
On the screen are seen two banknotes. 5 francs. One dollar. Joined by the mathematical symbol=

**32**

Advertisements. Those who buy a pair of shoelaces get the shoes free.
If you buy five francs worth of goods you get twenty francs change.
The newspaper boys gallop: read the wave!
                    Read the wave! !

**33**

In a sidewalk café. A lady and a gentleman enjoy coffee, cakes, whipped cream, etc.
Small talk. Calling the waiter, paying. The gentleman with a twenty-five centimes coin. The waiter gives him twenty centimes change.
The entire sidewalk café. People enjoy coffee, cakes, whipped cream. Bliss. The beatitudes.

**34**

At night.
A fence, posters.
Comes a bill poster. Industry. Before long the result is visible, a series of bills, each one separate as follows:

> ANNOUNCEMENT
> The Germans pay
> All Belgians will therefore receive those sums they are entitled to
> The wave of inflation rolls

We're heading for a peace time rate of exchange. Just a little more
patience
During this short waiting period, the best way to invest your money is
in
*Government Savings Bonds*
*The government is the best debtor.* Do not invest any money in industry
The Government pays more
Savings bonds up to 6% free of taxes. 5% discount
*Pass it on*

The billposter disappears to the left. Immediately from the right, billposter no. 2. Faster work: brushing, paste, sticking.

MESSAGE
The "Wave of Inflation" is swelling
In the meantime, the only sure investment is the
*savings bond*
What is the wealth of a country?     *THE STATE*
So buy savings bonds at $6\frac{1}{2}$% free of all taxes
Subscribers 10% discount

Disappears left. Now follow quickly in increasing tempo—accelerated motion—the third, the fourth, the fifth, the sixth billposter. Each one in his turn pastes over what the one before him put there. The text more and more laconic and emphatic with increasing percentages and discounts. 8%, $8\frac{1}{2}$%, 9%, $9\frac{1}{2}$%. The posting of the bills, i.e., the rising offers of the government, happens with such tempo that there is barely time for reading.

## 35

The Butte.° The Sacré Cœur.° The bells tolls jazz.
Notre Dame. The angel. Theban trumpets.
Panoramic view of Paris. Pilots. Leaflets.
Streets. Newspapers. *L'Intran.*°
                    Declaration of the government

The Anglo-Saxons are no longer buying our wines
They prefer their pale beer

> The French people will drink its wine
> *Drink*
> The heroes of the Marne, of Verdun, of Péronne° drink henceforth
> French wine
> French soil for the French
> 2 sous per liter
> Fecundity          Long live France

The People. Leaflets float above the people. Grabbing hands.

> Fight the high cost of living
> Buy only products which are bargains—
> What are those bargains?
> *Wine and        the savings bond*
> 7% free of taxes. Patriotic duty. Go to your bank now.

## 36

A map of Western and Central Europe. Berlin, Brussels, Paris. Three jazz groups are seen moving towards each other across the map.
In the lower left-hand corner appear two angels. One stays put. The other flies to the upper right hand corner, takes one end of a banner with it. In this manner the banner is stretched diagonally over the map.

JAZZ PACIFIES PEOPLE

## 37

Warsaw.
          A parade, sponsored by the government, in jazz form.
Schoolchildren.
          Soldiers.
                    The government. The clergy. Etc.
An enormous shield:
          *The government supports Dada*

DADA SAVES EUROPE

## 38

The carnival in Nice.

The parade. The main attraction of the parade is the victory float of

*THE SAVINGS BOND*

**39**

Monte Carlo.

Great celebrations. The prince of Monaco proclaimed the honorary president of the European Dada Republic.

**40**

The harbors. Hamburg. Antwerp. Marseille.

Empty steamers. The sirens whistle (sirens in the orchestra, jazz).

Back alleys stream into the streets.

The whorehouses open up.

The girls in their working clothes herd outside until they are in the arms of stevedores—harbor jazz. In the shipyards, on the ships. A Dutch salt throws his clay pipe away.

# Part Four

**41**

Brussels' Grand Place.° Mobs. The masses advance down the side streets. Festive mood.

A dais. The highest representatives of the nation arrive. The king, the ministers, the highest ranking clergy, the magistrate of the capitol, etc. Uniforms. Veils. Banners.

Orchestra high-bruited accompaniment, triumphal jazz, until the bells and kettledrums fall silent.

St. Gudule. Theban trumpets.

The people are attentive. The king stands straight. Short spiel. He grants the Secretary of the Treasury permission to speak.

The Secretary of the Treasury. Cheers. Hats. The Secretary speaks. The public's attention rises to approval. Inspiration.

"It is the goal of the government to develop the national economy to an even more favorable degree than has been the case up to now. The government has therefore stopped with a final issue of nonlimited

savings bonds, at 10%, free of taxes, and with 75% reduction for subscribers. Go to your bank now. In this way we will be able to realize the motto of our life: *every bourgeois independently wealthy.*"
Hats in the air.

Wild inspiration. Ecstasy.

The secretary of the Treasury carried around in triumph on strong shoulders.
The mayor—with renewed attention from the crowds—reads the latest municipal ordinance:

*The right* has been granted for the building of 2000 new dance halls.
Every house located in the center of town will be rebuilt as a dance hall.
*Appeal:* Yet one final costly duty: the building of dance halls.

## 42

A meeting of the French Academy. Recognition of the word jazz.

Solemnity.

The Chief of Staff.          The Archbishop.          The President.
as godfathers of the jazz child.

## 43

Downtown. Industrious anthill. Transformation of shops into dance halls. One house after another goes up ready with the announcement: opening the 5th, opening the 6th, opening the 7th, etc.
Meanwhile pilots drop leaflets.
News vendors gallop with victory headlines.
Read the new state sanction.
Ougrée closes.
Cockerill closes.
Espérance-Longdoz° closes.
News items which each time are received with thunderous approval.
Transformation of the national bank into GRAND NATIONAL DANCE HALL.

## 44

Dedication of the monument for the
UNKNOWN JAZZ DANCER

**45**

The first day of being independently wealthy. Jazz as national employment.

Strike of the thieves. Strike of the whores. Nothing doing, mister. I have savings bonds. Strike of the baby farmers.°

End of endless affairs. A thirty-year-old woman gives an old gentleman his walking papers; after that a youth of twenty gives her hers. Thieves simply refuse to steal purses.

Protest meeting of those who were cheated in this way. Reasonable distribution of national goods. Order of the day: rationing of the national resources.

**46**

A couple in conversation. The woman afraid. The man reassuring. Tomorrow I'll go get my interest on my savings bonds. Life is simple, dear wife.

**47**

Professional musicians also want to enjoy their savings bonds. Lay down their instruments. Momentary perplexity and disappointment among the celebrating public. Who will make music now? Jazz without music?

But two humanitarians, Messrs. Léon Bourgeois° and Romain Rolland,° save the day. (Jazz without music—the situation becomes explosive.) And the orchestra is made up of philanthropists and humanitarians from both continents, the heroes of humanity who offer themselves eternally. Bourgeois Léon. Rolland Romain. Duhamel Georges.° Wilson Woodrow. Moens Wies.° Havelaar the Just.° The Hasenschiller.° The charitable man of Klondike who lets his hump be turned into a street organ. And others. And the feast continues. While:

**48**

The residence of the Secretary of the Treasury. Office boys busily packing suitcases. The Secretary gathers papers. Preparations for an important journey.

Soft focus: souvenir, part of the jazz beginning is repeated. The Dada bar with the first timid jazz dancers. This is run slower—measure of contrast.

**49**

The small room of the little seamstress. Deserted. Almanac, waste-paper basket.

In the street, a blind man.

And in the orchestra just for a moment the sentimental tune,

When you think the moon goes down.

# Part Five

**50**

Dawn.

A shot which shows in succession the various treasury departments, taken as if all were on one street, by a camera placed in a car. Not separate views, but kinetic development.

The screen, divided vertically into three equal parts, shows three treasury departments, the German, the Belgian, the French. Out of each building comes a little fellow, the doorman. Simultaneous stage acting of the doormen on the three parts of the screen. Looking around for a moment. Then each of the doormen hangs a bulletin in a conspicuous place on the buildings which were entrusted to them. Satisfaction. Simultaneous rubbing of hands. Exit doormen. The three bulletins next to each other.

| |
|---|
| Wanted: serious young man |
| First-class references not necessary *Initiative* |
| Duties: Momentous communications to the public |

| |
|---|
| Le *Ministre des Finances* |
| demande |
| *jeune homme sérieux* |
| pour faire grave et intéressante communication au public |
| Initiative sine qua non |

*Ernsthafter Jüngling*
findet Stellung
beim Finanzministerium
nur *Initiative* erforderlich

## 51

On the screen remains only one ministry, the Belgian one, for example, which is also representative of the others.*

Jazz dancers who are still up walk by on their way home. Read nonchalantly what it says on the bulletin board. No interest. Mr. Joseph Caillaux° also among those who are going home. Young man with initiative? No. Though favorably disposed, this is no longer something for him. He has a smile on his face.

## 52

The music—through its being silent—announces. Silence is golden.

In *illo tempore*

Charlie Chaplin° appears on the screen. Hat, cane, shoes, mustache.

Reads the notice. Pulls the hat down over his brow and reads—more attentively—again. The hat pushed back again. Serious young man. Sure. That's him. He is it: the desired young man=Charlie.

Reports energetically to the doorman. Charlie's famous greeting. Hat. Hand on his heart: I am the young man without first-class references, but with initiative. The doorman refers him to the assistant. With the assistant. Same act. I am Charlie, the most serious young man on this globe. The assistant introduces Charlie to the Secretary of the Treasury. Charlie greets him, at a distance, most courteously; reserved, round smile on his lips.

The Secretary in travelling clothes. Suitcase ready. Surprised at the entrance of Charlie. But enormous shaking of hands after hearing the reason for his early visit. Embracing. Charlie adjusts his hat the way it's supposed to be.

The Secretary phones. In a wink the heads of state are present.

---

*The author uses the Belgian ministry because it is most readily available to him. If it is more profitable from a scenic point of view to choose another ministry as being representative, then there is nothing to be said against this mutation. The scenic appropriateness of this choice belongs in the domain of the director.

Triumphant reception of Charlie. Flattering words. You have an air of intelligence about you, my boy, etc.

The Secretary explains. For example, takes a pack of savings bonds and wants to throw them into the fire. Charlie restrains him. Stop it, I know what it is all about. Everything understood. Points forefinger at his eye. You either got eyes or you haven't.

The ministers, repeatedly bowing respectfully, exit. Run down the stairs. Jump in cars. Quick suitcases. Hop. Gone at 80 miles per hour. A brief backward glance.

Goodbye, you clods.

Charlie alone in the splendid Empire chamber. Act: Charlie as head of state. Bowler like Napoleon's hat.

## 53

The street around 10 a.m. The people together in the direction of the Treasury. Lively gestures, such as, Let's see what's up.

A panoramic view shows the dismantled Treasury, surrounded by the masses.

A small minority with large wallets. Others with thick packs under the arm. The majority, however, with a bag which can hardly be moved.

Also come rolling: carts, cars, trucks full with papers. A view from above of these vehicles.

The station. In the hall the notices:

> Savings bonds the best and most secure investment

Arrival of trains from the provinces. Getting off the trains, farmers dragging bushels and baskets filled with valuable papers. Gentlemen— village accountants and such—with travelling cases (beautiful pigskin leather).

Freight trains loaded with securities.

Along the great highways leading to the capital, moving vans transport state securities from the provinces.

## 54

Charlie on the balcony. The masses. Yelling. We demand the Secretary of the Treasury. Charlie calm: Ecce Homo. Among the masses: dismay, disapproval, fury.

Little or no applause.

Charlie reassuring, "I am a financial genius," invites the public to send a delegation to him.

## 55

The chamber. Delegation inside. With wallets, bags, baskets, bushels. Gesture of the leader of the delegation: if there are no more . . . .
The delegation throws stacks of papers on Charlie's ministerial Empire table.
Charlie
         very carefully takes one piece of valuable paper, by means of which he gets some fire from the fireplace. Lights an enormous cigar. Easy chair. Smokes in a jovial fashion. Crossed legs. Gestures with the palm of his hand—there's your solution, gentlemen.
"Don't ask me why I handle this savings bond so carelessly. Instead you should ask why I light a cigar—a cigar gentlemen!—so cheerfully."
Hands grasp for the cigarbox. Empty.
The last cigar on the continent, gentlemen.
Charlie to the window. He throws the burning savings bond outside.
The savings bond falls amidst piled-up savings bonds.
Charlie: True fireworks is to be magnanimous.

## 56

But this is a great advantage:
         the inevitable is quickly understood.
The people, hand in hand, resume their momentarily forgotten dance around the burning wealth of the *state*.
The humanitarians (see above) get the fire going, wave hats, coats, etc. Wave in jazz tempo. That is to say, the jazz is expressed plastically by means of a rhythmically equal exchange of short and long waving, from left to right, up and down, and vice versa.
Total jazz—music, dance, plasticity—also song.
Under the direction of Charlie, schoolchildren sing the new national anthem (in the orchestra, children's voices, clear).

| I am broke     | I love being bankrupt      |
|----------------|----------------------------|
| You are broke  | you love being bankrupt    |
| He is broke    | he loves being bankrupt    |
| We are broke   | do we love being bankrupt  |
| They are broke | do they love being bankrupt|
| You are broke  | you love being bankrupt    |

Bells toll. Flames engulf the buildings which attest to culture.

## 57

The body of a banjo, the tube of a saxophone. The little room from the first scene. The moon shines on the calendar.

One sole kid selling newspapers, gallops through the quiet streets.

*IT'S BANKRUPTCY*

---

1. Throughout the superior symbol ° indicates the presence of a note.
St. Gudule—A cathedral, now better known as the Cathedral of St. Michael, which dominates the skyline of Brussels' upper town. Right next to the church is The National Bank. The lower city of Brussels is dominated by the Grand Place, famous for its town Hall, and is the centre of business activities. This opposition between various sections of a city is also noticeable in the description of Berlin.
*Marie Claire*—A women's magazine.
Serpentine—Play on words. A verb meaning "to wind" and also an obsolete wooden wind instrument which coils like a snake and has a deep hoarse sound.
Easy chair—Play on words. In the original *bergère*, meaning both a large, stuffed easy chair, as well as a shepherdess, swain or nymph.
Matchiche—French phonetic transcription of the Portuguese word *maxixe*. Introduced into the French language around 1904, it means a South American dance imported from Rio de Janeiro.
Alt-Moabit—A district where the typical "Berliners" used to live. It is also distinguished for harboring a State Penitentiary and Courts. A seedy quarter. Presently it is quite close to what constitutes the center of West Berlin.
Patzenhofer—A brand of beer, a local Berlin variety.
Gallic Jew—An educated guess at identifying this mysterious figure: the French poet Max Jacob (1876–1944). Van Ostaijen knew and admired the work of Jacob, who died in a German concentration camp. He was a good friend of Apollinaire, a poet whose work Van Ostaijen praised and emulated.
Expansive—In the original *pofeties*, which is either an error for *profeties* (i.e. "prophetic") or a pun on *pof*. If the latter, it has the force of a "slap," a "shove," "smash" (a fist); or, in the expression *op de pof kopen*, to buy on credit, and in soldiers' slang to go AWOL. The latter meanings are appropriate in the context of a bankrupt Europe.
Garbaty—A rich cigarette manufacturer who bought works of art for his collection during the depression, at low prices.
Universal reason—In the original, *Weltvernunft*, where it has the typically abstract force Hegel has become infamous for.
Nietsche—This spelling of the name provides a nice pun. *Niets* means "nothing" in Dutch.

Bankruptcy—In the original *pleite*. The translation gives the literal meaning, but *pleite* was also a biweekly satirical periodical sponsored by the Berlin Dadas in circulation from 1919 to 1924.

Dolled up—In the original *Barbarrosados*; combination of Barbarossa and *dos* (the Dutch word for elaborate costume). Emperor Frederick Barbarossa (1120–1190) reunited Germany after the disastrous squabbles of Charlemagne's heirs. According to legend, he has been lying asleep for some eight hundred years in a cave in the Kyffhäuser mountains in Thuringen. When the ravens who nest around the cave depart the old hero will rouse himself and save Germany from her enemies. This is the conservative, chauvinistic, phoenix myth of a Germany rising from its ashes.

*La Juive*—A five-act romantic opera by Jacques Francois Halévy (1799–1862).

Tirpitz—Alfred von Tirpitz (1849–1930). For twenty-nine years, Tirpitz was Secretary of State for the Navy. He retired in 1916, involved himself with nationalistic and rightist politics, and became something of a Teutonic Barry Goldwater.

Zehlendorff—Berlin's Park Avenue.

To become Negroes—In the original *vernegeren*. Pun on the verb *negeren* (*negerde*, *heeft genegerd*) which means to pester, maltreat, bug someone. The Dutch noun *neger* means Negro.

Black-white-red flag—To show the disunity of regionalism in Germany, both politically and religiously.

Noske—Gustav Noske (1868–1946). German politician, important member of the Social Democratic Party, which took over when the Kaiser fled to Holland in 1918. The government sent Noske to Kiel that same year to restore order after the November Revolution. As supreme commander of troops loyal to the government, he brutally suppressed the abortive revolution of the Communists in Berlin during January of 1919. He performed an effective, ruthless, bloody job, and was probably one of the most hated figures in Germany at that time.

Polizei—At that time similar to our State Police.

Sipo—Stands for *Sicherheitspolizei*, an indefinitive and much feared strong arm of the Government. Akin to the F.B.I.

Sipol etc.—In the original *Sipol enz.* In Dutch *enz.* is an abbreviation standing for *enzovoort* which means *etc.* But in German *-enz* is a suffix which gives the noun it is added to an abstract connotation. In this case it has the force of indicating that *Sipolenz* is synonymous with *Polizei Krankheit*—i.e., the police is like a cancerous growth in society.

Bruited—Bruitism is a prominent feature of this script. The word derives from the French *bruit* (noise); Dada applied it to both words and music. Bruitistic poems used typography as a significant element; in public performances, poetry readings were interrupted by all sorts of noises, both human and mechanical. Bruitistic music—which began the trend later including *musique concrète* and electronic music—could be summed up as calculated cacophony.

Alexanderplatz—Part of Berlin, a combination of Wall Street and Times Square. See Alfred Döblin's famous novel, *Berlin Alexanderplatz* (1929).

Kurfürstendam—One of the main boulevards in Berlin, noted for its cafés, restaurants, places of entertainment, etc. Comes to life at night.

Potsdamerplatz—Center for political demonstrations in Berlin at that time.

Wittenbergplatz—Typical bourgeois area in Berlin.

Neukölln—The proletarian quarter of Berlin during Van Ostaijen's time.

Unter den Linden—Once one of the longest, broadest, and most imposing boulevards in Europe. Now the famous Wall cuts it in half at the Brandenburg Gate.

Zeughaus—A museum which was a national shrine where weapons and historical souvenirs from Germany's past were on grandiose display. Note that the three battles Van Ostaijen mentions (Ulm, Austerlitz, and Jena) were all lost by the German forces during the Napoleonic wars.

Schloss—I assume that Van Ostaijen is referring to the Charlottenburg Palace which has the goddess of Fortune as a weather vane.

The Wandering Jew—In the original, Van Ostaijen refers to a novel with that title by a Flemish author whom he disliked. I substituted Eugène Sue, whose novel on the same subject and with the same title is probably more familiar to readers.

Spandau—A beautiful section of Berlin, including, however, the Spandau Citadel, which was a state prison and treasury of the Kaisers, and has housed since 1945 Nazi criminals convicted at the Nuremburg Trials.

Belfry of Ghent—A tall, massive tower in the center of what was once an important city. The belfry is especially famous for its carillon of fifty-two bells, of which the largest weighs 13,310 lbs.

Roland's bell—The most famous bell associated with the Belfry of Ghent. Charles V had it confiscated after it was used to call the people of Ghent together in revolt against him. Important in this context as a special Flemish symbol, and as a symbol of revolution and liberation.

The Butte—Metonymy for Montmartre. Here mentioned not only for its artists, but also because it has been a center of revolt during Parisian uprisings and time of war.

Sacré Cœur—The famous, beautiful, and imposing cathedral on top of the *butte Montmartre*, whose white outline dominates the Parisian skyline. It is interesting to note that the church was built as a result of a vow made during the Franco-Prussian War of 1870–1871, and was constructed with money from public subscriptions.

L'Intran—Mass circulation newspaper.

Marne, Verdun, Péronne—World War I battles involving incredible casualties.

Grand Place—The rest of the script takes place in the unique square which is the heart of the old city in Brussels. It is a rectangular space, surrounded by architectural gems: the city hall, the House (said to be) of the King, and a number of guild houses. It is obviously *the* place for official and important functions in Belgium's capital.

Ougrée, Cockerill, Espérance-Longdoz—Three enormous Belgian steel corporations which were very powerful economic forces. They still exist in modified forms of trusts and limiteds.

Baby farmers—In the original *engelemaaksters*. This word means literally, "women who make angels," which was precisely what they did. The noun designates women who were either abortionists (of the butcher variety) or who would take in babies for a large sum of money, and promise to care for them. The babies were usually illegitimate and died very rapidly—that way the women could obviously make more money.

Léon Bourgeois—(1851–1925) a French politician and briefly prime minister towards the end of the nineteenth century. He tried to introduce financial informs including an income tax in 1896, and was replaced in the same year largely because of these measures. After the war he became an ardent internationalist and humanitarian and received the Nobel Peace Prize in 1925. For Van Ostaijen of threefold importance: financial reforms, internationalism, and his name.

Romain Rolland—(1868–1944), novelist, essayist and music critic, most famous for his (endless) novel *Jean Christophe*, published between 1906 and 1912. He was also a very ardent internationalist who pamphleteered and fought for Franco-German peace as well as friendship.

Duhamel Georges—Georges Duhamel, born in 1884, is particularly important in this context as a positivistic writer and a member of the Unanimists a society of writers who believed in placing the group before the individual. They held that one's essence should be submerged in a collective such as a factory, city, church, army, etc. The founder of the movement and its most forceful member was Jules Romain.

Moens Wies—Wies Moens (b.1898). The work of this Flemish poet was particularly repulsive to Van Ostaijen. Moens maintained an undaunted faith in humanity despite the horrors of World War I. A militant Catholic, Moens saw the poet as a political and social influence on the masses, and his verse was replete with bright humanitarianism.

Havelaar the Just—Just Havelaar (1880–1930), minor Dutch author, reflected the same optimistic humanitarianism as Moens, without the latter's force. In 1928 Havelaar was still hailing the arrival of "The New Man"—an endeavour one can only describe as stillborn. His idealistic innocence was remarkable in its refusal to see facts.

Hasenschiller—Nickname for Walter Hasenclever (1890–1940), a German writer most famous for his bathetic dramas. Member of the Expressionist movement.

Joseph Cailleaux—(1863–1944) a politician and Prime Minister of France. He initiated an income-tax bill similar to the one Bourgeois had tried to obtain (see above), which he managed to put through in 1909 after two years of struggle. He lost office in 1912 after infuriating nationalists by trying to effect an international settlement for a crisis which almost exploded into war.

Charlie Chaplin—An early Chaplin film, *The Bank* (1915), might have given Van Ostaijen the idea for the final section of his film. Chaplin plays a handyman who makes a mess out of the bank president's office.

ST. MARY'S COLLEGE OF MARYLAND
ST. MARY'S CITY, MARYLAND

058472